CARTRIDGE CARNIVAL

Center Point
Large Print

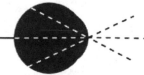

**This Large Print Book carries the
Seal of Approval of N.A.V.H.**

CARTRIDGE CARNIVAL

William Colt MacDonald

CENTER POINT LARGE PRINT
THORNDIKE, MAINE

This Center Point Large Print edition
is published in the year 2016 by arrangement with
Golden West Literary Agency.

First US edition: Doubleday, Doran & Co.
First UK edition: Hodder & Staughton

The text of this Large Print edition is unabridged.
In other aspects, this book may vary
from the original edition.
Printed in the United States of America
on permanent paper.
Set in 16-point Times New Roman type.

ISBN: 978-1-68324-114-0 (hardcover)
ISBN: 978-1-68324-118-8 (paperback)

Library of Congress Cataloging-in-Publication Data

Names: MacDonald, William Colt, 1891–1968, author.
Title: Cartridge carnival / William Colt MacDonald.
Description: Center Point Large Print edition. | Thorndike, Maine :
Center Point Large Print, 2016.
Identifiers: LCCN 2016024598 | ISBN 9781683241140 (hardcover : alk.
paper) | ISBN 9781683241188 (pbk. : alk. paper)
Subjects: LCSH: Large type books. | GSAFD: Western stories.
Classification: LCC PS3525.A2122 C37 2016 | DDC 813/.52—dc23
LC record available at https://lccn.loc.gov/2016024598

1. MURDER?

A glaring morning sun beat down upon Carnival and the surrounding country, reflected dazzlingly from the varicolored slopes of the rugged Carnival Mountains to the west, and bathed the streets of the town in torrid waves of heat that gave promise of becoming, by noontime, unduly oppressive. The vast sea of mesquite and cacti that bordered Carnival on all sides moved but slightly in the hot, irregular breeze that lifted sporadically across the dusty range. Already rattlesnakes were seeking the shadows of the red, yellow, and blue rocks that had moved down, in ages past, from the calico-patterned escarpments of the mountains. Small birds perched motionless in the lacy branches of mesquite trees; in the cloudless, blue expanse above, a pair of soaring buzzards scarcely stirred their sluggish wings.

That same reluctance of movement appeared to prevail in Carnival also. Along Main Street certain stores were being opened. There were but few people on the sidewalks. Here and there a cow pony switched a listless tail at the myriad flies buzzing about hitch rails or stamped fretfully in the dust of the unpaved thoroughfare. A group of cowpunchers lounged on the porch of the Bonanza Bar, at the corner of Main and Flagstaff streets; though the men spoke but little, there was an air of expectancy about them, a certain tense something in their slightest movements. Diagonally across Main Street, Gage Freeman emerged from the entrance of his general store and, broom in hand, made a few desultory sweeping motions in the vicinity of his doorway. After a moment he paused and mopped perspiration from his bald head with a blue bandanna.

A middle-aged, gray-haired man, dressed in "town clothes" and a broad-brimmed black hat, came along Flagstaff Street, carrying a small hand satchel. Turning east on Main, he nodded curtly to the cowboys on the Bonanza porch and continued on his way. The eyes of the cowboys followed him—followed, rather, the satchel the man carried.

Across the roadway Gage Freeman ceased his sweeping and hailed the bearer of the satchel: "Mornin', James. Figurin' to do some travelin'?"

James Sanford stopped momentarily. "Hello, there, Gage. Why, yes, I'm planning to catch the nine-seventeen for Capital City. I might do a little business up that way."

"Nine-seventeen, eh?" Freeman consulted his heavy silver watch. "You got better than an hour yet. Kate goin' to run the *Banner* while you're away?"

"I won't be gone long, Gage. Expect to be back tomorrow."

"Tomorrow, eh? By the way, James, that was a dang good piece you had in the paper yesterday— the one relatin' to law and order. The missus and I agree with you one hundred per cent."

The publisher of Carnival's local newspaper smiled appreciatively. "Glad you liked my editorial, Gage. I'm hoping to wake up a few folks."

"You will," Freeman said emphatically. "Conditions in Carnival are—" He broke off abruptly, conscious of the listening cowpunchers on the Bonanza porch, and finished lamely, "It's warm for so early in the year."

"Damned hot, I call it," Sanford replied. "Well, I'll be seeing you, Gage."

"So long, James. Take care of yourself."

Sanford moved on and again stopped, a few doors farther on, before the locked entrance of a good-sized rock-and-adobe building, the high wooden false front of which bore a sun-faded and sand-blasted sign reading: THE CARNIVAL BANNER. Sanford inserted a key in the lock, opened the door, withdrew the key to place it in the inner keyhole, and stepped inside, leaving the door standing open.

By this time Gage Freeman had resumed his sweeping. After a few minutes he stopped. "It's sure hot," he mused. "I wonder if James would care to take a beer with me before he leaves for the depot."

Freeman bent his gaze in the direction of the *Banner* building while he considered the idea. He could see, beneath the wooden awning that projected above the sidewalk in front of the newspaper building, that the door to the *Banner* office stood open. Even while he gazed, however, Freeman saw the door slowly swing shut; he could almost imagine he heard the key turn on the inner side.

"I reckon not," Freeman muttered disappointedly. "Probably James has some pressin' business to clean up before he leaves and doesn't want to be bothered." Making a couple of more desultory "swipes" with the broom, he concluded it was too hot for further sweeping and retired inside his store to await the coming of the first customer.

He had scarcely taken up a position behind one of his long counters when he heard a noise that resembled a revolver explosion. Freeman stiffened. "Was that a shot?" He started toward the doorway. There came a second, similar sound, though this time it wasn't so loud. For a brief moment Freeman thought he might be hearing an echo of the first shot, though he decided almost instantly the sounds were spaced too far apart for that.

Reaching his doorway, Freeman glanced involuntarily toward the Bonanza Bar, where the cowboys had been lounging, and was just in time to see one of the punchers leap over the porch rail and start on a run in a northerly direction along Flagstaff Street. The others punchers descended to Main and started east, glancing about as they moved, as though endeavoring to determine from what direction the shots had come.

By the time the punchers had drawn abreast of the *Banner* building a man had popped, hatless, out of the barbershop next door to the newspaper office. Gage Freeman heard him say, "I'd swear that shot came from Sanford's place." He looked wildly about and then swung toward the *Banner* door. Before he could reach it, however, the cowboys had gathered about the door and one of them was rattling the knob and knocking on the panel. The man from the barbershop brushed past them and tried to look in through the big front window, composed of a number of smaller panes, that stretched four fifths of the way across the building.

Men were hastening from all directions. A crowd gathered before the *Banner* building. Somebody mentioned sending for the deputy sheriff. A couple of men went sprinting east on Main Street. Gage Freeman left his store and hurried across the road. He noticed, as he pushed through the crowd, that the cowboys were still clustered about the closed door of the newspaper building, as though to prevent anyone from drawing near. That thought flashed through Freeman's mind, and then another: "But why should they?" There was a good deal of excited speculation in the crowd now.

Freeman worked his way through the jam until he'd reached the knot of cowboys. Standing directly before him was a wide-shouldered man with sandy hair, topaz eyes, and a close-cropped mustache, dressed in corduroy pants, white shirt, boots, and a wide-brimmed sombrero. A black string tie held his collar at the throat and a six-shooter was swung from the cartridge belt that encircled his hips.

Freeman said, "What's up, Rufe?"

Rufe Harper rested his cold yellow eyes on the owner of the general store. "Didn't you hear a shot?"

"I heard two shots, but—"

"No," Harper stated definitely, "you heard only one shot. I *know*. I heard it too."

"All right, have it your way," Freeman snapped in exasperation. "One shot, if you insist, but what did it mean? Is Sanford in there? What has happened to—?"

"We don't know what it means—yet," Harper said coldly. "We're not even sure it came from the *Banner* office. Now, wait a minute, Freeman. Don't go off half-cocked. Hell no, I don't know if Sanford is in there or not. We called to him, but no one replied. The door is locked, and until—"

"Damn it!" Freeman jerked out. "Let's break it open!"

"Hold your horses," Harper advised soothingly. "Anything that's done will be done lawfully. Deputy Bayliss will be here in a minute. If he says break open that door, I'll be more than glad to accommodate."

"But if Sanford is inside—wounded . . ." Freeman protested excitedly. "Maybe somebody's shot him. Whoever did it might get out the back door—Sanford might be bleeding to death. I insist you break that lock."

Harper laughed contemptuously. "Did you see anybody enter here—besides Sanford? You were on your porch when Sanford arrived. Hell! You were talking to him. I heard you. Well, did you see anybody go in after him?"

"We-ell," Freeman said uncertainly. "I was inside my store right after—"

"How do you know, then," Harper said triumphantly, "that Sanford didn't leave here for the depot? Do you want to be responsible for destroying his property? We don't even know that shot came from here. Maybe there wasn't any shot. It might have been some other noise."

"T'hell with that," Gage Freeman said angrily. "Break that lock; I'll take full responsibility."

One of the crowd pressed against the window raised his voice, his face flattened against the pane: "Looks like I can see a man's foot and part of a leg on the floor."

Someone else called, "Break down that door!"

"That's right, Harper," Freeman snapped. "Break it in, or I'm holding *you* responsible."

Harper laughed scornfully. "You'll hold me responsible? Responsible for what?" He made no move to do as Freeman requested, though the cowboys about him looked questioningly at their chief, while more precious moments were lost in argument. However, the crowd also took up the cry: "Break in that door!"

"If you'd just be patient until Deputy Bayliss gets here . . ." Harper commenced, then shrugged his wide shoulders. "All right, if everybody insists." Still he hesitated, frowning. Suddenly his face cleared as he glanced above the heads of the crowd. "Here comes Bayliss now. We'll have this door open in a jiffy."

"It'd be a good idea to have Doc Glover here too," Freeman commenced, "just in case there is anything wrong with—"

"I sent for Glover—same time as I sent for Bayliss," Harper cut in mockingly. "I'm not an entire fool, Freeman."

Deputy Sheriff Bayliss, a potbellied individual with walrus mustaches, came panting up to the scene. "What's wrong here?" he demanded importantly.

A dozen voices informed him. Rufe Harper added, "There was a lot of agitation, Deputy Bayliss, for breaking in this door, but I thought it best to wait until you got here before destroying private property."

"Quite right, too," Bayliss nodded. "All right, break 'er in, somebody."

The crowd surged forward as Harper turned and put one muscular shoulder against the locked door. Freeman's mind was working coolly now. He was sure Sanford would be found dead, or at least badly wounded, inside. Whoever did it would surely have escaped by the rear entrance. The thing to do was to get through to the rear as soon as possible and see if some trail might not be picked up, some clue found. Harper again lunged at the door. There came a sudden splintering of wood as the lock gave way. The door swung open. Instantly Freeman caught the odor of burned powder from the narrow corridor which lay ahead.

Harper was first inside, followed by the cowboys who had been clustered about him. Freeman came next. A sudden oath left Harper's lips as the men glanced through a doorway into the *Banner* office. There on the floor, not far from his desk, was sprawled the motionless body of James Sanford. A gun was clutched in one hand and he lay face down.

A heavy lump rose in Freeman's throat. He heard Harper snap, "Don't anybody touch that body!" as the crowd surged in from outside. Then Harper's further words: "It looks like suicide."

"Suicide hell!" Freeman groaned. He left the

office doorway and started through to the big back room where the printing press and other equipment stood, his eyes glued to the rear door beyond that opened into an alley behind the building. Apparently other men had the same idea. For a brief instant, in the narrow passageway between office and printing plant, the way was blocked by men. Harper's cowboys got through first; the rest of the crowd surged after them. Somehow Freeman squirmed and fought his way through and was first to reach the back door. Then his heart sank: he had expected to find the door unlocked, but it was bolted tightly shut. One thing was certain: the assassin hadn't made his escape through the rear door.

Rebellious frustration took hold of Freeman. Sudden anger surged in his heart. "It's locked!" he snarled furiously.

The whole building was filled with men by this time, though most of the curious were bunched about the doorway where the dead man lay. The men collected near the printing press looked curiously at Freeman. Several of them pressed forward to examine the bolted door. With a sinking heart, Freeman pushed back in the direction of the spot where the publisher of the Carnival *Banner* had breathed his last. Dr. Glover had arrived by this time and had turned the body on its back. One of the cowboys pushed past Freeman and said something to Rufe Harper, who was kneeling at the side of the doctor's crouching form.

Glover listened intently, then a frown crossed his face. "I hate to think so," he said slowly, "but if the back door and front door were locked, there isn't any other answer. Sanford committed suicide. Has anybody notified Kate of this yet?"

Nobody had thought to break the news to Sanford's daughter, apparently. Freeman said, "I'll take care of that. He lived next door to us." With eyes blinking rapidly, he left the *Banner* office and headed in the direction of his home, on Beaumont Street, one block over. Here, after breaking the news to his wife and requesting her to handle the sad matter of passing the information on to Sanford's daughter Kate, he returned to his general store.

By this time one of his clerks had arrived, and Freeman once more crossed the street to the *Banner* building, arriving there just in time to see men from the undertaker's bearing the body away. Deputy Bayliss was pompously ordering the throng of curious to leave the building and go about their business, but there was still a number of men, including Harper and his cowboys, clustered about the front of the building, discussing the tragedy.

Considerably shaken by the death of his old friend, Freeman stood uncertainly near the hitch rack, before the newspaper office, endeavoring to collect his thoughts. After a few minutes Freeman noticed, standing on the edge of the sidewalk a few feet away, a tall, lean individual in overalls, riding boots, woolen shirt, and black sombrero. Freeman wondered who he was; undoubtedly a stranger in town. The man was somewhere between twenty-five and thirty, with a firm chin, straight lips, and rather tousled black hair beneath the tilted-back Stetson. His face held a somewhat sardonic expression that was belied by the tiny laugh wrinkles at the corners of his level gray eyes. At his right thigh hung a Colt's forty-four six-shooter. Without knowing why, Freeman felt himself drawn to the man.

Even while Freeman stood staring at him the stranger vaulted lightly over the hitch rail and moved in the direction of a tethered buckskin gelding. Gathering the reins in his hand, the man slowly shook his head and said something that sounded like, "People are sure fools."

Freeman spoke without thinking: "Meanin' just what?"

The man standing near the buckskin raised his head in some surprise, then smiled. "Didn't realize I was talking out loud, mister. But I'll let it lay as is."

"Meanin' just what?" Freeman said again.

The man with the black hair looked keenly at Freeman. "Do you," he questioned flatly, jerking his head in the direction of the *Banner* office, "believe that was suicide?"

"Why—er—I—" Freeman felt bewildered. "Doc Glover allowed it was suicide."

"Your doc," the stranger said flatly, "is one of three things. He's stupid, he's crooked—or maybe he's just plain mistaken. That wasn't suicide by a long shot. That was murder!"

"By God!" Freeman burst out. "I knew it!"

Rufe Harper and his cow hands had moved closer while the two were talking. Now Harper spoke, coldly, venomously: "You're both fools. Any man who says Sanford didn't commit suicide is a liar!"

The stranger smiled thinly and cocked one quizzical black eyebrow in Harper's direction. "Y'know," he said easily, "I don't take kindly to that. Any man calls me a liar usually has to back his language with a fistful of shooting iron." He lounged carelessly against the saddle of the buckskin pony, thumbs hooked in cartridge belt. "Howsomever, I'm unknown to you, so I'm inclined to give you another chance. Mister, either apologize almighty sudden or fill your mitt. Now, think fast. I'm getting plumb impatient!"

2. STORMY KNIGHT

The buzz of conversation about the men had suddenly ceased. Several of the crowd moved warily to one side, eyes still intent on Harper and the black-haired stranger. Harper's hard tiger eyes bore into the stranger's level gray ones. The black-haired man spoke again, softly: "Think fast, mister—or fill your mitt."

Harper considered swiftly: he felt certain in his own mind that he could beat the stranger to the shot. And yet there was a definite air of confidence about the man that gave Harper pause. What was it the fellow had said? Oh yes, *I'm unknown to you, so I'm inclined to give you another chance.* What, exactly, did the man mean by that? Harper decided to go slow until he was certain of treading on safer ground. The stranger might be some famous gunman; then again he might be only bluffing. Was it worth taking a chance? The wily Harper figured it wasn't. Still, how was he to get out of this?

Harper's cowboys stood close, glaring at the black-haired man, ready to take up the boss's fight if necessary. There was Cameo Sloan, cobra-like and slim, with two guns; the bulky-shouldered 'Brose Echardt, foreman of Harper's Anvil outfit; Muley Porter, unshaven and always looking for trouble; Steve Gooch, of the belligerent jaw and hard eye; Squint Amber, undersized, sneaking, but deadly with a six-shooter. There were a couple of others as well, but none of the Harper men seemed to be getting any of the black-haired man's attention.

Cameo Sloan's swarthy features contorted angrily. He spoke from the corner of his mouth: "Say the word, Rufe, and I'll let him have it."

Harper's eyes never left those of the stranger. Neither did he reply to Sloan. It was never wise to rush hastily into anything; it might be best to learn first just what this fellow was doing in Carnival if possible. But how to back down gracefully Harper couldn't quite decide. Intervention by Deputy Sheriff Bayliss solved the problem.

"Look here, you two"—Bayliss finally found his voice—"I don't want any gun-slinging. I'm the law in Carnival and—"

"Hush up, Fatty," the black-haired man interrupted, gray eyes still boring into Big Rufe Harper's. "This has gone too far for you to stop. I've been called a liar, and I aim to have satisfaction one way or the other. I'm not standing for anybody—not anybody—cutting in on this game."

Harper forced a smile. "Deputy Bayliss is right, Mister Man. There's been enough trouble here for one day. It ill befits my position in Carnival for me to make rash statements when I judge you were speaking sincerely. Let's forget it. My name's Harper—my friends call me Rufe."

The tension instantly eased, though there were many in the crowd, including Harper's cow-punchers, who looked their amazement at Harper's backing down. The black-haired stranger nodded easily. "We all make mistakes one time or another," he said. "My name's Knight—my friends call me Stormy. Believe me, it's a misnomer. I'm all for peace myself, though"— his gray eyes twinkled—"I sure don't like to be pushed around none."

Neither Knight nor Harper had offered to shake hands. Right now Knight's fingers were employed in rolling a brown-paper cigarette. Harper said something in an aside to Bayliss. Bayliss nodded and raised his voice:

"Knight, none of us like to be pushed around. That's all been peaceably settled, now that Mayor Harper has consented—"

"*Mayor* Harper?" Knight cut in incredulously. "You mean he's mayor of Carnival?"

"Certainly," Bayliss blustered. "It's an affront to our civic dignity to have a stranger ride in here and question a statement made by our duly elected representative—"

"Cut the political speeches, Bayliss, and get down to brass tacks," Harper said contemptuously. He turned to Knight. "What the deputy is trying to say is you made a statement, a spell back, to the effect that James Sanford had been murdered. What you basing that on? . . . Bayliss, isn't that what you intended to ask?"

"Took the words right out of my mouth," Bayliss assented glibly. "And furthermore, Knight, I'm demanding to know what you're doing in Carnival. For a stranger you seem to know a heck of a lot when you state, flat out, that Sanford didn't commit suicide. Where did you get that fool idea? We all know Sanford was killed by a gunshot. The gun was still in his hand. Both the front and rear doors of his place of business were locked on the inside. No murderer could have done that and still escaped. Excepting for Sanford's dead body, there was no one in the building when we broke down that door."

Knight's gray eyes narrowed. "Shots have been fired through windows," he pointed out.

"Hah!" Bayliss exclaimed triumphantly, turning and sweeping one hand in the direction of the broad front window of the newspaper office. "Do you see any broken windows there? Perhaps"—chuckling—"you're maintaining the murderer fired his bullet through a rear window, said bullet dodging the printing press and all that other machinery in the back, then making a turn to enter Sanford's office and striking him plumb in the heart."

A guffaw went up from the crowd. Bayliss held up one hand for silence and continued: "No, it won't go down, Knight. I personally examined both front and back windows. None of 'em were broken. Now it's your turn to think fast, Mr. Stormy Knight."

Knight smiled good-naturedly. "Looks like what I bit off might take a mite of chewing. Let's go back a spell. You asked what I was doing in Carnival. Well, I just happened to be riding through. The crowd here attracted my attention. When I saw some hombres breaking down the door, I was just curious enough to see why. I followed on in. I saw the dead man on the floor; I heard what the doctor had to say. It was Harper who put out the suicide idea. The doctor fell into line—"

"It couldn't be anything else but suicide," Harper said earnestly. "Consider the circumstances, Knight. If I happened to be the first one to term it suicide, that's just because I happened to see the body first. Any sensible man would have done the same thing."

"No sensible man would jump to hasty conclusions," Knight said flatly. He drew deeply on his cigarette. "Are you maintaining the whole subject should be dropped on your say-so, Mister Mayor?"

Harper flushed and hesitated. "I'm not doing anything of the sort if something in the way of concrete evidence can be produced to show that Sanford was murdered. You've said too much, or too little, Knight. I'm demanding an explanation."

"Demanding?" Knight cocked that quizzical black eyebrow at Harper and smiled tolerantly. "Let's say I'm willing to give an explanation. You see, it's my contention that the murderer could have escaped by the rear door. When the front door was broken in, men swarmed inside. Was there anything to prevent the murderer having a confederate in the crowd? That confederate could have locked that rear door in the excitement."

Harper snorted skeptically and turned toward Gage Freeman. "Gage, you got anything to offer this amateur detective on that angle?"

"Reckon I have," Freeman said reluctantly. "Knight, it's a good idea. I had one like it myself, even before we entered the building. I made up my mind to be first to reach that rear door—"

"And it was locked when you got there?" Knight asked, a twinge of disappointment showing in his tones.

"It was locked—bolted tight," Freeman stated.

"Could someone have reached that door before you did?" Knight asked narrowly.

"Yeah, they could have," Freeman admitted, "but not without me seein' 'em. Once inside that front door, a man only has to take three-four steps and he can see straight through to the back."

Cameo Sloan said insultingly, "Some hombres couldn't see straight if you pointed it out to 'em."

"That was meant for me, of course," Knight said

pleasantly. "Just about two black eyes and you wouldn't see a-tall—and, so help me, another crack like that, mister, and your orbs are sure going to go into mourning."

"You looking for trouble?" Cameo snarled.

"Never had to look for it," Knight said lazily. "It just naturally seems to seek me out. Howsomever," he added, smiling, "I've managed to keep my health. Take my advice and you'll make sure of doing the same."

"Why, damn your hide—" Sloan commenced.

"Cut it out, Cameo," Harper said sharply. Sloan fell silent, though he continued to glare at Knight.

"Take the leash off, Harper," Knight chuckled. "I'd like to see if your friend Cameo is as tough as he thinks he is."

"Now looky here, Knight," Deputy Bayliss blustered, "if you're trying to start trouble—"

"Did I start this?" Knight asked blandly. "I was on my way to my horse, minding my own business. You hombres started firing questions at me. I've done my best to answer—and I'm still not taking any pushing around."

"You're finally convinced, though," Harper said, "that this was just an ordinary suicide, aren't you?"

Knight shook his head. "A damned clever murder," he contradicted.

"Hell, you're crazy as a hoot owl," Harper growled.

24

"Could be." Knight shrugged carelessly. "But before I agree with you I'd like to talk to that doctor. Where is he?"

"He left when the body was taken away," Bayliss said. "What you want to see Doc Glover about?"

"Maybe I'll tell you when I've seen him," Knight replied shortly.

"Knight," Bayliss said testily, "I don't like your attitude. You either know more than you're telling or you're a fool. For all I know, you've had something to do with this killing yourself."

"You admit it's a killing, then?" Knight said swiftly.

"Certainly he doesn't," Harper interrupted. "Bayliss knows it was suicide, nothing else."

"That's nice." Knight smiled thinly. "Then there's no reason to question me further, Deputy Bayliss."

Bayliss looked uncertainly from Harper to Knight. Finally, "Don't you be in no hurry to leave Carnival," he stated.

"You intending to arrest me?" Knight asked.

Bayliss shook his head. "Not yet, leastwise. But you stick around in case I want to ask any questions."

"Regarding what?"

"Dammit!" Bayliss exclaimed exasperatedly. "What do you think we've been talking about?"

Knight grinned. "Sometimes I'm not sure. Are you?"

Bayliss' face crimsoned. Abruptly he jerked around and bawled at the crowd: "Come on, get moving! The excitement's over. Clear the street. Hey, you, Johnson, get a hammer and some spikes. I want to nail up that door we broke down." He continued to shout further orders.

The throng commenced to disperse. Harper and his cowboys headed in the direction of the Bonanza Bar. Just before leaving, Harper glanced over his shoulder in Knight's direction. "I'll be seeing you again," he said cryptically.

Knight nodded. "Any time you say," he returned quietly. Once more he turned to gather up his pony's reins, then stopped. Gage Freeman was standing a few feet away. Knight smiled and said, "It's damn hot."

Gage nodded, catching the idea. "I was about to mention a bottle of beer—or whatever you say."

"Brew suits me. What's the best place in Carnival?"

"Let's cut across to the Pegasus Saloon," Freeman suggested.

Knight again tossed his pony's reins over the hitch rail and fell into step at Freeman's side. They had reached the opposite sidewalk when Knight stopped. "I still think it was murder," he stated doggedly.

"So do I," Freeman agreed, mopping his wet forehead, "but I'm danged if I can understand how—"

"How about that deputy? Is he on the square?"

Freeman frowned. "Oh, Bayliss is honest enough, I reckon. He's a blowhard, stupid; he lets Harper run all over him. However, I'd hesitate to call him downright crooked."

"We'll put him down as a fool. How about the doctor who examined the body?"

"Doc Glover? Square as a die. I've known Beriah Glover for a good many years now, and I'd stake my life on him."

"All right. But even an honest man can make a mistake. I want to talk to him. Can we postpone that beer a mite longer?"

"Hell yes, if it will help clear up anything. Doc ought to be home by this time. He lives over on Beaumont Street, right at the corner of Ogden. Got his office there too. Let's see if he's home."

Ten minutes later Stormy Knight was talking earnestly to Dr. Beriah Glover, a tall spare man with grizzled features and sharp blue eyes. Glover listened intently, frowned. "Jeepers!" he said irritably when Stormy had finished, "I never thought of that. Maybe I'm just a plain damned fool. Trouble is I took too much for granted. When Rufe Harper said it was suicide I took his word for it—but with those doors both locked from the inside—"

"I know," Stormy said. "That fact has got me pawing at the air too, but if we can clear up one thing at a time, maybe we'll get someplace."

"Right," Glover said crisply. "Just wait until I get my case and I'll be with you."

The three men left the doctor's home and walked briskly along a cottonwood-shaded street until they had again reached Main. On the way Glover said to Freeman, "You seen Kate yet?"

Somewhat shamefacedly Freeman shook his head. "I left that job to my missus."

"Can't say I blame you, in a way," Glover replied. "Your wife came with her to the undertaker's when I was there. I'd just got back to my office when you and Knight came in."

"How's Kate taking it?" Freeman asked.

"Like a champion, of course," Glover replied promptly. "You can't beat that girl." He added for Stormy's benefit, "Sanford's daughter. A likely looking girl, too. Oh, by the way, did you see anything of Sanford's satchel, Gage?"

Freeman frowned. "Say, I never thought of that. I remember he was carrying a satchel when he passed this morning. It's probably in his office."

"I certainly hope so," Glover said fervently. "Kate says he had three thousand dollars in it."

"Three thous—" Freeman's eyes bugged out. "Good God!"

"Now I'm sure it's murder," Stormy said softly. "Aces to tens that satchel won't be found in Sanford's office."

"As soon as Kate told me," Glover continued, "I

28

sent word to Bayliss to grab onto that satchel. I didn't mention there was money in it."

"Your messenger must have arrived after we left," Stormy said. "And I don't reckon it would do any good for us to go back to Sanford's office now. Either that satchel is still there, which same I doubt, or it was stolen when Sanford was killed."

"Just the same," Freeman said, "I'm going to get to the *Banner* office as quick as I can. Somebody has to look out for Kate's welfare. Stormy, you and Doc can go on to the undertaker's without me. I'll see you later." Without waiting for his companions to reply, Freeman turned and hastened west along Main Street. After a few steps he broke into a run.

3. STOLEN MONEY

It was going on eleven o'clock by the time Stormy Knight again bent his steps in the direction of the newspaper office. He strode along Main, thoughts intent on the tragedy that had taken place and the fresh information he now had to substantiate his murder theory. The sun, nearing meridian now, made the atmosphere almost stifling. Mostly, the townspeople were remaining indoors or seeking the shelter to be found on shaded porches or between buildings.

There was no one outside the *Banner* office when he arrived, but Stormy heard voices from within. The door, with its broken lock, still stood wide open. Stormy entered the short, narrow corridor that led back to the printing shop. From this point he could see the printing press and had an unobscured view of the closed rear door. Next he noticed a couple of men loitering back there. He hesitated but a moment, then, figuring they might be there under Bayliss' orders, turned right through the doorway into Sanford's partitioned-off office, which stretched nearly across the front of the building.

As Stormy came into the office he saw Gage Freeman and Deputy Bayliss standing there aimlessly. Freeman looked downcast, sorely disappointed regarding what had happened. The deputy's flabby features held an expression of irritation combined with stupidity. Freeman's eyes instantly sought Stormy's as the latter entered the office. Stormy nodded slightly, then asked, "Did you find that satchel?"

Slowly Bayliss shook his head. Freeman said, "It's gone, as I expected." Bayliss went on: "If there was ever a satchel here, I don't see how it could get out—"

"I keep telling you," Freeman said testily, "that I saw James Sanford carry that satchel into this office. The satchel's gone, and with it three thousand dollars."

"Probably," Bayliss said sarcastically, "the murderer who escaped—after locking both doors on the inside—made 'way with the money too— just walked right through the walls with said satchel in his hand and then vanished into thin air. Oh hell! There wasn't any murderer, and I don't believe there was any satchel either. Any fool can see this was a case of suicide."

"All right," Stormy said quietly, "we'll let the fools go on thinking that way. Let's pretend for a minute, Bayliss, that you're not a fool. What type gun killed Sanford?"

Bayliss said in some surprise, "Why, Sanford's own double-action, thirty-eight-caliber revolver. Everybody knows that. It was in his hand when he was found. He only bought that gun about three weeks ago—probably had suicide in mind then—"

"You insist it's a thirty-eight-caliber slug that killed him, though," Stormy cut in.

"Certain. I've got the gun right here in my hip pocket, holdin' it for evidence should anything come up. I've examined it thorough. One shell has been fired."

Stormy nodded. "I heard you say that before." He took from his pocket a small leaden object which he handed to the deputy. "Take a look and tell me what you call this."

Bayliss scrutinized the somewhat battered chunk of metal, then raised wary eyes to meet Stormy's. "Looks to me like it might be the lead out of a forty-five ca'tridge. Where did it come from?"

Stormy said calmly, "That's the slug that killed Sanford. Doc Glover probed it out, down to the undertaker's, a short spell back."

Freeman said eagerly, "You called the turn, then, Stormy!"

"I reckon," Stormy nodded.

"But how—" Bayliss commenced.

"Listen," Stormy said, "I was in this office when the doctor arrived. I saw him turn the body over, rip open the shirt, and examine the wound. No thirty-eight makes a wound as big as the one over Sanford's heart. I had a hunch then it was a forty-five did the business."

Bayliss looked somewhat bewildered. "Maybe it is murder," he blurted, then, "No, it couldn't be. Sanford was locked in here by himself. Cripes! My eyes must be deceiving me." He looked again at the lead bullet in his hand. "This has just got to be a thirty-eight."

"Weighs too much for that," Stormy said tersely. "Hell, man, look at the size of it." Bayliss didn't reply. Stormy went on, "Hang on to it for evidence, Bayliss. Doc Glover is aiming to hold an inquest tonight. He asked me to tell you to round up a coroner's jury for him. He stands ready to swear that the bullet he removed from Sanford's body was not a thirty-eight. Now how do you feel about my murder theory?"

Bayliss had no reply for that. Freeman said, "But, dammit, with both doors locked . . . ?" His voice dwindled off to silence. No one spoke for a time. Stormy rolled and lighted a cigarette and glanced about Sanford's office.

The office was oblong in form, with its walls running clear to the ceiling, and stretched along the big front window of the building. Next to the window was a long table, at the foot of which Sanford's body had been found. A deep red stain at this point was already turning a darker hue as it seeped into the bare plank flooring. On the table were a few books and newspapers. Across the office from the table a bookcase stood against the inner wall. At one end was a coat rack; beyond the bookcase, near the office entrance, stood a small sheet-iron stove which, naturally, held no fire at this season of the year.

At the farther end of the office stood a wide, roll-top desk, cluttered with pencils, loose sheets of paper, paste, a pair of shears. A swivel chair, now facing away from the desk, held a faded cushion on its seat. Stormy crossed over and seated himself on the chair. To his left he noticed a small drawer drawn partly out of the desk. The drawer held some papers and other odds and ends. He studied the floor a moment in thought, then glanced up, gazing straight ahead. Now he found himself looking through the open door of the office into the narrow passageway that joined the pressroom and the front door to the building.

"What you looking for?" Bayliss asked curiously.

"I don't know—for certain," Stormy replied, frowning. He glanced through the wide window to his left, as though to say something more, then paused as a noise from beyond the partition caught his attention. "Who's out there in that back room?"

"God only knows," Bayliss said wearily. "Folks keep wandering in and out. I've told 'em to keep out of here, but seems like they don't pay me any attention."

"They're full of a sort of morbid curiosity, I reckon," Freeman commented.

"I don't know what you call it," Bayliss said

aggrievedly, "but there was one queer-lookin' hombre, wearin' a hard-boiled hat, that I had to chuck out twice."

"Who is he?" Stormy asked.

Bayliss shrugged his shoulders. "You got me. I never saw him before. Stranger in town, I guess."

Stormy said, "Let's go see who's out there now."

The three men stepped into the narrow corridor beyond the entrance to the office and headed back toward the big rear room. Directly ahead was a tall, round-bellied cast-iron stove, cold at present. Beyond that was a table, and next stood the printing press, occupying most of a rear corner. There was a smell of printer's ink and grease in the room; ink stained the cleanly swept floor at spots. Across the room from the press, in the opposite corner, stood a type case and tall wooden stool. A few feet from the stool, ranged against the wall, was a shelved rack holding large stacked sheets of paper of varying size and weight. A few carboys of ink stood about. Standing near the front wall of the room—the wooden partition that formed one wall of Sanford's office—was a paper-cutting machine, and across the corner formed by the wooden wall and the outer adobe wall of the building had been built a triangular closet, the door of which now stood closed.

Stormy ran his quick gaze through the room, then it came to rest on a couple of men. One of them stood near the table, perusing a copy of the previous day's issue of the Carnival *Banner*, several of which lay stacked on the table before him. The other man stood near the printing press, gazing with evident fascination at the machine and apparently unconscious of the approach of Stormy and his two companions.

Bayliss ripped out a curse. "Dammit! I've told everybody to stay out of this building."

The man with the newspaper grinned. "All right, Bayliss. No need you gettin' peeved. I'm takin' this paper, if you don't mind; it's got a piece about my cousin in Corto City."

"Take it and get out!" Bayliss snapped. The man departed leisurely, reading the paper as he went. Bayliss turned his attention to the individual near the press. "You again! I already run you out twice. What do you want in here?"

"Don't want anything from you," the man replied coolly. He gestured toward the printing press. "I'm just trying to figure out how this thing runs."

He was a medium-sized, narrow-shouldered, wiry individual in shabby town clothing. A black derby hat, rapidly turning green, was plastered on one side of his head of stringy brown hair. When he talked his Adam's apple bobbed loosely above a soiled celluloid collar. He needed a shave, and his long nose had a distinct alcoholic glow. In direct contrast to this, the man's eyes showed character: they were sharp and intelligent looking.

Bayliss swore again. "What t'ell do you care how it runs?"

The man murmured cryptically, "The power of that press is indeed strange, Mr. Deputy Sheriff."

"By jeez!" Bayliss snorted. "That press is no stranger than you. What's your name?"

"My name's Wrangel—Quad Wrangel. I'm new to Carnival. Just got in late last night."

"Meaning," Bayliss growled, "that you bummed your way on the freight that passes through here. There's no late passenger train stops. Well, we don't like bums in this town. You catch yourself a job, pronto, or move on. Now, get out of here!"

"But, Deputy, I'm—"

"Get out, I said!"

Wrangel shrugged his skinny shoulders. "You win," he said briefly, and took his departure from the building. Bayliss glared after him. "More damn hoboes hit this town," the deputy complained.

But Stormy wasn't listening. He had already crossed to the closet in the corner and opened the door. After a moment he closed it. Freeman said, "We, also, thought of looking in there for that satchel, Stormy. And we looked on top of that paper rack too. We even looked in the stove. The money's plumb gone."

Frowning, Stormy returned to the center of the room. In the rear wall a large window composed of many panes of glass, similar to the window in the front of the building, threw light on the printing press. All the panes were intact. Placed high in the wall, above the type case, was a small window; a second small window let in light above the table next to the printing press. Stormy gazed at them, brow furrowed with thought wrinkles.

Freeman guessed what was on his mind. "It's no good, Stormy," he said. "None of these windows were made to open. They're built in tight. Any air gets in comes through the doorways."

Stormy shrugged disappointedly. "I reckon I'm stopped for the time being. Next best thing to do is go get my dinner."

"That's the right attitude," Bayliss nodded. "Forget this idea of murder. It couldn't be anything else but suicide."

Stormy looked disgustedly at him and headed for the street without saying anything. Freeman and the deputy followed behind, Bayliss mentioning something that had to do with nailing up the front door of the building until the new owner took charge.

Stormy whirled sharply. "Who's the new owner? Won't Sanford's daughter continue to publish the paper?"

"Don't reckon so," Bayliss replied. "That girl couldn't run it alone. Ten to one Rufe Harper will buy her out. He's been trying to get Sanford to sell for a long time now."

Stormy continued on until he reached the sidewalk. "So it's like that, eh?" he said softly, half to himself. Freeman looked queerly at him. Stormy gave him a half-smile. "C'mon, Gage, let's find that Pegasus Saloon you mentioned a while back. I'm plumb dry."

The two men crossed the street. Even before they entered the saloon Bayliss was busying himself with hammer and spikes at the front door of the *Banner* building.

4. POWDER SMOKE!

The coroner's inquest Dr. Glover had called for that evening was completed and the verdict in—a verdict of "Suicide." Stormy wasn't completely surprised; it had been about what he expected. He, Dr. Glover, and Gage Freeman stood talking before the frame building, flattered by the designation of Town Hall, in which the inquest had been held. A few lights still shone along Main Street. A number of pedestrians were to be seen hastening toward their homes or dropping into one of the saloons for a nightcap. Big Rufe Harper and his crew were even now entering the Bonanza and lining up at the bar to drink and discuss the inquest. Other men, in other bars, were arguing the pros and cons of the evidence that had been brought out. It was near ten o'clock.

"Well," Dr. Glover sighed, "I guess there's nothing we can do about changing the verdict."

"This town," Freeman said wrathfully, "is ninety per cent jackass."

"Aren't you putting your estimate rather low?" Glover smiled. "I did hope, though, the size of that bullet would convince the jury it wasn't suicide."

Stormy said, "The doors being locked on the inside was the fact they couldn't get around. And your jury didn't give much consideration to that missing satchel, either."

"I was the only one could swear I'd seen that satchel," Freeman said moodily. "I think if we could have had Kate there to swear that her father had three thousand dollars in—"

"I just couldn't insist on that girl being present," Glover cut in. "She's going through enough as it is."

"Stormy," Gage said bluntly, "I had a feeling you didn't testify to all you knew."

"Let's just say," Stormy said slowly, "that I testified to all I had proof of. After all, this inquest isn't final. When—and if—I get some real evidence, there can still be an arrest made. But let's drop the subject for now. I'm plumb dry for some more of that Pegasus beer."

Freeman and Stormy said good night to the doctor, then strolled along Main Street until they'd reached the Pegasus Saloon, which was operated by One-Horse Shea, a gray-haired man with an affable manner and a white apron tied about his generous middle. There were only a few customers in the bar when they entered, among them Quad Wrangel, whom Stormy and Freeman had encountered earlier that day in the press-room of the *Banner*. Wrangel looked up from the glass of whisky before him and nodded. Freeman and Stormy returned the greeting.

"What'll it be, gentlemen?" Shea asked. "Glad

to see you again, Mr. Knight. Hope you got that room at the hotel all right."

"I did, One-Horse. And my pony is being taken care of at that livery you recommended. I'll take another bottle of that Texas beer." The drinks were served, and Shea moved away, down the bar, where he stood talking with Wrangel. Stormy continued to Freeman, speaking low-voiced, "Gage, you had to get back to your store today, but I've been wanting to ask you a few things."

"One of 'em bein', I suppose," Freeman said a trifle bitterly, "just why Carnival has a man like Rufe Harper for its mayor. Well, I said a spell back that this town was ninety per cent jackass. That still goes—and I'm including myself among the ninety per cent. I'm as much to blame as anybody. Our last mayor died. Harper had just come here and bought the Anvil Ranch and allowed as how he had money to spend in developing a town business too. We didn't know him then like we do now. That's three years ago. He himself suggested that we appoint him mayor until next election. I took it up with the town council—I'm chairman—and we decided to appoint him."

"And he's held office ever since?" Stormy asked.

Freeman nodded. "When election came Harper had his votes lined up, and any opposition there was was snowed under. It was simply that none of the honest men in town were interested enough to pay any attention to what was going on. So damned busy chasing the almighty dollar and having fun that a lot of 'em didn't even vote. Harper got stronger and stronger, and now he practically runs Carnival—makin' money, too, what with his ranch and gamblin' interests. Oh, he's the big boss here all right."

"Where does James Sanford fit in?"

"Sanford distrusted Harper from the first, but he couldn't make us see it. James had a mighty good head on him. He's fought Harper and his schemes from the beginning—through the Carnival *Banner*, of course. That newspaper is the one thing that has kept Harper from getting the complete upper hand on us. Harper tried to buy him out a year ago, so the paper could be run along the lines the gambling interests favored. That didn't work. Six months ago somebody broke into the *Banner* building and used a sledge hammer on the press. Sanford got going again— Oh hell! We're licked this time, I'm afeared."

"No chance of his daughter carrying on?"

Freeman shook his head. "That paper needs a man at the helm. Kate's smart, but there's a limit to what a woman can do. I suppose she'll sell out to Harper now. It's about all she has left to do. But if her dad had lived just a mite longer we could have really cleaned up this town—and it sure needs cleaning."

"Sanford's wife dead?"

43

"Died when Kate was a little girl," Freeman replied.

One-Horse Shea came waddling down the bar. "Ready for anything more?" Both men shook their heads. Shea continued, "I understand you're taking over the *Banner*, Mr. Knight."

Stormy smiled. "Who you trying to kid now, One-Horse?"

"It's a fact," Shea said earnestly. "It's rumored all over town that you're buying the newspaper. A couple of fellers in here earlier mentioned it." He jerked one thumb in Quad Wrangel's direction. "I was talking to him about it just now."

Stormy's jaw dropped. "Somebody's gone plumb batty."

Quad Wrangel joined, them. Stormy questioned him. Wrangel said, "Sure, I heard it in the Oasis Saloon, the Bonanza, and a couple other drinking places. Don't tell me it isn't true?"

"That's exactly what I am telling you," Stormy snorted. "What would I do with the Carnival *Banner*? I know nothing about running a newspaper. I just read 'em. Do you think I'd put money into a business I know nothing about?" He cocked a quizzical black eyebrow at Wrangel and laughed. "Somebody's running a whizzer on you, Wrangel."

Wrangel shrugged his shoulders and sauntered back to finish his drink. Then he left the saloon. Freeman and Stormy decided to have another bottle of beer. After a time Quad Wrangel reentered and ordered a drink. Stormy moved a few paces away from the man, not wishing to become involved again in a discussion regarding the rumored purchase of the *Banner.* A half hour passed while Stormy and Freeman discussed the situation in Carnival. Stormy was just reaching for Durham and cigarette papers when Rufe Harper burst in, his face like a thundercloud.

"I want to talk to you, Knight—private," he growled.

Stormy eyed him a moment, then stepped to the center of the room. "If you'll hold down your voice, I reckon this is private enough to suit me," he said coldly, shaking tobacco out of the Durham sack into the paper. "What's on your mind?"

Harper lowered his tones, though they still shook with anger. "How much will you take for it, cash on the barrelhead?"

Stormy looked quizzical. "How much will I take for what?"

"The Carnival *Banner.*"

"I don't own the *Banner.*"

Harper snapped irritably, "You bought it, didn't you?"

"You're wrong," Stormy shook his head. "I don't know where the rumor started, but I haven't any intention of running that newspaper—now or any time."

A look of relief crossed Harper's features. "Is

that straight?" He took a quick, eager step toward Stormy.

Stormy moved back so suddenly the Durham sack slipped from his grasp and fell to the floor. Even as he stooped quickly to retrieve the tobacco there came the sharp sound of splintered glass. A six-shooter roared in the alley back of the Pegasus and a leaden slug whined viciously through the space occupied by Stormy but an instant before. A dull thud followed as the bullet buried itself harmlessly in the front wall of the saloon.

For just a moment there was a shocked silence in the room. Stormy was still crouched close to the floor, reaching for his tobacco. When he came up his fist came with him, swinging hard in a blow that caught Rufe Harper on the side of the head. Harper floundered back then, abruptly, sprawled on the barroom floor.

"Framing me into a position for a killing, eh?" Stormy said grimly. Whirling swiftly, he leaped to the rear door of the saloon and landed outside. An acrid whiff of powder smoke greeted his nostrils. It was dark in the alley. Stormy hesitated to accustom his eyes to the low visibility. Footsteps sounded ahead. A running shape dodged through the gloom. Instantly Stormy started in pursuit, triggering two shots from his six-shooter as he ran. Both shots apparently missed, as a moment later Stormy thought he saw his assailant dodge out of the alley to cut between two buildings in the direction of Main Street. Back of Stormy men were emerging from the Pegasus and yelling for him to wait.

"Wait hell!" Stormy panted, and plunged on. He had just reached the corner of the first building, where his prey had turned, when he ran into a heap of rubbish stacked back of a door. His right spur became entangled in a piece of wire fencing, and Stormy, losing his balance, plunged face downward on the earth.

As he struggled to arise a dark figure moved quickly around the corner of the building, gun in hand. As the heavy six-shooter barrel crashed against Stormy's head he felt consciousness vanishing. Quite suddenly everything faded out and he lay motionless. . . .

Stormy regained consciousness to find himself stretched out on a table in the Pegasus Saloon. He struggled to arise and grinned feebly. "What happened?" He was wringing wet about the face and shoulders. Groggily he shook his head. "Did you catch him?" he asked as his mind cleared.

"Didn't see anybody to catch," Freeman spoke. "By the time Wrangel and I and a couple others arrived there wasn't anybody there but you—out cold. We carried you back, and One-Horse has been dousing water on you. There's a nice lump on the back of your head."

"I tripped and went down," Stormy explained, "then somebody hit me a crack. I saw his legs just before I passed out. I reckon he escaped over to Main Street then. How long have I been this way?"

"Only about twenty minutes," Wrangel said. "That deputy sheriff was in here. He blew off a lot of hot air and then went looking for whoever fired the shot—"

"I told Bayliss," Freeman cut in, "that it looked like Harper had maneuvered you into position for that shot. Bayliss pooh-poohed the idea."

Stormy forced a feeble grin. "Where's Harper now?"

Freeman chuckled. "He left with Bayliss, nursing his jaw and vowing to square accounts with you."

"I hope I'm in shape when the time comes," Stormy observed. He accepted the glass of whisky Shea held out. After downing the liquor he felt stronger and made his way to the bar. The excitement gradually died away. Neither Bayliss nor Harper returned. Wrangel said after a time, "Here's your Bull Durham you dropped, Knight."

Stormy said "Thanks" and, accepting the proffered sack, rolled a cigarette and lighted it. "I'd sure be a goner now if I hadn't dropped my makin's," he commented, thrusting the Durham back into his coat pocket. As he did so his fingers encountered a folded sheet of paper which felt strange. Wondering what it was, he drew it out and unfolded it to see handwriting on one side. A look of astonishment crossed his features as he commenced to read:

For the sum of one dollar and other valuable considerations, I do hereby sell, transfer, and assign . . .

The written words blurred before Stormy's eyes. The cigarette fell from his gaping mouth. He gasped, "I'll be damned!"

Freeman glanced curiously at him. "What's wrong with you, Stormy? You sure look upset. That a bill you forgot to pay, or a letter from a deserted woman?"

"Nothing so simple as that," Stormy replied, frowning. He continued reading, then heaved a long, perplexed sigh as he noted the name, *Kate Sanford,* signed at the bottom. The paper he held in his hand was a bill of sale for the Carnival *Banner*, made out to one Stormy Knight!

Slowly Stormy refolded the paper and slipped it back into his pocket. The other men in the saloon were gazing inquiringly at him. Stormy forced a thin laugh and turned to Freeman: "Gage, I reckon I'll run along to my room at the hotel. Do you feel like taking a short walk before you head home?"

"Glad to accompany you," Freeman nodded. The two said good night and headed for the street.

Wrangel gazed after them until the swinging doors at the entrance had once more come to a stop. "Now what do you suppose got into Knight?" Wrangel asked of the room in general. "He acted like he'd had a shock."

One-Horse Shea swabbed at the bar, then commented sarcastically, "Maybe if you'd been shot at and been whanged on the head, you'd feel shocked too. It took more than a feather to raise that lump on Mr. Knight's skull, remember!"

5. "IT'S YOUR MOVE!"

In his hotel room, the following morning, Stormy shaved with more than usual care. He donned a clean shirt and neckerchief, brushed dust from his boots, and in other ways made himself presentable. Then he descended to the hotel dining room and ate a sizable portion of ham and eggs, washed down with copious draughts of black coffee. The headache of the previous night had vanished, though a small swelling still remained at the back of his head. Physically he felt perfect, though he was none too confident regarding the business that lay ahead.

Ten minutes after leaving the hotel Stormy found himself on Beaumont Street, searching for the Sanford residence. He finally located it—a small frame dwelling at the corner of Flagstaff Street, surrounded by a whitewashed picket fence. An ancient cottonwood spread wide limbs above the front yard. Stormy pushed through the gateway, ascended the porch steps, and knocked at the door, which was presently answered by a motherly looking woman in an apron. Stormy made himself known, then said, "You're Mrs. Freeman, I reckon. Gage said you were staying with Miss Sanford. I know this is no time to be calling, but could I see her for a minute or so? It's quite important."

"Oh, Gage told me about you." Then, dubiously, "About Kate, I don't know what to say. I do know she wants to thank you for what you tried to do about her father's— Well, look, Mr. Knight, you just come into the parlor. I'll go ask her."

The parlor was a pleasant, comfortably furnished room with a fireplace in one corner and a carpet spread on the floor. A couple of framed pictures ornamented the walls. Stormy stood uneasily twirling his sombrero after Mrs. Freeman had left. He wondered what Kate Sanford would be like, how she'd accept this visit. A step at the doorway caused him to turn.

Stormy caught a quick breath. This was almost more than he'd bargained for. Kate Sanford was tall and slim, with wavy tawny hair hanging to her shoulders and long-lashed hazel eyes. She was clothed in a dress of some soft brown material, and there was lace at her throat and wrists. Even the evidences of her grief failed to mar the girl's sheer loveliness. Her voice was low and throaty. "You're Mr. Knight?"

Stormy gulped. "I sure hate to bother you at a time like this, Miss Sanford, but—"

"Let's not talk about that. I'm in your debt for what you've tried to do—tried to prove—where my father is concerned. I'd feel sorry if you hadn't come. I still hope some clue will come to light—"

"That's not what I came to talk about, either, Miss Sanford. I don't know just how to say this,

52

but—well, I asked Gage Freeman not to mention the bill of sale to you. Told him I'd take care of it myself. Now I wish I hadn't. He might have smoothed the way a mite. I don't know just how you got that paper into my pocket, but"—stammering—"I just can't do it, that's all, and I thought you should know at once—"

"Whatever in the world are you talking about?" Kate Sanford looked bewildered. "Maybe you'd better sit down and we can get this straightened out."

Doggedly, Stormy remained on his feet. "It's the *Banner*. I'd give anything to be able to take over for you, but I don't know anything about getting out a newspaper. I'd—I'd—" Stormy floundered some more. "Well, it's just that I don't know anything about printing or publishing a newspaper."

Kate Sanford's hazel eyes opened wide. "Why on earth should you be expected to? I appreciate, more than I can say, your efforts on Father's behalf, but that's no sign I expect you to take on all my troubles. And what did you say about a bill of sale?"

Stormy's jaws clamped tightly. Just what sort of queer runaround was this? He wondered momentarily if the tragedy had unsettled the girl's mind. "Look," he ventured warily, "you made out a bill of sale selling the Carnival *Banner* to me."

53

The lovely hazel eyes looked startled, then a look of indignation crossed the girl's features. "I did nothing of the sort!" She paused a bit grimly. "I don't understand this, Mr. Knight. Are you playing some sort of game? You wouldn't—no, you couldn't be working with Rufe Harper. But I would like an explanation of your words."

"All right, I'm crazy then," Stormy said exasperatedly. He plunged one hand into a pocket and produced the questionable bill of sale. "Here you are," he stated, thrusting the paper at her.

The girl eyed him steadily a moment, then accepted the bill and glanced through its contents. She looked up. "Where did you get this?" she asked calmly. Stormy told her. She continued, "But how could it have got into your pocket without your knowing?"

"That's something I hoped you'd tell me," Stormy answered. "Next you'll be telling me you never wrote it."

"I'm telling you that now."

"What!" Stormy exclaimed. "You claim you never—"

"It's not my writing," the girl insisted. "I never sign my name Kate.' I always write 'Katherine.' I don't understand this. Rufe Harper must be back of it, somehow. For a long time he's been trying to buy the paper. Maybe he thinks he can use you as he's used other tools."

Stormy smiled. "Harper knows me better than

that. I'm the one man he wouldn't want to see in control of the *Banner*. Why, only last night I had an argument with him when he'd heard a rumor I was going to buy the *Banner*."

"But who could start such a rumor?" Kate said incredulously.

"It's more than I can figure out. Nor can I see a reason for it. . . . Do you plan to continue publishing the paper?"

"I don't see how I can. Harper was here last night, insisting that I sell to him. I said no, but I don't know what else I can do. Father borrowed three thousand dollars against the *Banner*. That has to be repaid." She sighed. "So I guess Rufe Harper will get his way after all."

About that time Stormy went completely overboard. He'd come here to convince this girl he couldn't run a newspaper and that he didn't intend to have anything to do with a newspaper. He knew he was making a fool of himself, but his emotions, sympathies, call it what you will, ran away with him. "Look, Miss Sanford," he said earnestly, "your father has made a long, hard fight against Rufe Harper. All his good work will be wasted if you turn the paper over to Harper—"

"But I don't see how I can continue—"

"Wait a minute until I finish. This bill-of-sale thing is something I can't figure out, but if you didn't do it, somebody else did, and for his own advantage. Maybe Harper's back of this in some way I don't understand. We'll let that ride until such time as I can figure out his moves. Meanwhile we both know that nothing will hurt Harper more than for the *Banner* to continue the fight it has been making for law and order in Carnival."

"But I'm trying to tell you—"

Stormy interrupted. "You say that's not your writing on that bill of sale. Do you mind showing me just how you'd sign it?"

Without thinking, Kate seized a pencil that lay on the mantel over the fireplace and signed "Katherine Sanford" under the original signature on the bill, then handed it to Stormy. "See the difference in the writing—" she commenced.

Stormy smiled and took the paper. "Thanks. That makes it legal now."

Kate frowned uncertainly. "I—I don't understand."

"I'll make it clear. You can't quit now—after your father carried the fight so far. I may sound like a fool, but with your help I'll publish the *Banner*."

"But you say you know nothing about getting out a newspaper." The long-lashed eyes were wide, uncomprehending.

"Less than that even. But with your help we'll get the paper out on schedule."

"You forget," Kate wailed, "there's three thousand owing—"

"We'll cross that river when we come to it."

"We should have a typesetter. I can set, but I can't do everything. It costs money to hire help."

"That's another river to cross. Are you with me?"

"Do—do you think we could do it?" Kate asked hopefully.

"Yes—but I don't know how—yet. Just one thing, if you want your payment for the paper now, you're out of luck. I can't get the money that soon."

"That"—and Kate smiled faintly—"is the third river we'll have to negotiate."

"You'll do it, then?" Stormy asked eagerly.

The girl crossed over, placed both hands on his shoulders, and looked steadily at him. Her voice broke a trifle. "Stormy Knight—I think we're both a—trifle crazy—but I'll do it. It's the sort of thing I've wanted to do. I—I don't feel helpless anymore."

Five minutes later, when Stormy left the house, he was still in a daze. "Of all the fools," he told himself, "one Jonathan Stormover Knight is the foolest! I've sure let that girl in for something. She don't realize how damn dumb I am about printing a newspaper. A typesetter, she says. Where am I to find a typesetter? Maybe I could learn to do it. No, that would take too long. Whew! What a mess this will be."

Cursing himself for an idiot, he turned down

Flagstaff Street and thence to Main. Just as he rounded the corner he saw Big Rufe Harper approaching. Stormy's mind cleared instantly. "I may not know anything about publishing," he chuckled joyously, "but here's something I can handle. Harper is just my dish! And will he be burned to a frazzle when I tell him!"

Harper came striding angrily up to Stormy. Before he could speak, Stormy got in the first word. "Hold it, Harper! I know you're rarin' to tear me apart for that bruise I put on the side of your cheek. We'll get to that later."

"We'll take it up now," Harper snarled.

"Hold it, I said. Last night I gathered the idea that you wouldn't like the idea of me owning the Carnival *Banner.* Is that correct?"

Harper paused warily. What was this about? His brows drew down in a heavy frown. "That's plenty correct. I aim to control the *Banner* myself. You go messing into that business and I'll make you regret the day you were born."

Stormy produced the bill of sale, signed by Kate Sanford. "Take a look at this, Harper. That's my answer to your threats. Now, you'd better make up your mind whether you're just trying to bluff me or if you want more trouble. It's your move, Harper! I'm hoping you'll fight!"

6. CHALLENGE!

Harper eyed Stormy steadily a moment, as though trying to measure the extent to which he'd back up his words, then lowered his eyes to the bill of sale held out for his inspection. He started to take the paper. Stormy said quickly, "Hands off! You can read it as is."

Again Harper lowered his gaze. As he scrutinized the words on the paper a slow wave of crimson spread over his features. Then he went white. Involuntarily his right hand started to stray toward the gun at his hip. Swiftly Stormy switched the bill of sale from right to left hand. "You want to draw, Harper?" he challenged.

With an effort Harper got his feelings under control. He forced a harsh laugh, raised his hand again, and took a long black cigar from a vest pocket. Savagely he bit off one end and struck a match. He puffed hard for a moment, then laughed harshly. "Draw? Why should I draw against you? I don't settle my arguments that way, or if I do, it takes more than something like this to make me burn gunpowder."

Stormy nodded and put away the bill of sale. "Sort of inclined to pull iron for a minute, though, weren't you?" he taunted.

"Don't talk like a fool, Knight. Last night you

told me you weren't interested in buying the *Banner.* How come?"

"That," Stormy pointed out, "was last night—before you tried to get me shot."

"Look here, Knight," Harper said wrathfully, "I had nothing to do with that. Probably wasn't meant for an attempt on your life, anyway. Ten to one it was some cowpuncher, feeling his oats on redeye and triggering lead just to hear the explosion. Accidentally a shot happened to enter the back window of the Pegasus Saloon—"

"Accidentally!" Stormy snorted. "And I suppose somebody accidentally hit me over the head with a gun barrel too. Probably said somebody was ust waving his six-shooter around careless-like, and I happened to get in the way!"

"Whatever happened," Harper said testily, "you had no reason to swing on me. I'm not forgetting that."

"Good! Then you'll be remembering that I landed the first punch in this brawl you and I have mixed into. I'm still awaiting your next move."

"Look here, Knight"—Harper forced a tone of honest sincerity into his words—"if it had been planned to kill you last night, why didn't that feller—whoever he was—throw a slug of lead into you instead of hitting you on the head—as you claim?"

"He didn't dare shoot again," Stormy replied promptly. "Men were coming close behind me, from the Pegasus. A gun flash might have lighted his face. He'd have been recognized. He was planning to make a getaway over to Main Street. Another shot might have drawn people toward him. By cracking me on the head he prevented my catching him."

"Got it all figured out, ain't you?" Harper sneered.

"I've given the matter a mite of thought," Stormy admitted.

"T'hell with it," Harper said suddenly. "Let's forget the whole business, along with that wallop you managed to land on me last night. Knight, you and I could be friends—"

"I doubt that."

"—and there's no need of us squaring off every time we see each other, like a couple of strange Injun dogs. I'll admit frankly I wanted the *Banner.* You beat me to making a deal with Kate Sanford. You deserve to make a nice profit. What did you pay her for the paper?"

"I'm not saying, just now."

Harper nodded. "That's up to you. However, I'll pay you a thousand dollars more than you laid out for the paper—and put the cash in your hand today."

Stormy shook his head. "No, you won't."

"You want more money? A thousand makes a pretty nice profit. You'll find nothing but grief if you try to run that paper yourself."

"That a threat, Harper?"

"You know damned well it's not. But you don't know what you're up against. It takes work to get out a newspaper."

"I'm not selling, Harper."

Harper flushed angrily. "Maybe before you're through with the business you'll wish you'd *given* the *Banner* away!"

Stormy smiled thinly. "Before I'm through with you, Mister Mayor, you'll wish I had too."

Harper started to reply, checked himself, turned and stalked angrily into the Bonanza Bar a few steps away.

Stormy walked on, musing seriously: "One of these days when I start poking sticks at the tigers that-a-way, one of 'em will bust out of the cage and settle my hash. I wonder if I'll ever learn to keep my big mouth shut? I got trouble enough without going out of my way to ask for more."

He decided he wanted to talk to Gage Freeman and crossed the road to enter the big general store. Freeman was still busy with his morning rush of trade, however, and Stormy left the store without interrupting him. On the street once more, Stormy stood undecided. Glancing across the street, he suddenly became aware that he was gazing at the *Banner* building. A feeling of awe swept over him—awe mingled with a sinking feeling in the vicinity of the stomach.

"Holy smoke!" he whispered. "That's mine. And I got to prove I'm man enough to run it. Oh

Lord!" The words ended in a groan. "How the hell do I start in?"

At this point a drink seemed indicated. Stormy glanced around. Next door to the general store was the Pegasus Saloon, on whose wooden false front was a faded sign depicting a rearing bronc equipped with upstretched wings. "Nothing stronger than beer, now, you fool rannie," Stormy warned himself as he entered the barroom.

It was pleasantly cool in the saloon after the heat of Main Street. Quad Wrangel stood talking at the bar with One-Horse Shea. Wrangel was the only customer, but another man at the rear window was just finishing installing a pane of glass to replace the one shattered by last night's bullet. Wrangel and One-Horse both spoke to Stormy, inquiring after his health.

"It's not my health that's bothering me," Stormy said gloomily. He took up a place at the bar, some distance away from Wrangel, where his thinking wouldn't be disturbed. One-Horse served him with a bottle of beer, then withdrew, sensing that his customer wanted to be alone.

Stormy sipped the cool, foamy suds in moody silence. From time to time he glanced around the barroom. The numerous pictures of prize fighters, burlesque queens, and race horses offered no solution to his problem. By the time the window-glass man had completed his job and departed, Stormy's beer was gone; he still felt in the dark.

Finally he decided to consult One-Horse and called to him down the bar. One-Horse waddled up. "Another beer?"

"No, I want to ask you a question."

"Glad to give you any information I can."

"One-Horse," Stormy commenced, "you knew James Sanford quite a spell, didn't you?"

"Cripes a'mighty, yes! It was Sanford suggested the name for this place when I first opened up. There was hardly a day passed when he didn't come in for his touch of bourbon. He'd talk about what a good paper he was going to give Carnival someday—a daily it was to be, instead of just once a week—and about printing and such. I didn't understand half the things he said, but it was always good to hear him talk. He was high-educated, Mr. Sanford was."

"A little learning is a dangerous thing," Wrangel offered, coming along the bar, whisky glass in hand. He was slightly unsteady.

"So's too much whisky," Shea grunted shortly.

"That's open to argument," Wrangel commenced. "Now I—"

"I still maintain," Shea said stubbornly, "that too much whisky's a dangerous thing—as well as too much talking." He jerked one thumb toward Wrangel and said to Stormy, "Quad, here, don't realize you and I are talking private."

"It doesn't make any difference," Stormy said morosely. "I don't care who hears my troubles right now. Tell me, One-Horse, where did Sanford get help when he needed any?"

Shea looked a bit bewildered. "Why—I dunno. There was just him and Kate run the paper. And they had young Horace Brigham to assist."

"Who's Horace Brigham?"

"Old man Brigham's son."

"And Mrs. Brigham's, I presume," Stormy said ironically.

"Yeah, sure," Shea said, surprised.

"This Horace Brigham," Stormy asked. "Is he a typesetter?"

"I don't figure so. No, Kate and Mr. Sanford set type. Horace just sort of—well, just sort of helped out. He swept, delivered papers, and so on. He's just a kid, trying to get along."

Wrangel asked a bit uneasily, "Did you find a murder clue that points to a typesetter?"

Stormy shook his head and again addressed himself to Shea: "Look, if Sanford had wanted to find a typesetter—whatever that is—where would he go to hire one?"

Shea looked blank. "I ain't the slightest idea."

"What," Wrangel queried cautiously, "would he want with a typesetter?" The conversation seemed to have a sobering effect.

Stormy released a slow, exasperated breath. There was a dangerous gleam in his eye. He turned savagely on Wrangel. "What in the devil do you think a publisher would want with a typesetter?

Someone to sweep the floor, or lay eggs, or something? No, he'd want him to set type. Maybe you have different ideas, though."

Wrangel suppressed a hiccough. "Look, Mr. Knight, this is getting beyond me."

"Beyond *you?*" Stormy glared. "Where do you think it leaves me?"

"But," Wrangel said earnestly, "Sanford's dead. He has no use for a typesetter."

"But I'm not dead," Stormy burst out. "I need somebody that knows something about printing. I need help, I need—I guess I need my brain examined," he concluded feebly.

Wrangel eyed him warily. "Don't tell me you've taken over the *Banner*."

"No, dammit, it's taken me over. I've got to run a newspaper. I don't know anything about publishing. Kate Sanford will help, but she can't do everything. I've got to stand on my own hind legs and make a showing. If I don't get help someplace, I'm due to blow my top. Is all this clear to you gentlemen?"

One-Horse nodded, his eyes wide, his jaw sagging. An expansive smile spread over Wrangel's features. Quickly he swallowed his drink of whisky and announced, "Mr. Knight, I'm your man."

"Shh-shh!" Shea shook his head admonishingly. "Can't you see Mr. Knight is bothered? This is no time for joshing."

But Stormy had caught the idea. He seized

Wrangel by the coat lapel. "Don't tell me you're a typesetter!"

"Sometimes I think I invented typesetting," Wrangel bragged. "If there's anything I don't know about printing—"

Shea asked blankly, "How come you never mentioned that to me, after all the time you've spent drinking in here?"

"I've got a one-track mind," Wrangel replied. "I don't like anything to interfere with my drinking. No man can talk and savor his liquor at the same time."

"Have you ever worked on a newspaper?" Stormy demanded.

Wrangel looked disgusted. "Have I ever worked on a newspaper? Yes, all over these United States, from coast to coast and from border to border. Why, when I was in Dallas I run—"

"It looks like you don't stay long in one place," Stormy commenced disappointedly, then paused. "Never mind that. You're hired if you can run that printing contraption across the road."

"Never yet saw one I couldn't run," Wrangel boasted. "When do I start?"

"Just as soon as you have a drink with me. I can enjoy my beer now. One-Horse, you've got to join us." Bottles and glasses were placed on the bar. Stormy raised his beer in a toast. "Here's to the Carnival *Banner*," he proposed.

"Long may she wave," Wrangel added.

The three men drank deeply.

7. THE BULLET CLUE

After dinner at the T-Bone Restaurant, adjacent to the newspaper building, Stormy and Quad Wrangel borrowed some tools from One-Horse Shea with which to open the entrance door of the *Banner* headquarters, which Deputy Bayliss had nailed shut the previous day. The work was accompanied by considerable profanity on Wrangel's part. "You could tell a blunderer drove these nails," he panted. "Two out of three are bent and hammered flat. Give me a man who can drive a nail straight, every time."

"Sometimes I wonder if Bayliss could do anything straight," Stormy said.

"He's a blowhard, if there ever was one," Wrangel nodded, "but I don't know if I'd put him down for a crook. Probably got a political pull that keeps him in office."

"Said pull having to do with Mayor Harper, I imagine. I wonder if the sheriff at the county seat knows what's going on here. Somehow I doubt he does."

Wrangel swore and wrenched out the final spike, pushed open the door. "Well, here we are."

Stormy said, "Looks like we'll be needing some repairs right off. Return these tools to Shea, then see if you can buy a new lock someplace. I reckon you can find a hardware store."

"Sure. I can get a lock at Jarvis' Hardware and Gun Store."

"You seem to know this town pretty well."

"It doesn't take me long to learn a town. By the time I've covered all the saloons and talked to folks, I know what's what."

"And you do like to cover the saloons, eh?" Stormy grinned. "Just remember to do your drinking and sobering up outside working hours, and you and I will get along fine. Here's five dollars. That should cover a new lock."

Wrangel departed. Stormy entered the building. He cast a glance into the office but continued along the short, narrow corridor until he'd reached the print shop proper, where he examined the place thoroughly, looking under the paper-cutting machine, table, and other equipment. Eventually he arrived at the closet built across an inner corner. Here the light wasn't too good. Stormy mused, "It would be a good idea to cut a window into the wall about here. This corner could stand a heap of lightening up. But I'm getting ahead of myself. The first thing to do is figure out where that satchel of money went to."

Opening the door of the closet, he struck a match and carefully surveyed the interior. There was a shelf at the top, with nothing on it. Below ran a row of clothes hooks; nothing was hanging on them. Stormy struck a second match and glanced at the floor. An old newspaper and a cigarette butt lay there; nothing else. There were cobwebs in the corners. The match flame burned down. Stormy straightened up, looked thoughtful, and slowly moved out to the center of the floor. "Dammit," he growled, "it would have simplified matters could I have found a trap door in this floor, but I reckon the place is built too close to the ground for that." Nevertheless, he examined the floor carefully, but found nothing to justify his hopes.

He made his way back to the office. Here the first thing that struck his gaze was the ugly dark stain on the floor boards. "I'll sure have to do something about that before Miss Sanford comes in," he muttered. "Seeing her dad's blood every day wouldn't help things for her." At that moment Quad Wrangel returned. Stormy asked, "Did you get a lock?"

Wrangel nodded. "Jarvis is going to send a man down to install it. There'll be some repairs on that door, besides, for the man to handle. I figured it best to let Jarvis take care of the whole thing. It'll cost you four bucks." He handed Stormy seventy-five cents in change, with the explanation, "I thought I ought to buy a drink when I was in the Pegasus—you know, to sort of repay Shea for loaning us his tools."

"That's a good idea," Stormy nodded. "I'll take

the two bits out of your first week's wages."

"Aw, say," Quad protested, "after me coming on the job to help you out?"

"Nobody's drinking on my money unless I invite him," Stormy said firmly.

"That's downright ungrateful," Wrangel protested sadly. "And," he went on, "you haven't said yet what my wages are to be."

"We'll talk about that when I see how much you know. Yesterday, when Deputy Bayliss threw you out of here, I heard you tell him you were trying to figure out how that printing machine runs. If there's any doubt in your mind, you'd better get back there and study on it a spell, because, s'help me, if you let me down now, I aim to cut off your head and throw it in your face!"

"Hey," Quad said in some alarm, "maybe you got me wrong."

"Maybe we're both thinking that," Stormy replied pleasantly. "It's up to you to show me you know your business. How long since you worked, anyway?"

"We-ell, let me see. It's just about—er—just about—let me see. I was in Kansas City in February. Before that I worked on the *Star* in Denhamville—there was that session in Louisiana—"

"Forget it," Stormy broke in. "I can see you've spent more time settin' 'em up than you have setting type. Okay, I'll give you a chance. Get out in that printing room and see what you can learn—first get me a bucket of water and some soap and sharp sand—"

"Now don't you go to scouring that press," Quad said. "I'll take care of that."

"I'm not thinking of the press." Stormy pointed to the bloodstain on the floor. "That's got to come out before Miss Sanford comes in. See what I mean?"

"I get you, Mr. Knight." Quad hurried away and within a short time returned with the necessary articles, after which he retired to the pressroom, while Stormy proceeded to scrub at the spot on the floor.

The ominous dark stain had seeped deeply into the wood, and it was hard work. Finally, so as to get at it better, Stormy moved the long table away from the window. Then he started to work again. It was when he had stopped to take a brief rest and smoke a cigarette, seated on the floor, that he noticed the small hole in the baseboard, about three or four inches from the floor.

A thrill ran through Stormy. "Hmmm! That's interesting. Entered at an angle, I'd say, so it can't be too deep imbedded."

Taking his barlow knife from his pocket, he opened it, then shoved closer to the baseboard. For ten minutes he dug industriously and at the end of that time was rewarded by uncovering a small, cylindrically shaped chunk of lead.

"The slug from Sanford's thirty-eight," he whispered elatedly. Then he frowned. "But why did it enter so close to the floor? The gun must have been almost flat when it was fired. Could reflex action on Sanford's part have triggered that weapon after he fell to the floor? Could be. But I wonder."

Brow furrowed with thought, he speculated on the problem, remembering the position in which the body lay when it was found and the way the dead hand clutched the butt of the gun. Finally he gave up and put the bullet into a pocket for future reference. "I'll have to give it some more thought," he mused, renewing his scrubbing activities. Ten minutes more and there was only a slight stain left on the whitened wood where he had been working. Stormy took a long breath and straightened up, realizing his back was commencing to ache.

Wrangel entered the office, looked at Stormy, and grinned. "I'll bet a long cold beer would go good about now."

Stormy grinned back. "Just when my spine has become unhinged you arrive to tempt me in my weakened condition. But my rule of no drinking during working hours still holds."

"I was afraid you'd say that," Quad said ruefully. "Y'know, I think we could mix some printer's ink with a mite of grease and stain that spot you've been scouring to about the same tone as the rest of the floor. That would save further work."

"Now you've really started to earn your pay," Stormy nodded gratefully. "Take that pail and stuff out of here and we'll try your idea."

Quad did as ordered and within a few minutes returned with a smeary-looking gob on a piece of rag. Getting down on his knees, he worked at the spot a few minutes, then rose. "What did I tell you?" he said triumphantly. "You'd never know there'd been a bloodstain there. Too bad I didn't think of it before; you'd have been saved some backbreaking toil."

"Yes," Stormy admitted, thinking of the thirty-eight slug in his pocket, "but I reckon it was all worthwhile. I did a good job." Wrangel had failed to notice the small spot on the baseboard where the bullet had been dug out. Stormy continued, "Help me lift this table back next to the window."

When that had been done Quad said, "I've been studying that press. I think I've figured out how it works."

"No thinking, Quad. You've *got* to make it work."

"Oh, I'll make it work, all right, but that press is a bastard—and I'm not swearing—if there ever was one. It's made from parts of different machines. Looks like it started out as a Washington, but it's part Columbian, part Albion, part Stanhope, part Wharfedale. The platen is from an old Merlin. The hand lever is—"

"This is all Greek to me," Stormy frowned.

"Those are names of different makes of presses," Quad explained. "Hell! There's parts on that press I never did see any place before. The idea of 'em looks right good, too."

Stormy said, "Maybe I can clear up a few things. Some time ago, Gage Freeman tells me, somebody broke in and used a sledge hammer on that press. Sanford suspected Harper of being back of it, the idea being to put Sanford out of business. Sanford couldn't afford a new press, so he repaired what he had, getting spare parts from Capital City and places back East, then had the parts machined so he could adapt them. Parts he couldn't replace he had the local blacksmith forge, incorporating some of his own— Sanford's—ideas into 'em. Gage said Sanford intended to patent three or four of his ideas someday."

Quad nodded. "That explains a lot."

"The question is, can you run it?"

"Cripes, yes! I knew I could run it. But presses break down every so often. I wanted to make sure I knew how to fix it. We'll run it, all right, and run Harper right out of the country with it. Y'know, I sure admired the way you stood up to Harper yesterday when he called you a liar. I was scared you'd get shot up or something."

Stormy laughed. "*You* were scared? What did you think *I* was—enjoying myself at that gathering?"

"You sure didn't look bothered."

"Sheer bluff, Quad. And I got away with it."

"Not all bluff." Quad shook his head. "Y'know, sometimes when a man needs courage it comes to him."

Stormy eyed this queer specimen of a man who had, in a large measure, come to his rescue. A drinker the man undoubtedly was, with his skinny frame, stringy hair, and unshaven jaw, but a man to be counted on for all that. "Quad," Stormy said warmly, "we'll lick Harper, with your help, but you've got to figure there'll be powder burned before we get through."

"It won't be the first time I've sniffed powder smoke," Quad said quietly. "When the time comes, I've a sawed-off shotgun that may come handy."

"The hell you say!" Stormy was struck by a new thought. "Where'd you sleep the past two nights?"

"At the hotel. I put up there as soon as I got into Carnival. Haven't paid anything yet, though, and I don't know how much longer I can get away with it."

"Broke, eh?"

"Except for my bourbon money."

Stormy smiled. "We'd better get that wages question settled, so you can have an advance—" He broke off, glancing through the office window. "Here comes that fat deputy."

Bayliss strode in, looking very much concerned.

"What the devil does this mean? I nailed that door up yesterday. You're trespassing on private property."

"Bayliss," Stormy said, "you remind me of a cow's tail—you're always behind. For your information, I've taken over the *Banner* and—"

The deputy's eyes bugged out. "You're runnin' the newspaper? But I thought Big Rufe Harper—"

"Harper had the same cowish qualities I mentioned a moment back. I got ahead of him—somehow."

Bayliss looked put out. "Rufe ain't going to like this when he hears about it."

"Cripes! I told him this morning."

"You did?" the deputy gasped, jaw dropping. "And you're still—"

"I'm still alive, if that's what you were going to say," Stormy nodded.

"You know damned well I wasn't going to say that," Bayliss protested. He looked serious. "I'm afraid this will mean trouble. You've made a bad mistake, Knight. I'm not going to stand for any fights in Carnival."

"Meaning, I suppose," Stormy snapped, "that you'll take Harper's side in any fight that comes up."

"I take no man's side. I enforce the law. But you must have realized this would lead to trouble."

Stormy said disgustedly, "Oh hell."

Sensing the contempt in Stormy's tones, Bayliss

77

turned away, then his eye fell on Wrangel, whom he hadn't recognized at first. "You again, eh?" he snorted. "Didn't I tell you we don't stand for bums in this town? Want I should throw him out, Mr. Knight, like I did yesterday?"

"Bayliss," Quad said belligerently, "how would you like to have me knock you out from under that tin badge you're wearing?"

"You can't talk to a sworn officer of the law like that," Bayliss squealed furiously. "You're under arrest."

"Cut it out, both of you," Stormy said sternly. "Now you listen to me, Bayliss. I don't intend having you coming in here interfering with my help."

"Your help?" Bayliss asked, eyes bulging.

"Certainly. The *Banner* couldn't be published without the assistance of Mr. Wrangel. He's in charge of all printing activities. And get it through your thick skull that he's not a bum. I've stood just about all I'm going to from you, Bayliss."

"Yes, Mr. Knight," Bayliss said humbly. "I'm sorry."

"Never mind your apologies. You came in here without an invitation. I don't want you here at all. Now get out!"

"Yes, Mr. Knight," the deputy mumbled, and stumbled toward the exit from the office.

"We'll send for you when we want you, Deputy," came from Wrangel in an imperious voice.

"Oh yes, Bayliss," Stormy called as the deputy reached the doorway. "Do you know a button by the name of Horace Brigham?"

"Sure. He's a kid that used to work for Sanford. You missed something? Want him arrested?"

"Don't be in such a damn hurry to arrest somebody," Stormy said sternly. "You get over to Brigham's and tell that kid he's needed here, on his job. And get a move on!"

"Yes, Mr. Knight." The deputy hurried away.

The instant he was out of earshot Stormy and Quad exploded into gales of laughter. "My gosh!" Stormy chortled. "Did you ever see such a feeble excuse for a deputy sheriff?"

"I never did." Quad shook his head. "Shucks, that potbellied so-and-so will take orders from anybody."

"I reckon Harper must have broken his spirit."

In a few minutes Quad went back to his press and Stormy seated himself at Sanford's desk. There were certain papers, no doubt, that should be gotten together and given to Kate Sanford. The girl would probably want to go through the desk herself. Stormy gazed somewhat helplessly at the mass of material in the drawers and on top of the desk—a couple of scribbled articles on bovine diseases, an old galley proof, bills stamped "Paid," and bills still unpaid, pencils, erasers, circulars from ink and paper companies. Stormy shook his head and thought of Quad.

"Maybe," he muttered, "there's something about this printing business that drives men to drink."

A step at the doorway caused him to whirl in the swivel chair. A gangling boy of sixteen or seventeen, with tow hair, was somewhat timidly entering the office. "You Mr. Knight? Deputy Bayliss said you wanted to see me at once."

"Yes, if you're Horace Brigham." The boy nodded. Stormy went on, "I remember you now. You testified at the inquest as to what you did here the night before Mr. Sanford was shot."

"That's right. It's just like I said then. After I finished delivering some papers I come back here. Miss Kate and Mr. Sanford left for home, and I started to clean up the press and sweep out and so on. I finished up about nine or nine-thirty. Then I locked up and went home—"

Stormy interrupted. "That's not what I wanted to see you about. You see, Miss Sanford and I are going to continue publishing the paper. I'm counting on you to help us, if you want to stay on."

"Yes sir, I do." Horace Brigham looked relieved.

"All right, that's fine. You'll find our new printer out in the back. His name is Quad Wrangel— Mr. Wrangel to you. Go out and tell him you're his helper. He'll explain, better than I can, what you're to do."

"Thank you, Mr. Knight." The boy hurried out to make Wrangel's acquaintance.

At suppertime, when they were leaving, Quad said to Stormy, "I think I'm going to learn to love that press."

"Good. How's that kid going to make out?"

"He's all right. Smart boy, Horace is. But I'm talking about that press. It was wrecked once. I'd hate to see it wrecked again."

"What's the answer?"

"Suppose, for the time being, I move a cot in and sleep here. I can bring my shotgun along and—well, I have to sleep someplace. There's no use of paying a hotel bill, and I don't think it safe to leave this building unguarded."

Stormy nodded slowly. "It's a good idea, Quad. We'll see if we can dig up a cot for you. I'm glad you thought of it."

Quad chuckled. "There'll be nothing like a couple of charges of buckshot to discourage anybody that comes sneaking around with sledge hammers. Me, I'm sick of being known as a bum. Some folks are sure due to change their minds!"

8. "GET HIS NERVE!"

Rufe Harper stood at one end of the bar in the Bonanza, moodily staring into a glass of liquor. The Bonanza Bar wasn't quite as good a saloon as One-Horse Shea's Pegasus, but it was Harper's property and he and his gang preferred to do their drinking there. It consisted of one room, with the long counter stretching across the rear wall. A door to the alley opened in the right-hand corner. There were a few round tables and straight-|backed wooden chairs standing about. The bar mirror was flyspecked, and the bartender, Joe Wiley, was a shifty-eyed individual with scanty hair and a soiled apron about his waist.

Rough footsteps were heard at the entrance, and 'Brose Echardt, foreman of Harper's Anvil Ranch, came in, followed by five or six of the Anvil hands. Echardt swung his bulky-shouldered form alongside Harper's. "Jeez, boss, ain't you et your supper yet?"

Harper shook his head. "Haven't felt like eating, 'Brose. I'll get a snack later. I've been thinking a bit."

"About which?"

"Nothing that matters much, I guess. I can work it out, in my way. 'Brose, you'd better get back to the ranch and take the boys with you—no, wait, don't take all of 'em. I might want somebody here."

The other men had lined up at the bar by this time, and Joe Wiley was busy serving them. A short laugh twisted Cameo Sloan's swarthy features. "I know what's eating you, Rufe. You're burned up because Knight beat you to getting the *Banner*." Sloan was inclined, in his attire, to tend toward the flashy type of raiment. His shirt was a robin's-egg blue; there was a yellow neckerchief at his throat. On each hand was a large cameo ring, and a pair of pearl-handled six-shooters swung from the crisscrossed cartridge belts that encircled his slim hips. "Mebbe," Sloan continued, "we should settle his hash pronto."

"I'd like a hand in that," crooked-nosed Steve Gooch put in.

Harper glanced at Sloan. "I'm not saying you're wrong, Cameo," he admitted heavily. "It was just our luck to have Knight come in this way and upset the applecart. Of course you know and I know we can get the *Banner* eventually."

"Why not right now?" the undersized Squint Amber demanded.

"Shut up, Squint," Harper said roughly. "I'll do the thinking for this crowd—and the talking. Sure, Knight could be taken care of, but I'm not sure I want things that way right off. He made us look bad yesterday. There are folks in Carnival doing a little thinking—folks that never did any thinking before."

Joe Wiley was going about the barroom, lighting the oil lamps in the brackets. Harper went on, "Of course maybe we've nothing to worry about. I don't figure Knight knows anything about running a paper. Bayliss says he's hired that tramp Wrangel to do his printing, but there's more than printing to getting out a newspaper. You've got to know how to mold public opinion to your thoughts, and that can only be done according to how good your articles are—and I don't meanthe pieces about who died and who got married and who was in a train wreck and so on."

A rather stupid-looking puncher with dull eyes, named Muley Porter, put in, "Aw-w, Rufe, who wants to read a newspaper, anyway?"

Harper turned sharply on him. "I said I'd do the talking for this bunch, Muley."

"All right, Rufe," Muley said good-naturedly. "No offense meant."

Harper went on, "What I'm trying to say is, maybe we'd better not interfere with Knight's publishing. He may do such a terrible job that nobody will want his paper. Then he'd just be a big flop. In other words, give a man enough rope and he'll hang himself. When and if that happened, we could take over the paper without being criticized by the public. We can only push this town so far. We've got to take things easy, more or less."

Nobody spoke for a time. Another round of drinks was set out. Cameo Sloan broke the silence at last. "I think you've got the right slant, Rufe, but I've been thinking we might help Knight's downfall a mite."

"In what way?"

"Intimidation."

"Meaning what?" Harper growled.

Sloan explained, "Three or four of us might corner Knight and get real tough with him—make him understand he isn't wanted in Carnival. If we could throw a scare into him, it might affect what he says in his paper."

"Who do you suggest?" Harper asked. "It might work."

"I'll take on the job. Give me Steve and Squint and—"

"Steve and Squint and you should be able to handle it. If you take too many, it will look like we've ganged up on him. That's why he got away with what he did yesterday. He was a stranger and we were all making war talk against one man. Naturally the crowd's sympathies went to the underdog."

"Aw-w, Rufe," Muley Porter put in, "you don't think three against one is a gang-up, huh?"

Harper flushed angrily. "I told you to keep your trap shut, Muley."

"Okay, Rufe. I didn't mean nothin'."

Harper took a bottle from the bar and gestured

toward one of the tables. "Let's talk it over a mite, Cameo," he suggested, "where we won't be interrupted by imbeciles."

He and Sloan left the bar. The others stood there, drinking and talking. Eventually Harper called Amber and Gooch to join him and Sloan at the table. The four conversed earnestly for several minutes, then they came back to the bar. Harper, by this time, looked more cheerful.

Harper turned to Echardt. "Cameo, Squint, and Steve will stay in town, 'Brose. You and the other boys better slip back to the ranch. First thing tomorrow you'd better slap a new brand on that bunch of Rafter-O stuff, then throw 'em in Hidden Arroyo until the new brands have healed a mite. After that, push 'em north as fast as you can."

Echardt nodded understandingly. "All right, waddies. We're drifting. Rufe, will we see you tomorrow?"

"Tomorrow or next day. I'll keep in touch with you."

The punchers' spurs rattled across the flooring as they followed the foreman through the doorway. There now remained at the bar only Harper, Sloan, Amber, and Gooch. They ordered another drink. Harper lighted a long black cigar. Sloan said, "What you thinking about now, boss?"

"Pudge Bayliss. I'd just as soon you didn't pull anything when he's around."

Sloan laughed carelessly. "I reckon we can count on him to back any play we make."

"I'm not so sure. We've had Bayliss on our side because we've been running things. Hell! Right now he acts half scared of Knight. Trouble with Bayliss, he'll do whatever the strongest man tells him—the man who's with him at the time."

"Maybe," Sloan suggested, "we should try to get a new deputy in here—one who will think our way."

Harper puffed out a cloud of gray smoke and shook his head. "You're wrong, Cameo. While folks don't have much respect for Bayliss, they figure him honest at bottom. That gives us a break, because we can pull the wool over his eyes any time we like."

"I reckon you've got the right slant at that."

"Sure I have. Bayliss is one of the best cards in this hand we're holding."

Harper left the bar, crossed to a side wall, and slipped into the long-skirted coat he usually donned in the evening. Settling his sombrero on his head, he said, "I'll leave things in your hands, Cameo. I'm going to get some supper, then drift over to the Pyramid. The games will be opening soon. You'll find me there—afterward. Now, go after Knight. Get his nerve!"

"I'll have good news for you," Sloan promised.

"That's fine. Just about what I expect from you."

"Take care of yourself."

"You do the same. Don't underestimate Knight any. He could be dangerous if you gave him a chance."

Sloan laughed confidently. "Did you ever know me to give anybody a chance, Rufe?"

"Can't say I have. I've known the time when I felt none too confident for the safety of my own carcass when you were behind me." Harper's lips were smiling, but his eyes were hard.

Sloan exploded in a gale of laughter. "Damn'd if you aren't a card, Rufe," he chuckled. "You know me too well to say a thing like that."

"That's exactly why I'm saying it," Harper said tersely. "Just don't mess things up, that's all." Without waiting for a reply, he strode through to the street.

Steve Gooch said queerly, "What's wrong with him lately?"

"Jittery," Sloan said shortly. "He's always this way when things go wrong—gets suspicious of everybody."

"If you ask me," Squint Amber said, "ever since that satchel disappeared he's been edgy as—"

"Forget that satchel," Sloan said sharply. "There's a job ahead. One more drink and we start. This night should show us just how much, or how little, Mr. Stormy Knight can take. I've a hunch his spine might come unglued if the going got real tough."

"He didn't show evidence to that effect yesterday or this morning, according to Rufe. I think he might be rugged, Cameo, if we pushed him too hard."

"Trouble this morning was," Sloan said, "that Rufe didn't push him hard enough. From what I picked up, Knight did most of the talking and Rufe never did get started. Sometimes I wonder about Rufe."

"Meaning," Squint Amber said nastily, "that you wonder if Rule is strong enough to head a gang like ours—and if maybe he's got your job?"

Sloan darted a quick sidewise glance at Amber. "Sometimes, Squint," he said savagely, "you talk too much for your own good. I wouldn't want that repeated."

"Especially in front of Rufe, eh, Cameo?" Gooch said slyly.

"Let's forget it," Sloan said roughly. "Joe, set 'em up again. We'll drink damnation to one Stormy Knight."

9. GUN-WHIPPED

Stormy and Quad ate supper at the hotel, then arranged with Ethan Whitlock, proprietor of the hostelry, to get a cot for Quad that could be moved down to the newspaper building. This accomplished, Stormy suggested they take a walk about town, to get acquainted. Carnival, Stormy realized, was a much more prosperous-looking settlement than he had at first thought. Both sides of Main Street were lined with stores. There were several saloons, a bank on the corner of Main and Ogden streets. Two livery stables, a gun and hardware shop, two pool halls, a women's wear establishment known as Euphemia Jones' Paris Emporium. A photograph gallery stood across from the post office, and on either side of the photo gallery were the town hall and jail and deputy sheriff's office. Five or six restaurants, including one Chinese and one Mexican cafe gave proof that Carnival citizens wouldn't go hungry. A men's clothing store was run by one Otto Schmidt; next door was a mining supplies and assay office. A huge barnlike structure, named the Pyramid, was given over to gambling. The Pyramid, Quad explained, was owned by Rufe Harper.

"Harper," Stormy said, "seems to have his

finger in a lot of pies." He paused. "I wonder why Harper named it the Pyramid."

"The clients," Quad observed dryly, "are supposed to pyramid their winnings."

"That's good come-on talk," Stormy chuckled. "I don't suppose the suckers ever stopped t think that a pyramid is big where it starts and gets smaller the farther it goes."

Quad laughed. "Make a note to put a paragraph in your paper to that effect. Maybe it will open folks' eyes."

They didn't enter the Pyramid, but continued on until they reached the Pegasus Saloon. When Stormy suggested it was about time for an after-supper libation, Quad was quick to assent. There were several men at the bar when they went in. One-Horse Shea performed certain introductions. Stormy received congratulations on his acquisition of the Carnival *Banner.*

A well-fed-looking man with muttonchop whiskers and a portly expanse of fancy vest offered to buy Stormy and Quad a drink. "It may be," he said genially, "that you didn't get my name and business when One-Horse introduced us. Meeting so many all at once is likely to—"

"Your name is Trent, isn't it?" Stormy said. "I think One-Horse said something about a bank."

"Ah yes, that's correct. Trent. Morgan Trent—at your service, I hope. My bank—the Stockmen and Miners'—will be pleased to assist you in any financing you may require. Carnival needs new blood. I'm glad to see you here—you and Mr. Wrangel."

Shea served drinks. Stormy and Quad drank Mr. Trent's health. Trent continued, "It was a blow, James Sanford's death. Why he should commit suicide is more than I can comprehend. I knew him well. He had no worries, so far as I know, and with so much to live for—Kate, for instance. A beautiful girl. No, why James should have killed himself I simply cannot understand. Or perhaps"—the banker's shrewd eyes studied Stormy—"you are one of those who think it was murder."

"I am," Stormy nodded. "In fact, I think I was the first to call it murder. I still think so, despite the verdict of the coroner's jury."

Trent nodded agreeably and lighted a fat cigar after offering similar smokes to Stormy and Quad. Quad accepted; Stormy rolled a cigarette. "I remember now," Trent went on, "you did create quite a stir with your charge of murder. Perhaps you're right. I sincerely hope so. Between you and me, James Sanford wasn't the man to commit suicide. If he had troubles—and he has had plenty in the past—he would have faced them like a man. Suicide is the coward's way."

"What," Stormy asked bluntly, "is your opinion of Rufe Harper?"

Trent lowered his voice but replied promptly,

"He's a blight on Carnival. It was a sorry day for the town when Rufe Harper arrived here. He took us all in—all except James Sanford. Sanford was smart. Of course I must ask you not to quote me. Harper does his banking with me. It ill behooves one businessman to adversely criticize another. Nevertheless, I could do without Rufe Harper's business. By the way, speaking of business, I expect to leave my ad with you."

"Ad?" Stormy looked blank.

"He means his advertisement in the *Banner*," Quad explained.

"Quite so," Trent smiled. "You know, advertising the benefits of the Stockmen and Miners' Bank. My ad appears weekly. Sanford made me a flat rate. If the price isn't right, drop in and see me. I'm sure everything will be satisfactory all around."

"I reckon," Stormy nodded.

"Did Kate—er"—Trent looked uncomfortable—"speak of any outstanding obligations when she made the paper over to you? . . . No, never mind, Mr. Knight, don't answer. I'll talk to Kate myself, when she has recovered from her shock. . . . No, no, thank you, no more to drink. I must be on my way home, or Mrs. Trent will 'take after me,' as she terms it. She doesn't approve of my drinking at all."

He smiled slyly and, fetching a clove out of his vest pocket, ground it between his big teeth.

"Well, good night, gentlemen. Drop into my office when you find time, Mr. Knight. I'd like to get better acquainted. Too, I might put you in the way of some profitable investments."

"Much obliged," Stormy nodded. "Good night."

Quad said, when the swinging doors had closed behind Trent, "Pompous old duck, ain't he?"

Stormy smiled. "Bankers have to put up a front, more or less. He talked like he didn't care much for Rufe Harper."

"I haven't found anybody yet that does," Quad grunted, "excepting Harper's own gang."

Stormy swung around to face the room, elbows resting on the edge of the long counter, one boot heel hooked over the bar rail, and commenced to question Quad on matters pertaining to printing. Quad replied to the best of his ability, speaking of typefaces, papers, headlines, and so on. Finally Stormy shook his head ruefully. "The deeper I get into this, the more trouble I see. I should stick to something I know."

"With Miss Kate to help," Quad said, "it'll come easier than you think."

He paused as One-Horse Shea appeared and tapped Stormy on the shoulder. One-Horse looked worried as he jerked a thumb toward the entrance. "I don't like it, Stormy. Those three never bring their trade here. It looks like trouble to me. That's Cameo Sloan in the lead. Squint Amber and Steve Gooch with him. You know they're Harper's men, of course."

A silence fell on the room as Sloan and his two companions advanced. Halfway along the bar Shea tried to head them off: "What'll it be, gentlemen?"

Gooch and Amber didn't reply. Sloan snapped nastily, "We don't like the custom you keep, One-Horse. We didn't come here to drink and we're particular who we drink with. Is that clear?"

"Now I don't want any trouble in the Pegasus—" Shea commenced.

Stormy cut in, smiling thinly, "I don't reckon there'll be much trouble, One-Horse. These hombres probably came to see me. Well, what's on your mind, Sloan?"

"Just this," Sloan rasped. "Yesterday, Knight, you made a few statements I didn't like. Rufe Harper didn't want trouble, and because of that I kept quiet."

"And now," Stormy said easily, "Harper's taken the leash off his dog, after all, eh?" He was watching Sloan's hands closely. Sloan made no attempt to draw, though his fingers twitched as though he'd liked to have jerked out the long-barreled pearl-handled guns and started throwing lead then and there.

"I wouldn't talk like that was I you, Knight,"

he said, his swarthy features flushing dully. "I came here to talk business."

"But Harper sent you, eh?" Stormy said.

"Big Rufe had nothing to do with this. He's a busy man. I'm just trying to save him trouble. He can't give personal attention to everything that comes up."

"Oh hell," Stormy said wearily, "what's your business? I'm sick of this palaver."

Sloan nodded shortly. "I'll get to it. Knight, you might be wise to transfer the Carnival *Banner* to Rufe Harper—"

"Why?" Stormy cut in.

"Rufe's an established citizen here, besides being mayor. He has the town's respect—"

"That's open to argument." Stormy smiled thinly.

"We won't argue it now," Sloan replied testily. "The point I'm making is, you know nothing about publishing a newspaper. It's pretty damned difficult to please everybody, and the way I look at it, you won't be pleasing anybody. The thing for you to do is to sell out and get out!"

"Suppose I don't see it that way?" Stormy asked lazily.

"You'll make enemies and find yourself in trouble. There's some things you can't buck, Knight."

"Meaning Rufe Harper and his crowd, I suppose. Well, Harper doesn't scare me, and neither do you, Sloan. I expected trouble when I took over the *Banner.* The sooner it starts, the sooner it will be over. There's your invitation, Sloan. From now on it's up to you."

"By God!" Sloan spat furiously. "You don't know what you're saying. You act like you were willing to cross guns with me. Nobody but a fool—"

"Certainly I'm willing to cross guns with you," Stormy snapped. "You and your pards came here with the intention of throwing a scare into me. You didn't think it would go this far. All right, you started this; you'll take the consequences. Go ahead, Sloan, pull your irons any time you like!"

Stormy was still standing, back against the bar. His right thumb was hooked in cartridge belt. His lips were smiling, but there wasn't any smile in his eyes. They were hard, relentless.

Sloan backed away a step. This was more than he had expected. He cast a quick glance at Gooch and Squint Amber. They stood waiting, ready to back up any signal Sloan gave them. But Stormy's belligerent attitude had taken some of the courage out of Sloan. He wasn't at all sure he wanted to engage in a gun fight right now. He glanced nervously about the room; the other customers had scattered hastily to one side, expecting any moment to see lead fly.

Slowly Sloan shook his head. "There's a law

against gun fights in this town. I don't want to be accused of breaking any laws, Knight. Don't get the idea I'm afraid of you. I'll meet you any time, any place, but right now's not the time—"

Quad Wrangel laughed harshly. "That's a contradiction that should make an item for the *Banner*."

Sloan cast a look of hate at Wrangel, then his gaze, reluctantly, came back to meet Stormy's steely gray eyes.

"Go ahead, draw, Sloan," Stormy invited easily.

Sloan backed another step. "I'm not a fool; you got friends here and—"

Stormy said disgustedly, "Oh hell." His right hand seemed to flick, and his gun was out, covering Sloan, Amber, and Gooch. The three gave a rather startled gasp at the speed with which Stormy's gun had filled his hand.

Without removing his gaze from the three, Stormy spoke to Wrangel: "Get Amber's and Gooch's guns, Quad. Give 'em to One-Horse to keep until tomorrow."

"Now, look here—" Amber commenced to protest.

"Shut your trap, Amber," Stormy snapped. "I'm just making sure you and Gooch won't cut in when Sloan and I get to work."

Quad did as ordered and turned the guns over to One-Horse. While this was going on, Sloan's face had turned a pasty white. "When Harper hears about this—" he started.

"Cut out the talk, Sloan," Stormy said, the words like icicles. "You've still got your two guns. I've got my weapon. You've made a heap of talk. Let's see you back it up. There's something between you and me that can be settled right now."

Abruptly Stormy thrust his forty-four back in its holster, then flung wide his arms. "All right, Sloan," he challenged. "I'm ready for you. Jerk your irons!"

Sloan's eyes widened, then narrowed. Two guns against Stormy's one. Sloan's heart pounded faster. Slowly his fingers started to curve above his pearl gun butts. Stormy's arms remained as before, wide from his sides. There was a half-contemptuous smile on Stormy's lips. It was that smile that finally broke Sloan's nerve. Stormy looked too sure, too confident.

Suddenly Sloan flung his own arms wide. "No, no," he choked. "I'm not drawing. You're aiming to pull some trick. But I'll get you yet, you—" The name he called Stormy was vile, vicious.

The smile vanished from Stormy's face. He went white about the lips. "Now, so help me," he exclaimed wrathfully, "you've got to fight, loan. Draw, or I'll beat the living hell out of you!"

Sloan continued to shake his head as he backed

away. There was sheer terror in his features now, as he took each stumbling step. The man's face was ashen; his eyes bulged with panicky fright. He tried to speak, but the words wouldn't come. He could only shake his head and back another step, intent now on reaching the doorway and making an escape.

Stormy leaped like a tiger and closed in on him. "Draw, damn you!" Stormy urged.

Desperately Sloan made a halfhearted gesture toward one gun, then a sob broke in his throat. Stormy stopped, then like a flash his left hand swooped down and jerked one of the pearl-handled weapons from its scabbard. Swiftly raising the gun, he slammed the barrel smartly across the side of Sloan's head. It wasn't a crushing blow; just hard enough to knock Sloan staggering against the wall. Again the gun barrel fell, and again and again, as Sloan's head was knocked from side to side.

A customer in the Pegasus gasped: "By jeez! He's gun-whuppin' Sloan with his own weepon!"

The barrel of the pearl-handled six-shooter was landing on Sloan's shoulders and arms now. The only sounds heard were the steady crack-crack of the gun barrel and Sloan's cries for mercy. Suddenly the man slumped to the floor and crouched groveling at Stormy's feet. Only then did Stormy stop, as the righteous anger commenced to fade from his face. "All right, Sloan," he said disgustedly, shoving the pearl-handled gun back in its holster, "you can get out now. And consider yourself lucky."

Sloan commenced to crawl on hands and knees toward the doorway. Blood was running from his nose; one eye was swelling shut. Stormy turned toward Amber and Gooch. "You don't need to wait until tomorrow for your six-shooters. You can get 'em from One-Horse now, in case you'd like to take up Sloan's fight later. And get Sloan out of here; he's stinking up a decent barroom."

Cautiously Gooch and Amber approached the bar, received their weapons, and placed them still more cautiously in holsters. Neither spoke a word as they went to the half-conscious Sloan and, taking an arm on each side, carried the beaten man through the swinging doors to the street.

A number of pent-up breaths were suddenly released throughout the Pegasus. "Cripes! What a beating!" a man ejaculated.

One-Horse looked with some awe at Stormy. "It's a wonder you didn't knock Sloan senseless with that gun barrel."

"Didn't want to knock him senseless," Stormy returned. "I didn't hit him hard enough for that. I just wanted to give him a beating he'd remember. He wasn't hit any harder than he'd been if I'd used my fists, only"—Stormy smiled slightly—"it's a mite easier on knuckles that-a-way."

"I'm getting the idea now," Quad chimed in. "So long as you didn't knock Sloan unconscious, he still had a chance to use his other gun—if he'd had the nerve. Man alive! It will take Sloan a long time to live this down."

"That's what I intended," Stormy nodded. "I admit I did sort of lose my temper for a moment."

Quad laughed. "Lost your temper? Lord! I'd hate to see you get really mad sometime."

Meanwhile Gooch and Amber had half carried the bruised and battered Sloan along the darkened street, until they'd reached the Pyramid Gambling Saloon. They left their beaten companion sprawled at the edge of the sidewalk while they entered the building to tell Rufe Harper what had happened. To their amazement, Harper threw back his head and laughed uproariously, then followed them out of the Pyramid.

Light streaming from the building threw the huddled figure into bold relief; by this time Sloan was sitting up, head cradled on his knees. Harper laughed again as he gazed down on his defeated lieutenant. Sloan lacked the courage to protest.

"I reckon this should be a lesson to you, Cameo," Harper said curtly. "I knew what you were up against; I had Knight picked as tough from the first. But you think you know it all. This serves you right. You've been getting pretty cocky lately—getting the idea you'd be a better man to run the gang than I am. Well, I thought I'd let you try out one of your smart schemes. You got exactly what you had coming. So far I'm still boss. Maybe you'll remember that from now on. When the time comes to stop Knight we'll stop him—but it will be done my way. What was it you said a spell back about giving a man enough rope to hang himself?"

Sloan didn't reply, though a moan left his lips.

Harper continued, "Get your horse and get out to the ranch. Unless you want to be a laughing-stock, you'd better stay out of Carnival until your features heal a mite. We'll square this job—but it will be squared my way, when the time comes. I think now you realize who's boss. It won't be too long before Knight realizes it too. I aim to cut a notch for that hombre."

10. STORMY MAKES A DEAL

The following morning the funeral of James Sanford took place in the Boot Hill, north of town. Nearly half the merchants in Carnival closed shop to attend the ceremonies, and the procession of buggies, riders, and surreys that wound up the road to the fence-enclosed cemetery was a long one. Stormy saddled up his buckskin gelding and attended, though he remained back from the crowd and made no move to speak to Kate Sanford, who had arrived with Gage and Mrs. Freeman. Stormy's heart leaped when he saw her. Kate saw him looking her way and raised one hand in a short wave of greeting. The girl was dry-eyed, pale, but her dark clothing served only to accentuate her loveliness.

Back in town once more, Stormy turned his pony in at the Yucca Livery and hastened toward the *Banner* building. The door was open when he arrived, and he heard the clackety-clack-clack of the press which Quad had been trying out. After a moment the noise stopped, and Stormy heard Quad giving orders to young Horace Brigham, who had come in the back way after the funeral ceremonies were over.

Stormy sat himself down at the office desk. Within a few minutes Quad entered. "How'd it go?"

Stormy said, "About as buryings usually go. People said the usual things. There was less weeping than usual, I guess. The reverend made his talk short and to the point. He sounded sensible. . . . Everything all right here, I suppose."

Quad nodded. "No sign of trouble a-tall."

"I didn't think there would be, but I didn't want to take a chance of leaving nobody here. Harper might have got an idea of breaking in and doing some damage. I'm just probably overcautious."

"Maybe it will pay to stay that way for a time. Shucks! It's all right with me. I'd sooner stayed here than go to the funeral anyway."

Stormy nodded. After a moment he said, "I heard the press running when I came in. Work all right?"

Quad said, "Sure. After I'd turned it over a few times yesterday, I was pretty familiar with it. This morning I just wanted to make sure. I'll run off some proofs after a while, now that Horace is here to help. I've got the kid learning to set type now. Might as well break him in as far as possible, in case anything ever happens to me."

Stormy cocked a rueful black eyebrow at Quad. "Nothing had better happen to you. We've got a job to do."

"Exactly what I've been thinking. You know, there's a newspaper to be published next Tuesday. What have you got to go in it? This is Friday, you know."

Stormy looked startled. "Ye gods! What would I put in it? I was figuring we could wait until Miss Sanford returned—"

"How do you know when she'll return? We can't wait for her. She may not feel like working for a month. You can't let Carnival down. People want the news."

Stormy groaned. "I knew damned well I should never have gone into this business. What'll we do, Quad?"

Quad took pity on him and grinned. "We'll make out. I've already got page four set."

"You have! Well, well—say—what did you put in it?"

"The usual matter. Wait, I'll try not to be too technical, so you'll understand. There are certain ads, for instance. They stay set in type from week to week. And then the last couple of days I've picked up a few items of interest. Nothing important, of course; things like how there's to be a church social held, and about the Perkinses' daughter being home for a visit, and how the Camerons have a new baby—stuff like that. Then there's state news from other towns—"

"Where do you get that?"

"I went to the post office this morning and asked for the *Banner*'s mail. You'll find a couple of personal letters to Sanford and his daughter on your desk there. And there were several newspapers. I clipped out a few items. Got Horace setting 'em up now. He's pretty slow but he'll learn. Oh yes, I set in your name as publisher on the flag head—you know, the heading on the editorial page that tells who's the owner, editor, and so on. Do you go on as editor too?"

Stormy said irritably, "How the devil do I know? An editor has to write, doesn't he? What do I know about writing?"

"You talk like you'd had an education."

"Sure"—wrathfully—"I went to college, but that doesn't make me a writer."

"Any fool can write," Quad said, grinning. "It's the printer that makes a newspaper. There's nothing to writing. All you have to do is know how to spell and string words together. Most of the time your typesetter will take care of your bad spelling too. So you see it's a cinch."

"I deny that," Stormy said heavily. "Tell me what to do and I'll try to do it." He rose and paced nervously about the office.

"In the first place, I don't suppose you plan any radical changes in the *Banner*, such as changing the name or anything of the kind. You probably want it to run as is."

Stormy nodded. "Changing sounds like more trouble. We'd better let it stand as is."

"In the second place, you've got to get your lead story lined up—"

"My what?"

"The principal story of the week, the same being, of course, the death of James Sanford. Then there'll be his obituary . . ." Quad paused a moment. "You'll probably have to see Miss Sanford and get all the details. We'll dope out a head for the story—"

"Quad, you're getting ahead of me."

"You know, a banner—er—a headline that will extend clear across the page in big black type. Something like, 'James Sanford Dies Suddenly' or 'Pioneer Publisher Passes—'"

"Cripes!" Stormy broke in. "Everybody in town knows that Sanford is dead. Why bother publishing the fact?"

Quad groaned. "Nevertheless, it has to be published. It has to be a matter of record, for one thing. Folks like to read about it."

"I don't know why they should."

"Stormy," Quad said wearily, "if nothing but cheerful news appeared in the papers, there wouldn't be near so many sold. People are funny; they like to read about fires and floods and murders and fights over women and horse races and—and—well, everything. You'll have to put in a couple of paragraphs about the funeral this morning. And any names you put down, see they're spelt right. Who attended the funeral this morning?"

Stormy shrugged his shoulders. "I only knew a few of the people. There were Miss Sanford and

Gage and Mrs. Freeman and that banker—er—Morgan Trent. And let's see . . ."

"You," Quad said flatly, "are a hell of a reporter."

"I'm not a reporter a-tall."

"You don't need to tell me. Look, Stormy, you write up the story of what happened to Sanford as well as you can. There's one rule you must follow in writing news—tell who, what, when, where, and why, if possible—" He broke off to explain more fully. "Anyway, make a stab at it. I'll look your stuff over and help you out, before it gets set up. If you can pick up any other items while you're sauntering around town, do it. But just remember that we've four pages of space to fill—and the paper has to be out next Tuesday."

Stormy looked aghast. "Lord help us!"

"Another thing," Quad continued. "When you find time you'd better write the story of what you did to Cameo Sloan last night."

"Hey! We can't put that in the paper."

"T'hell we can't! That's news. You put a quietus on one of Harper's gunmen. You want to let folks know you aren't afraid to buck Harper. That's the way you'll get support."

"But—but it will look as if I was boasting about winning a fight. And you really couldn't call it a fight."

"Forget it," Quad said disgustedly. "I'll compose the story of Sloan's downfall myself. I can do it.

But it's your place, as owner, to do the write-up on Sanford. Take a look at last week's paper. See if you can't pick up some idea on how newspaper writing is done. Then get busy with paper and pencil."

Without another word, Quad turned and departed for the print room. Stormy smiled ruefully. "I'm commencing to wonder if he's working for me or I'm working for him." Dropping into the swivel chair at the desk, Stormy reached for one of a small pile of newspapers stacked on the table and opened it.

The Carnival *Banner* was a four-page affair printed, then folded, on both sides of a single sheet. Each page was a trifle less than twelve by eighteen inches in size and carried five columns of printed matter. At the top of the page, in bold type, was the name, CARNIVAL BANNER, with below, in smaller print, the date and place of publication, volume number, price, and so on.

Below this came the headline, running the full width of the page, in heavy black letters: Cattle Thieves Still Rampant. Two columns, extending halfway down the page, related the loss of a bunch of prime Rafter-O cows stolen from Hoddy Oliver, local rancher. There was also a statement from Deputy Bayliss to the effect that arrests could be expected in the near future.

Other stories on the page carried news of a storm in the neighboring county to the east; a recent train wreck on the T.N. & A.S. Railroad came in for several paragraphs; the passing of one of the county's retired cattlemen was noted; a story devoted to the expansion and building activities of Carnival took up its share of space; a number of lines of type told of prospecting work in the Carnival Mountains.

The news carried over to pages two and three, where the items were shorter and carried word of interesting local happenings, including fights, scandals, weddings, real-estate deals, social activities, as well as advertisements. Page four was largely given over to ads, in boxes; there was a column of short county items, and a list of those who had died, been married, or born recently.

Stormy came back to page two where, beneath a small ruled box giving Sanford's name as editor and publisher, Katherine Sanford, assistant editor, was a two-column editorial beseeching the citizens of Carnival to strive harder for a law-and-order regime. The editorial scorched Rufe Harper, "our marauding mayor," and Pudge Bayliss, "dull-witted deputy," in no uncertain terms. The writing was trenchant, clear, and to the point. As he read the editorial Stormy found himself admiring the dead James Sanford; the printed word gave Stormy a definite impression of just the sort of man Sanford had been and the life he had lived.

Stormy finally refolded the paper and put it down. Then, with a long, reluctant sigh, he turned back to the desk, drew a sheet of paper toward him and, with a stubby bit of black pencil, started writing an account of James Sanford's death. Once started, he found himself growing angry; the words poured from his pencil in an indignant stream. He was still at work when Quad and Horace Brigham went out to dinner; several sheets of paper had been filled by the time they returned.

Eventually Stormy put down the pencil and leaned back in his chair. "Whew!" he breathed. "I feel like I'd done a job of work. Reckon I'd better go get me a bait—and a bottle of One-Horse's beer wouldn't go bad either." Rising from the chair, he left the scattered sheets of paper on the desk, donned his sombrero, and stepped out to the sun-bathed street.

It was nearly two o'clock by the time he returned. As he stepped into his office he stopped short at sight of the tawny-haired, gingham-clad figure seated in the swivel chair. "Hey"—Stormy's tones voiced his surprise—"what are you doing here?"

Kate Sanford swung around in the chair to face him. The girl smiled slightly. "Why shouldn't I be here?"

"But—but—" Stormy stammered.

"I suppose you expected me to stay home and mourn. Not for Kate Sanford, Stormy. I'd go crazy sitting around that empty house, just thinking—" Her voice faltered.

Stormy jumped into the breach. "Don't think I'm not glad to see you," he said quickly. "I'd about reached the stage where I'd start pulling out my hair in chunks." He removed his sombrero and tossed it on the table, then grinned. "If you look close you'll see I'm getting gray already."

"Regret your bargain, cowboy?"

"I'm hanged if I do," Stormy said stoutly, and added, "though I admit it's a right big job for me—" He broke off, noticing the blue-penciled sheets on the desk. "You been reading that stuff I was writing—trying to write?"

Kate nodded. "I'm sorry Dad isn't alive to see the nice things you've said about him."

"We-ell, you see, I'd heard Gage Freeman talk and One-Horse Shea and others. I read one of his editorials and really felt like I knew him myself. But what's all that blue-pencil scribbling?"

Kate explained. "I was just trying to whip it into shape a little."

"I butched up the job, eh?" Stormy's face fell.

"You did a grand job, Stormy," Kate said warmly, "only there's some editing necessary. There are things you couldn't be expected to know about. You've given the facts as they're generally known. That's what we'll print. Your own ideas we'll leave for editorials—"

"But, look," Stormy protested, "you won't want to be writing that piece about your dad. It's—it's—"

113

"Too personal?" Kate shook her head. "I can handle it, Stormy. Dad taught me to take the detached attitude in writing news. If necessary, I can be the hard-boiled newspaperman he tried to make me. It's what he'd want me to be. Besides, there are certain facts regarding Dad's life that only I know. They'll have to go into the article. But remember this first lesson in news writing: save your indignation for your editorials."

"Which same I doubt I'll ever write."

"You'll learn," Kate said confidently. She came back to the writing he'd done. "By the way, you suspect Dad was killed by somebody else, don't you?" Stormy nodded. The girl continued, "I noticed you didn't say much about that. What you wrote I changed to 'foul play suspected' and let it go at that, which is practically what you said."

"I figured it best not to talk too much about that," Stormy explained. "Let the matter be forgotten, while I dig up more evidence."

"Do you think you can do it?"

Stormy nodded, then, remembering Quad, said, "I suppose Gage told you I'd hired a printer."

"Told me last night," Kate replied. "I went out in the shop as soon as I returned and introduced myself. He and Horace seem to be getting along fine."

"What do you think of Quad?" Stormy queried.

"Type lice all over him," Kate responded promptly.

Stormy gulped. "I guess he has been a sort of tramp, but he shaved this morning and, so far as I know, has had only one drink today."

Kate laughed. "Stormy, there are no such things as type lice. That's just an expression Dad used to use when he meant a printer knew his business thoroughly. Golly, Quad's a jewel. I just hope we can keep him. Printers like Quad come through here several times a year, but they never stay long on a job. Train whistles in their heads, or itching hoofs, I guess."

"I'll keep him if I have to hog-tie him," Stormy promised. "Look here, Kate, there's something I've got to take up with you. You've turned the paper over to me, but no price has ever been mentioned. If you're to help get out the paper, there'll have to be a salary for you too."

"Let's forget the money end of it for the time being," Kate proposed. "We'll see how things go. There's a matter of three thousand dollars standing against the *Banner.* That will have to be repaid. But until things work out a little, let's not talk of money. I have enough to get along on. There'll be more coming in from the next issue."

Stormy slowly nodded his head. "Tell you what, I'll make a deal with you. Just sell me a half interest and we'll be pardners. You handle the editor job. The way I size up things, you and Quad and Horace can get out this paper without my help—or interference. If there's any prestige in having a man's name on the second page as publisher, leave mine there, but let's have it understood that you're half owner and editor. And don't worry about the money to keep going. I'll have some shortly; sent a wire to my bank back home last night."

"You really want it that way?" Kate asked seriously.

"Never wanted anything so bad in my life."

Kate stuck out her right hand. They shook on the deal. Stormy held her hand a trifle longer than was necessary. He cocked one black eyebrow at her. "Pardner?" he said.

"Pardner," she nodded.

Stormy heaved a long sigh of relief. "Now I can leave all this business to you and Quad. I knew I was getting in over my head."

"You don't get out of it that easy, Mr. Stormy Knight. I think we'll make a reporter of you. You can pick up news items and bring them in. You'll get ideas to write up—"

Stormy laughed. "You sure are optimistic."

"You're the optimistic one. You've gone into a business without even asking to see the books. You've probably no idea regarding our circulation—no, wait—I mean by circulation the number of papers we sell each week." She gave

116

Stormy certain facts and figures, adding, "There's an out-of-town distribution too."

Stormy made rapid calculations. "Well, that doesn't sound bad," he smiled.

"Remember," Kate warned, "we don't sell every paper we print, but we get rid of most of 'em. But there's stock to pay for—no, I mean paper stock. And ink. Wages for Quad and Horace. There are other expenses too, not counting the money you and I take out. And don't forget taxes on this building."

Stormy's face fell. "Maybe I jumped to conclusions."

"On the other hand," Kate continued, "there's a pretty steady revenue from our ads. And some job printing. You know, circulars, handbills, and so on. That boosts profits."

"Say! Can't we persuade more people to advertise?"

"Spoken like a true newspaper publisher," Kate smiled. "Try it sometime. There's a big field to work on."

"I might even take an ad myself."

"What would you advertise?"

"Our newspaper, of course," Stormy grinned.

Gravely Kate shook her head. "Wouldn't do. Then you'd have to buy a paper every Tuesday, just to see if your ad got a good position. It wouldn't be right for a publisher to have to pay for his own newspaper." A ghost of a twinkle appeared in her hazel eyes, then she sobered suddenly. "I'll have to go to the bank tomorrow, or next day, and talk to Mr. Trent about that three thousand dollars. Dad borrowed it from the bank, you know, with the *Banner* as security."

"Was that the three thousand that disappeared— the money in the missing satchel?"

Kate nodded. "You've probably wondered what Dad was going to do with the money. You see, for a long time he'd wanted a bigger press, a power press that could be run by steam. He dreamed of publishing a better, larger paper. Well, there was such a press as he wanted, to be auctioned off in Capital City. Dad had word that there wouldn't be many bidders and that he could probably get it for three thousand dollars. The terms of the auction called for cash in full when the sale was made. That's why he was carrying that money with him."

Stormy nodded comprehension. "I'd wondered a heap about that. I've a hunch we'll find it yet— that and the satchel. There's a heap of business I don't understand yet, but I will—sure as shooting."

"Did you ever discover how that bill of sale got into your pocket?" Kate asked.

Stormy shook his head. "Somehow I can't believe Harper had anything to do with it. I can't understand why he should, unless he figured to get me involved in some way, so he could take the paper from me instead of you. We know he wants the *Banner*. I'm sure looking forward to the time when he gets his comeuppance."

"You're not the only one in town who feels that way," Kate said soberly. "Dad thought he could lick him with the *Banner*. Now I'm not so sure. I'm afraid there'll be shooting, too. Stormy, if anything happened—" She broke off.

"Now don't you start worrying," Stormy advised. "This will all work out all right." He grinned suddenly. "I'm sure glad I made a deal for you to handle the paper. Any shooting that comes up won't drive me crazy, anyway."

"You'll do your part on the paper too," Kate said seriously. "I'm counting on that. Bucking Harper will take everything we've got. You had some trouble with Cameo Sloan last night—no, don't deny it. Gage told me. When I arrived today Quad was doing a story on it."

"I wasn't going to deny it," Stormy said, "but I can't see any reason for printing it in the *Banner*."

"I'm going to write the story myself," Kate said firmly. "Quad gave me all the facts. Meanwhile don't underestimate Sloan. Dad used to call him the Sidewinder. He's dangerous!"

11. CORNERED!

The next day, about ten o'clock, Stormy walked into Gage Freeman's general store. Gage was busy with a customer at the moment, but within a few minutes he hurried around the end of his counter, leaving his clerk to attend to other customers.

"You seem sort of busy," Stormy said. "Maybe I'd better drop in again."

"Thought you looked as though you wanted to see me about somethin'," Gage responded. "I'm always busy on Saturday. I'll be right busy all day, in fact, so you'd better talk now if it's important. Oh, say, that gun whipping you gave Sloan has caused a lot of talk."

"For or against?" Stormy smiled.

"For you, of course," Freeman replied. "Folks are glad to see there's somebody here that Harper's crowd hasn't been able to bluff. But you want to watch out for Sloan's next move. He's treacherous."

"Quite a few people have been telling me that."

"It's true. I saw him ride into town this morning, so keep your eyes extra peeled."

"I'll do that. What I wanted to see you about, Gage. Can you remember just what happened when Sanford was shot? I know you told me before, and I heard your testimony at the inquest, but I'd like you to go over the story again."

"Why, sure." Freeman launched into a recital of the happenings as he remembered them. "It was the noise of the shot that drew me to the doorway. Then I thought I heard a second shot, but I was probably mistaken. I glanced toward the Bonanza Bar and saw Muley Porter—one of Harper's cow hands—leap over the porch railing and head at a run up Flagstaff Street—"

"Why should he go that way?" Stormy cut in.

"You'll remember he testified at the inquest that he thought the sound of the shot came from that direction. Muley's kind of a big dumb ox, anyway."

"Must be something wrong with his ears. The rest of Harper's gang, as I understand it, headed toward the newspaper building."

"That's right. Rufe got there first, and it seemed to me he wasn't any too anxious to see that door opened too soon—though I can't see why."

"I don't either—yet—but I hope to. Now let's go back a spell. You say you think you heard two shots. You didn't mention that at the inquest."

"I'm not sure I did, Stormy. One or two others thought they heard two shots, but Harper insisted there had been only one. I guess we all took his word for it. Some other noise, like a shot, might have been heard."

"The first shot sounded like a forty-five, though, eh?"

"I'd swear to that."

"The second didn't sound the same?"

Freeman shook his head. "It wasn't as heavy."

"Could it have been made by Sanford's thirty-eight gun?"

"Could've been," Freeman admitted after a moment's pondering.

"In fact," Stormy said slowly, "I think it was. We know the thirty-eight had been fired—"

"Yes, but when? There was one empty shell in the cylinder. It was mentioned at the inquest, remember, that Sanford might have had his hammer resting on an empty shell, like cow hands do, and never carried more than five loads in his gun."

"Not in this case." Stormy shook his head. "I've talked to Kate about it. She says her dad only got that gun because some friends insisted—"

"I was one of them," Freeman interrupted.

"—that he have something to protect himself if Harper started trouble sometime. Sanford, apparently, wasn't afraid of anything of the sort, and only bought the gun to satisfy his friends. Kate says he loaded six cartridges into the gun, then dropped it in his desk drawer and forgot it. He never carried the weapon."

"Then when was that one shot fired?"

"The morning Sanford was killed, the way I figure."

"You mean he really did kill himself?"

"On the contrary. Look, Gage, I haven't everything worked out in my mind yet. When the details dovetail I'll talk more about it. That's about as much as I can say now. Thanks a lot."

"You're welcome. How're things at the *Banner*?"

Stormy smiled. "You'll have to ask Kate or Quad. I've turned the job over to them. They seem to be making out all right. Me, I'm just a publisher. I don't work at it."

He left the general store and started across Main Street, threading his way between ponies and horse-drawn wagons coming into town. A voice hailed him. Stormy glanced around and saw Big Rufe Harper approaching. "I want to see you a minute, Knight."

Stormy halted at the edge of the sidewalk. "All right, you see me. What's on your mind?"

"You had some trouble with Cameo Sloan—and Gooch and Amber—in the Pegasus night before last."

"No trouble for me," Stormy replied briefly. "Sloan started running off at the head and he got what he asked for. I was glad to oblige. His pards scarcely opened their traps. Harper, next time you send a crew to throw a scare into me, you'd better send more than three men. It might be a good idea to come yourself."

Harper smiled genially. "From what I hear, that would probably be the wise thing to do. However, Knight, I'd like to have you believe I had nothing to do with that business."

"You sure would," Stormy chuckled ironically, "but I'm not that dumb."

"I'm speaking truth, Knight. That was Sloan's own idea. He dragged Gooch and Amber along with him. I've questioned them. They didn't want to go with him. I had nothing to do with it."

Stormy asked, "Must I call you a liar, Harper?"

Harper's eyes narrowed. "It might not be advisable. Howsomever, I'll let it pass. I'd like to be friendly. You and I got off on the wrong foot to start with."

"And it was your toes got trod on," Stormy laughed softly. "No, Harper, it doesn't go down."

"Look, Knight, you probably won't believe me, but I'm glad you gave Sloan that beating. He had it coming. I'm speaking straight when I say that. Frankly, if you don't want to be friends with me, that's all right. I won't force the issue. But believe me when I say I had nothing to do with Sloan's trouble at the Pegasus."

Somehow Stormy gathered the impression that Harper was pleased over the beating Sloan had received. Stormy couldn't understand it. There was something queer going on here. Finally he shrugged. "Okay, Harper, I'll take your word for it. To tell the truth, it looked kind of dumb on your part—if you were responsible—to send Sloan after me in such a fashion. I didn't figure you thought I was that easy."

"I don't," Harper replied frankly. "It served Sloan right. I told him to keep out of town until his face had healed up, so you won't be bothered with him for a spell. I gave him hell, in fact."

"I heard he was in town this morning."

"He was," Harper answered promptly. "Came in against orders. I sent him sloping back to the ranch after I'd given him a good dressing-down. Just in case you should have any more trouble with him —or with any of my men—let me know."

"I'll do better than that. I'll hold you responsible for anything that happens from now on."

"Oh, look here, Knight," Harper protested, "you can't do that. My hands are right high-spirited and they get out of control sometimes."

"They're in your pay, Harper. What I said stands. From now on I'm holding you responsible—you personally."

Harper commenced angrily, "Now you listen here—" He stopped abruptly, growled, "Oh, to hell with it," and walked swiftly away in the direction of the Bonanza Bar.

Stormy gazed after him a moment, then laughed softly and continued on his way to the newspaper building. Arriving there, he glanced through the big front window before entering. Kate wasn't at the desk; the office was empty. "Probably out in the pressroom, with Quad, taking Rufe Harper to pieces," Stormy speculated. "If I go in, they might make me do some writing." He decided to continue on along Main Street.

He wandered around for another hour or so and talked to various people. Then, after eating his dinner at the hotel dining room, he returned to the *Banner* office once more. The office was still empty, but he found Kate, Horace, and Quad out in the pressroom.

Horace was industriously toiling at the paper-cutting machine, trimming stacks of stock to the required size. Quad was standing before the type case, his nimble fingers picking type from the multi-partitioned shallow boxes and arranging the letters in the stick, or small hand tray, he held in his left hand. Kate was seated at a table across the room, surrounded by a litter of papers and proofs, while she worked on a dummy page. The three scarcely noticed Stormy, so busy were they, when he walked in.

"Hey, don't you folks ever eat dinner?" Stormy asked.

Kate hardly raised her head. "My grief! Is it dinnertime already?" She continued working.

Stormy wandered over and glanced beyond Quad's shoulder, marveling at the speed with which the type letters grew into words and words expanded to line after line in the stick, under Quad's skillful manipulation. Stormy tried to read what Quad was setting. Suddenly he frowned.

"Quad!" Stormy protested. "You'd better watch what you're doing. You're all mixed up."

Quad worked swiftly on, without stopping. "What's wrong now?" He shot a quick glance at the copy he was following.

Stormy shook his head. "I knew I should have stuck around or things would go haywire. You been drinking? What's wrong! Can't you read? You've got all those words running backward!"

Quad chuckled. "You telling me how to set type?"

"But can't you see what you're doing?" Stormy persisted. "It's the Chinese that read backward—not us."

Quad continued working without a break. From the vicinity of the paper-cutting machine there came a muffled snicker. Kate glanced around, smiling, from her table. "Type has to be set that way, Stormy. You see . . ." She rose and came over to explain certain technical matters. Stormy heard her through in a sheepish silence. "Someday," he said, "I'll learn to keep my big mouth shut. Quad, I owe you a drink."

Quad put down his stick so fast he nearly pied the type. Then he picked it up again and grinned. "I'll get it when I go out to dinner."

"I said *a* drink, remember," Stormy warned. He turned to Kate. "I got two ads," he announced proudly. "That is, just one new one. Fitz's Barbershop. You're to write it up, Kate."

Kate shook her head. "*I* should write an ad for a barbershop! All right. We've tried to get Fitz's ad for a long time. You're a salesman, Stormy."

"I'm no salesman. Fitz buttonholed me on the street. I think we're getting the ad because he doesn't like Harper."

Quad said, "I knew you'd be a good influence here."

"What's the other ad?" Kate asked.

"I saw Euphemia Jones, of the Paris Emporium. She just received a shipment of twenty new bonnets and wants them mentioned in her regular ad. She said you'd know what to say, Kate. And she'd like it fixed up sort of fancy."

"Darn it!" Kate wailed. "She would have to have a change just when we have all page three set. Oh well, I'll take care of it. We'll give her an ornamental border. Quad, we can give her a border of hearts-and-roses dingbats, can't we?"

Quad looked dubious. "We're sort of shy on hearts. Maybe I could run in some stars to make up for 'em."

Kate nodded. "That'll be fine."

Stormy asked, "Did you say page three was all ready to print?"

Kate nodded. "It was, until you got here with Euphemia's change."

"There's plenty of time, isn't there?"

"Heavens no! We've lost a couple of days. We're going to have to put in some work Sunday. Pages two and three have to be printed Monday."

"You mean we do those before we do page one and—"

"We have to do it that way," Kate interrupted to explain. "Monday we print pages two and three; Tuesday we turn the sheet over and print one and four on the blank side. Then we fold them and they're ready to go. We leave the printing of pages one and four until the last, in case something important comes up we want to put on page one. We'll probably work late Monday night too."

Stormy scratched his head. "Maybe we'd all better go get a drink. I'm getting dizzier every minute."

"And I'm getting hungrier!" Kate exclaimed. "I'm eating dinner at Mrs. Freeman's today. I think I'll just slip out the back way, here, and across the alley. I can cut through Mr. Trent's yard to Beaumont Street and I'm practically at the Freemans'. Bye-bye!" She started toward the alley doorway, then paused. "Stormy, I've written the editorial for the next issue. I wish you'd look it over. It's on the desk in the office."

"Shucks! If you wrote it, it will be all right."

"You look it over before it goes into type," Kate said firmly. "I'm not going to take all the responsibility." Without awaiting further protest, she vanished.

Quad slipped an apron over his head. "I guess Horace and I had better eat now too. C'mon, kid. You can cut that stack of stock after you've had your chow."

A few minutes later Stormy found himself alone in the building. He wandered idly about, smoking a cigarette; for a time he studied the press, trying to understand the intricacies of its rollers, wide type bed, cogs, levers, and so forth. He sauntered over to the table and gazed at the dummy page upon which Kate had been working. There was a strong smell of printer's ink in his nostrils.

He strolled through to the front, where the entrance door stood open, casting a glance into the office as he passed. There were more people on the street by this time. Evidently the whole countryside came in on Saturday afternoon, as was the case in most cow towns. Stormy pinched out the fire on his cigarette and snapped the butt across the sidewalk to the dusty roadway, then turned and entered the office.

On the desk he found the copy for the editorial Kate had written. He read it through approvingly. It was an attack on the current political situation as administered by Mayor Rufe Harper and his crew, and called for a shake-up in the forces of law and order. The story commented but briefly on the passing of Kate's father. Stormy nodded. "This is all right," he muttered, "though if I was writing it I'd stick in a few 'damns' and a couple of 'hells.' It would make the piece stronger."

He reread the editorial, nodding his head in satisfaction. Three quarters of an hour had passed since he was left alone. Stormy finally put down the sheets of paper. "Someday," he mused, "it's going to be possible to persuade more people with a piece like this than with all the Colt guns manufactured."

A slight noise at his rear caused Stormy to glance back over his shoulder. Then he spun around in his swivel chair to face the office doorway. Immediately he realized he was cornered.

"Stay right where you are, Knight," came the cruel tones. "One move and you get it right now!"

Just beyond the doorway stood Cameo Sloan, a long-barreled six-shooter in each hand, the muzzles of which were bearing directly on Stormy's body. There was a maniacal gleam in Sloan's bloodshot eyes. He laughed harshly. "I'm going to kill you, Knight!"

12. A SLIM CHANCE

Stormy eyed the man with a calmness he was far from feeling. His own gun was holstered, wedged against the side of the chair, making a quick draw impossible. And Stormy knew he wouldn't dare try to shift position. Sloan's face still bore strong evidence of the beating he'd received two nights before. One eye was nearly swollen closed; the right cheekbone was split open; court plaster crisscrossed a couple of spots on his forehead.

Stormy said quietly, "You can't get away with this, Sloan. You shoot me and you'll be caught before you've gone half a block."

"Do you think I care for that?" Sloan snarled. "All I want to do is wipe you out, you interfering bustard. Go on, reach for your gun. I'll drill you before you can touch gun butt, and you know it."

"I suppose you're correct." Stormy nodded easily, stalling for time. People were passing along the street outside, but, situated as he was, Sloan couldn't be seen from the sidewalk unless someone approached the front entrance or stopped to deliberately gaze through the wide window of the office. Stormy went on, "You'd better think twice, Sloan. This will mean your finish as well as mine, if you shoot."

"Shut up!" Sloan rasped. "I'm doing the talking now. You had your say a couple of nights ago. Now it's my turn. No man is going to gun-whip Cameo Sloan without paying for it—and you're going to pay plenty."

Stormy continued, "You'll swing for it, Sloan." His eyes were boring steadily into those of Sloan. "It won't feel nice when that rope tightens around your throat. Your breath will be cut off. You'll feel yourself strangling." Stormy braced himself for a sudden leap from the chair. "It's pretty bad being hung, Sloan. I saw a fellow hung over in Texas one time. It took him a long time to die—"

"God damn you, shut up!" Sloan screeched crazily. "I can take that, that hanging. All's I want to do is kill you. And you're going to get it right now, you—"

The words ended in a torrent of profane abuse. One gun barrel tilted slightly. Stormy's gaze caught the slight movement as Sloan's finger commenced to tighten about the trigger. Stormy gathered his muscles, left the chair in a swift leap. But the move came too late to prevent Sloan firing. There were two shots, close together. Powder smoke stung Stormy's nostrils.

But even as Sloan pulled triggers his aim had been distracted: from the direction of the print shop a dark object had come hurtling into the corridor to land with a sound of shattered glass against Sloan's left temple, cutting a slash in his cheek as it struck and broke. A viscous black fluid mingled with the blood and drenched the man's features as he toppled sidewise and slumped to the floor near the office doorway.

Stormy halted abruptly, then stepped quickly over the broken glass and ink on the floor to kick the twin six-shooters from Sloan's nerveless fingers; Sloan had been completely knocked out by the blow. Next Stormy whirled to see Kate Sanford leaning limply against one corridor wall. The girl's face was drained of all color and held traces of the sheer terror which had gripped her but a moment before.

"Kate!" Stormy exclaimed. "Did you throw that—that—"

Kate nodded and forced a weak smile. "I'd returned from dinner by the rear door. As I entered the print shop I heard Sloan talking. For a minute I was petrified. I crept nearer, trying to think of some way to stop him. Then I saw a quart jar of ink on the table. I seized it—threw it as hard as I could . . ." Her hazel eyes went to the limp form sprawled on the floor, and a hint of hysterical laughter rose to her lips. "Looks— looks like Sloan has—printer's ink—in his blood."

"Steady, girl," Stormy said sharply. "Sloan's not dead, just unconscious. How did that jar of ink happen to be there?" The unimportant question was asked in an effort to quiet Kate's nerves.

Kate swallowed hard. Some of the color returned to her face. "We had a carboy nearly empty, so I told Horace, only this morning, it would be necessary to pour the remaining ink into a jar so we could return the carboy for more ink. That—that jar was the only thing I could see to throw. It was a slim chance, but I just had to take it or see Sloan shoot you."

"Lady, you sure have one fine throwing arm," Stormy grinned. He went to the girl, but she put out one protesting hand. "I'm all right now. Kind of shaky for a minute, though."

While they were talking, shouts had sounded along the street. Quad came dashing in at the front entrance. "What the hell!" he exploded. Then, "Sorry, Miss Sanford. But what's happened here?"

Other people, drawn by the sound of the shooting, were crowding in behind Quad and gathering in front of the newspaper building. Horace Brigham arrived and went white at sight of Sloan's figure stretched on the floor.

Stormy explained to Quad, "Sloan sneaked behind me and was figuring to do a rub-out job. Just a split instant before he pulled trigger Kate heaved a jar of ink at him. It landed hard and put him down for the count."

Quad smiled grimly. "Sort of jarred the coyote, I'd say."

A groan burst from Sloan's lips and he opened his eyes. Stormy moved back and kicked the man's six-shooters, on the floor, still farther out of reach. "If you're ready to get up and finish what you started, Sloan," Stormy said coldly, "just say the word and I'll let you have your guns."

Sloan cursed feebly, started to raise himself, then abruptly closed his eyes and collapsed back to the pine flooring. Stormy turned away in disgust. More and more people were crowding into the corridor. Stormy asked them to move back. He heard Big Rufe Harper's voice inquiring what had happened, and a moment later Harper, unceremoniously thrusting others aside, shouldered his way inside to face Stormy.

Stormy said, "Remember what I said about holding you responsible, Harper?"

Harper's yellow eyes narrowed angrily. He cast a quick glance down at Sloan, then asked, "Dead?"

"Knocked cold," Stormy replied tersely. "He tried to bump me off from behind. Miss Sanford hurled a jar of ink that collided with his head."

Harper shot a look at the girl. "Nice throwing, Miss Sanford," he complimented. "I reckon Sloan had it coming—"

Stormy broke in, "I'm expecting you to say you had nothing to do with this, Harper."

"Exactly what I am saying, Knight," Harper

insisted. "You're not holding me responsible for this. I had nothing to do with it. I didn't even know Sloan was in town. This morning I told him to go back to the ranch. I know he started, but he must have come back."

"That's my guess too." Stormy smiled sarcastically.

"Dang it!" Harper insisted. "I'm talking straight, Knight. What Sloan did he did on his own responsibility—and anything he does from now on will be the same way. I'm through with him! He had his orders. He chose to disobey. Hold me responsible if you like. That's up to you. What you aiming to do about it? If it will make you feel any better you can bring charges against me, but if you do, you're a bigger fool than I take you for. This is as much a surprise to me as it was to you—probably bigger. You at least knew that Sloan was out to get you if he had a chance. I never dreamed he remained in town after I sent him away. Now, believe me or not, as you like, but I still insist—"

"All right," Stormy conceded grudgingly, "you don't need to make a speech about it, Harper." Despite his own feelings in the matter, Stormy commenced to feel that Harper was, for once, speaking the truth. "I'll take your word for it. But don't get the idea I trust you any more than I ever did."

"I'm not asking you to," Harper snapped. "You

137

play your game and I'll play mine. We'll see who comes out on top—"

"Meanwhile," Stormy interposed, "suppose you drag this carcass out of here. Sloan's conscious now; he's just faking."

"Drag it out yourself," Harper rasped. "Didn't you hear me say I was through with the double-crossing scut?" Turning, he shouldered his way back through the crowd and disappeared.

Almost instantly Deputy Sheriff Pudge Bayliss came puffing importantly through the crush. "Make way for the law, make way for the law," he demanded. "What's all this about, Mr. Knight? Big Rufe tells me Sloan tried to kill you. Want I should place him under arrest?"

"What do you think?" Stormy said ironically. "Didn't you ask Harper first what you should do?"

"Yeah, I did." Bayliss seemed somewhat bewildered. "But Rufe said he didn't give a damn—beggin' your pardon, Miss Sanford."

"Well, I don't either," Stormy snapped. "You claim to represent the law here in Carnival. What do you think you should do with the coyote?"

Bayliss looked uncertain. "Lemme see, could you lay a charge of murder against him?"

Stormy smiled ironically. "Who did he murder?"

"We-ell"—lamely—"Sloan tried to kill you, didn't he, Mr. Knight?"

Stormy said impatiently, "Oh, cripes, Bayliss!

138

Murder and attempted murder are two different things. Just take Sloan out of here, that's all I ask. Throw him in the jug."

"I know what." Bayliss suddenly brightened. "I'll put him in jail on a charge of disturbing the peace."

Stormy said with grave sarcasm, "Don't you think that's a mite drastic, Bayliss?"

"I don't know as it is," Bayliss said seriously. "Mr. Harper refuses to be responsible for him, and if you ain't no definite charge to place—"

"Bayliss," Stormy said testily, "you're just too brainy for the kind of job you're holding—"

"Thank you, Mr. Knight."

"—and I'll be surprised if you hold said job much longer. Now get Sloan out of here and down to your jail. I'll be along later, and we'll put our heads together and maybe—if you'll try real hard—you can think up a charge to lay against Sloan. But right now all I want is to see him out of here. Is that clear enough for your thickheaded noodle?"

"Yes sir, Mr. Knight."

"Get busy, then!"

While curious faces crowded in at the entrance Bayliss strode over to Sloan and, seizing the man by the collar, heaved him upright. Sloan swayed a bit uncertainly, but his eyes were clear now and he darted a look of hate at Stormy.

"You, Cameo," Bayliss said sorrowfully, "don't

you feel ashamed of yourself, creating all this bother? Mr. Harper didn't like it a-tall."

"In fact, Sloan," Quad put in, "you deserve a right smart spanking, at least—but, Deputy Bayliss, don't you lay an angry hand on that man. With your temper—"

Boisterous guffaws burst from the onlookers. Bayliss glanced around, somewhat puzzled. Stormy swore disgustedly under his breath, then said to Bayliss, "Go ahead, get Sloan out of here and put him behind bars, or you'll answer to me, Bayliss."

The deputy tightened his grip on Sloan's arm. "Come along now, Cameo. I don't want no resisting of the law, mind you."

"Hell, who's resisting?" Sloan growled. "All's I want is a doctor to fix this cut on my face. Don't forget to bring my guns, Bayliss."

"Oh yeah, I nigh forgot them," Bayliss said obediently. "Just a minute—"

By this time Stormy's temper was ready to snap. "I'll take care of the guns, Bayliss. Just get moving— Oh, hell's bells!" he burst out angrily. Stepping quickly forward, he spun the deputy and the prisoner around, seized them both by the collars, and hustled them, through the crowd, out to the street. "Now, keep going, nitwit," he ordered. "Quad! You go along with Bayliss and see that he actually puts Sloan behind bars."

"I'll do it and glad to," Quad nodded. Scooping

one of Sloan's guns from the floor, Quad hastened to follow the somewhat bewildered deputy and his ink- and blood-smeared prisoner.

Still growling wrathfully under his breath, Stormy returned to the office, after requesting the crowd to scatter. The order was scarcely necessary; the throng had already started to break up, fully half of the men following Bayliss, Quad, and Sloan in the direction of Carnival's jail. As he re-entered the office Stormy picked up Sloan's other gun from the floor and tossed it on the table near his desk. Then he dropped into his swivel chair, his features contorted in angry exasperation.

He heard Kate call to Horace to come and clean up the glass and ink on the floor, then the girl entered and seated herself on the table near Sloan's gun. The girl eyed Stormy smilingly. "If angry," she counseled, "count ten; if very angry, count a hundred."

"In my case," Stormy growled, "a million wouldn't help! That Bayliss! In all my life I have never seen a dumber, no-good, useless, inefficient, ineffectual, weak, idiotic, imbecilic, half-witted—" He stopped for sheer lack of breath.

Kate's long-lashed eyes twinkled. "To be brief, you haven't any use for him."

"Kate," Stormy broke out, "that Bayliss makes me so damned mad . . ." He paused, then, doggedly, "I'm hanged if I'll apologize for the profanity, either."

"Not necessary," Kate smiled. "You're entitled to one 'damn' after what you went through. Well, on your own head be it. You would be a newspaperman. I warned you you'd have troubles."

Stormy grinned suddenly. "You know, I was right riled for a minute or so."

"That so?" Kate said dryly. "If that's the case, I'd hate to see you get real mad sometime."

"Something else," Stormy said suddenly. "I don't think I've said 'much obliged' yet, for saving my life. You did, you know." He abruptly got to his feet and took one of her hands. "Kate, I think you're just about the most wonderful—"

"Stormy," Kate reminded quickly, "do you think Horace is doing a good job of cleaning that floor? And you know, we're both near the window. People can see from the street. They might think you were getting emotional or something. And I hadn't the least idea of saving your life when I threw that jar of ink. I always did want to throw something at Cameo Sloan—and besides, I didn't want the *Banner* to lose its publisher just after you'd come into the business."

At that moment Quad re-entered the building. Stormy dropped back to his swivel chair. "Did Bayliss get him into a cell, Quad?"

Quad nodded. "Turned the key on him too. I made sure of that. In fact, Bayliss almost bawled

142

Sloan out for creating a disturbance. I sort of threw a scare into Bayliss."

"How?" Stormy asked.

"Told him you had a terrific temper and that if Sloan made an escape or wasn't treated exactly the way a would-be killer should be treated, you'd probably throw a whole flock of lead through Carnival's deputy sheriff. Bayliss turned sort of green when I said that, so I think the idea will stick with him."

"Trouble with Bayliss is he doesn't know where he's at now that Rufe Harper refused to help Sloan," Stormy said.

"Regardless of who helps who or who doesn't," Kate put in, "we can't sit talking all day. There's a paper to get out." She slid down from the table and smoothed out her skirt. "And, don't forget, we've just gained another item for the *Banner*. 'Gunman Fails in Murderous Attempt.' Write it up, Stormy."

"I'll be hanged if I will," Stormy snorted. "I'm in the paper enough already— But wait!" He grinned widely. "We'll play it up from your angle, Kate, and tell what a good throwing arm you have. Sure, I'll write it. Let's see—'Furious Female Flings—' No, won't do. 'Furiously Flinging Female Foils Fiendishly Fatal—'"

"Too long," Quad cut in, chuckling. "Why not 'Flinging Female Foils Fiendish Foe'?"

Kate stamped her foot. "I won't have it!" she

protested. "I don't like being written up as a 'female.' Even filly would be better—or feminist. And besides, we can drop the whole matter. I'll do the story myself. Meanwhile, Stormy, it would help a lot if you'd make up a list of our subscribers in alphabetical form. It's something we've always needed. And there are a few bills to be added up and paid. Those papers at the right side of your desk, Stormy. Take care of 'em, will you? Come on, Quad. The print shop's waiting for us."

"Slave driver!" Stormy jeered as the two left the office. The smile faded from his face as he swung around and contemplated the papers Kate had laid out for him. "This," he growled, "is one hell of a job for a gun-totin' cow hand."

Despite himself he became interested, however, and the sun had dropped below the Carnival Mountains before he realized the day was done.

13. DEPUTY BAYLISS RESIGNS

The editor and printing force of the Carnival *Banner* worked steadily all day Sunday, and by ten o'clock Monday morning Kate announced that the situation was well in hand and that—this with a long sigh of relief—the paper would be issued on time, Tuesday, as usual. Shortly before noon Monday they started printing pages two and three. From the press came a steady clackety-clack-clack as young Horace Brigham manipulated the long lever that set the machinery in motion.

Stormy stood by, watching with a certain fascination as Kate fed the large blank sheets of paper into the machine, which returned them, printed on one side, an instant later. Another sheet would be fed in, Horace would give a sturdy pull on the hand lever, and again a printed sheet would emerge to be seized by Quad and given a sharp scrutiny before it was placed on a stack of near-by similar sheets. Now and then a halt would be called while Quad made some minor adjustment on the press's "innards," as he called them.

"You three sure got teamwork," Stormy chuckled. "This goes faster than I thought it would."

Without raising her eyes from the work, Kate said, "We can turn out about two-fifty to three hundred an hour this way. With the power press Dad intended to get, that figure could be moved up to a thousand. But this is all right. We should be able to start the pages one-and-four run late this afternoon—"

Quad broke in to say, "Horace, when your arm gets tired, sing out and I'll take over. You can feed and Miss Kate can inspect and stack."

"Aw, I never get tired, Mr. Wrangel," Horace said.

Stormy asked, "What can I do?"

"Bring over some more of that cut stock and place it on my table," Kate replied. "After that you're at liberty. If you behave yourself, seeing you're the publisher, we'll let you help fold the papers tomorrow. Right now there's nothing much—"

"Hold it!" Quad interrupted. "Time to ink that roller again." The press stopped. "Miss Kate," Quad continued, "next time you buy ink, try ordering from the Kansas City Type Foundry. The linseed they use gives a mite heavier ink— and say, if you ever want a red for heads, you can't beat Kansas City's red."

"I'll keep it in mind if we ever go in for two-color printing," Kate nodded.

Stormy waited until the press had started once more, then announced his intention of leaving.

"I'm expecting a telegram at the depot," he explained. "I'll be back after a spell."

He paused in his office a moment and, seeing Cameo Sloan's twin six-shooters on the table, took time to thrust the pearl-handled weapons into a lower drawer of his desk. "Gosh," he muttered, "I'd plumb forgot about Sloan, we've been so busy. Reckon while I'm out I'd better drift down to the jail and check on him and Bayliss. Sloan might be persuaded to talk a mite."

He left the office and walked along Main until he'd reached Ogden Street. Here he turned and found the railroad station at the end of the street. Entering, he learned that a telegram awaited him from his bank. Thrusting the paper into his pocket, Stormy once more headed outside. His next stop was at the Stockmen and Miners' Bank, where his business was quickly transacted, though Banker Morgan Trent showed an inclination to detain him in conversation. Stormy pleaded a matter of hurry-up business, again shook hands with Trent, and left the bank.

By this time it was well past noon, and Stormy dropped into a small restaurant run by a Chinese, to get dinner. Leaving the restaurant a half hour later, he turned his steps in the direction of Main and Lincoln streets, on the corner of which stood the deputy sheriff's office, with the rock-and-adobe constructed jail at its rear. An angry voice assailed Stormy's ears as he approached the open doorway of the office. Stormy frowned. "Sounds like Rufe Harper. Boy, he's sure giving Bayliss a tongue-lashing for something."

The voice halted abruptly as Stormy stepped inside Bayliss' office. Bayliss was huddled at his desk, looking extremely frightened. Towering above him was Big Rufe Harper. Harper's face was flushed with anger, and his powerful hands opened and closed convulsively as though he'd like to tighten them about Bayliss' fat neck. He swung savagely around as Stormy came in, and his yellow eyes flashed hotly.

"Don't let me interrupt a little social discussion," Stormy said easily.

"Social discussion hell!" Harper raged. "This—this fool—"

"I'll concede that," Stormy smiled. So far Bayliss hadn't said anything, only shrunk a little deeper into his chair.

"There's some things you don't have to concede," Harper snapped. "You heard what this damn fool has done?"

"If it makes you mad, I'm not worrying," Stormy grinned.

"That's what you think," Harper snorted. "Maybe you won't feel so good about it when you hear Bayliss has let Cameo Sloan escape."

"T'hell you say!" Stormy's jaw dropped. "When did this happen, Bayliss?"

"Last—last night," Bayliss quavered. "I wasn't careless nor nothin'. It was just that Cameo had been so friendly that he took me by surprise, and after I'd had the doctor fix his cut and fed him good meals. I was waiting for you to lay a charge, Mr. Knight, and you didn't come—"

"I'll lay a charge, all right—a charge of dynamite under you, one of these days," Stormy said grimly. "How'd he get away?"

"It was right after supper last night," Bayliss explained. "I'd come into his cell to get his supper dishes and take them away. And then, while I had both hands full of dishes, the dirty crook hit me. When I woke up the cell door was open and he was gone. It was dark by that time. He took my gun too. I'll never trust him again."

"Did he get away on a horse?" Stormy asked, steely-voiced but calm.

"I don't know. He didn't take my horse, least-wise. It was at the livery. And nobody's made a complaint of losing a horse."

"Didn't you even try to get on his trail?" Stormy asked.

"How could I, Mr. Knight? I didn't even know what direction he took."

Stormy heaved a long, exasperated sigh. "And you haven't done anything about it yet, I suppose."

Bayliss squirmed uncomfortably. "We-ell, I thought of telling you, only I knowed you'd be mad. Then I heard that Mr. Harper was down to the Bonanza Bar, so I sent word would he please come and see me on a matter of importance—"

"And the damned fool has the nerve to ask me if I know where Cameo is," Harper burst out. "I told him I was through with Cameo."

"Just why you so riled about his escape?" Stormy asked directly.

"Why shouldn't I be riled?" Harper stormed. "Cameo worked for me—until I cut him loose. Folks will get to thinking I had something to do with this escape—"

"Didn't you?" Stormy interposed.

Harper's topaz eyes glinted furiously. "You know damn well I didn't. I said Saturday that I was through with Sloan. I meant that. But, after all, I'm mayor of Carnival. We should have a good administration here. How's it going to look when the news gets out that Cameo escaped jail?"

"Like a Harper administration isn't worth a hoot in hell," Stormy replied coldly. "I'll say this for you, Harper, if this is an act, you're doing a good job. But I don't think it is an act. For once I'll give you the benefit of the doubt."

"To hell with that palaver," Harper said roughly. "What we need here is a new deputy sheriff."

"Maybe you've got an idea, at that," Stormy nodded. He cocked one black eyebrow at Harper and added, "A dang good idea."

"Now, look here," Bayliss pleaded. "There's

nothing against my record up to now. All I asks is a chance—"

"You've had your chance—" Harper commenced, then switched abruptly into a fit of cursing that fairly shriveled Bayliss. Finally Harper swung disgustedly about and lurched out to the street.

There was a moment's silence when he had left, then Bayliss said wanly, "He's right mad at me, ain't he?"

"Well, I wouldn't say he loved you like a brother. Look, Bayliss, why should he get so mad at Sloan's escape?"

"I ain't got the least idea, Mr. Knight."

"He's mad at Sloan too. Could it be he's afraid that Sloan will spill something about the crooked stuff Harper has pulled in these parts."

Bayliss' eyes widened. "Crooked stuff? What crooked stuff? I never heard that Rufe Harper was crooked."

"You've never seen any evidence of it, any place, any time?" Stormy demanded searchingly.

Bayliss' eyes met Stormy's in a blank stare. "I never have," he said frankly.

"Poor eyesight." Stormy sighed deeply. "Anyway, Bayliss, it's not your honesty that's to be questioned. It's a matter of poor health, I'm afraid."

Bayliss laughed. "Not on your life. I'm sound as a dollar."

"I remember once a feller passed a counterfeit dollar on me," Stormy mused.

"Huh? What you talking about?"

"Skip it, Bayliss. Look, I've got to write a piece for the *Banner.* Let me have some paper and a pencil."

Still not comprehending, Bayliss furnished the requisite articles from his desk. Stormy took them and wrote steadily for several minutes. Now and then he paused to chew on the end of the pencil or to wet the point, but finally he finished. "Bayliss," he said, "I figured it was about time there was a piece in the paper about you."

Bayliss' face lighted up. "Well, that's fine!" he exclaimed. "Y'know, old man Sanford never did write anything nice about me, and I've served faithfully in my office—"

"Maybe that's the trouble," Stormy cut in, "you didn't get out of your office enough. Here, read this." He tossed a couple of sheets of paper across to the deputy.

Bayliss seized the papers eagerly. Then as he started to read his face fell. "Why—why, this"— he gulped—"this says I'm resigning as deputy— because of poor health and bad eyesight—why, this isn't true. I've worked for this county like it was a sacred trust—and now you're trying to make me resign because of poor health. There's nothing wrong with my health, Mr. Knight."

"There could be," Stormy said coldly. "You could have a nervous breakdown, or even worse"—letting one hand drop to the butt of his forty-four—"you might even be took bad with a case of lead poisoning."

Bayliss paled. "Mr. Harper might not like this."

Stormy spoke sternly. "Rufe Harper isn't going to know about this until you've left. If I hear of you going to see him, it will be a different sort of notice that will appear in the paper—only you won't be alive to read it."

Bayliss collapsed. "I'll—I'll do as you say," he moaned.

"You're using sense. I'm giving you an easy way out. All I'd have to do would be to drop a word to the governor and you'd be snatched out of office so fast it would make your head swim. Now, you get busy and write out your resignation. I'll see that it's sent to the sheriff. Then you pack your things, get on your horse, and beat it out of town just as fast as the good God will let you. And don't talk to anyone before you leave."

"Yes, Mr. Knight."

Bayliss wrote out the resignation, then rose and started to pack his few belongings in a small hand grip. Stormy asked him for the key to the office. There weren't any prisoners in the jail cells at present.

"You get in touch with the sheriff when you reach the county seat," Stormy ordered. "Let him know where he can find you if you're wanted. You may be needed to testify later."

"Testify on what?"

"We'll talk about that when the time comes. Now, get started. I'll send a telegram informing the sheriff of your resignation. I've got to go down that way anyhow. Come on, get a move on."

Five minutes later Bayliss had procured his pony from the Yucca Livery across the street, mounted, and was riding swiftly out of Carnival. Stormy watched the man until he had vanished around a far turn in the road. "Maybe I should feel hurt he didn't even say good-by to me," Stormy said to himself. "Danged if the poor cuss didn't look like he was ready to burst out crying. Probably figures he can square everything when he reaches the county seat and get back to his job. Well, I figure to stop that too."

He locked the door of the sheriff's office, then headed once more in the direction of the railroad station. Here he sent two telegrams, in addition to the resignation he wired, over Bayliss' name, to the sheriff of the county. With that much accomplished, he returned to the newspaper building.

Kate, Quad, and Horace were still at work when he entered the print shop. "Hold everything," Stormy announced. "I've got a story for tomorrow's paper."

The press stopped abruptly. The three stared at

154

him. Kate shook her head. "You may have a story," she said firmly, "but not for tomorrow's issue of the *Banner.* We're all set up—"

"Haven't started to print page one or four yet, have you?"

Kate eyed him narrowly. "Mister, it would have to be a mighty important story— Here, let me see it"—snatching the folded sheets of paper from Stormy's hand. She started to read, cast a quick glance at Stormy, then continued reading. "What's this—Bayliss is resigning because of poor health and bad eyesight? Stormy, what is this?"

"Just what it says. His bad eyesight wouldn't let him see anything crooked that took place and he was afraid of poor health if he stayed—you see, Sloan made an escape and I . . ." From that point Stormy went on and told what he'd done. When he had finished:

"You know what I think you are," Quad chuckled. "I think you're just a big bully, going around scaring the mentally deficient individuals of Carnival."

Stormy nodded sheepishly. "I felt like a dog, getting rough with Bayliss in such fashion. Ordinarily he'd be harmless, but as it was, I had to work fast. If I'm not mistaken, Harper plans to pull some political wires and get a new deputy appointed here—some man not so honest, but less stupid than Bayliss."

"But, Stormy," Kate frowned, "we should have a deputy here. With no law at all—"

"There'll be one here," Stormy grinned, "before long. I pulled some wires of my own, sent a telegram to the governor asking him to appoint a new deputy—"

"The governor!" Kate exclaimed. "Do you think he'll pay any attention to you?"

Stormy's eyes twinkled. "Anyway, it's worth trying. If any trouble arises through Carnival being without a deputy, the governor can't say I didn't warn him."

"Seems to me," Quad frowned, "you're running kind of roughshod over things—taking affairs in your own hands this way, without authority."

"Would you sooner I'd just sit back and let Harper run things?" Stormy demanded. He turned to Kate. "The question is, are you going to run that story? I don't want to have to get rough with you, but I must remind you I'm the publisher of the *Banner.* Think what a bombshell it will explode under Harper when he reads of Bayliss' resignation."

Kate nodded reluctantly. "We'll run it—darn it all! It's too important to be left until next week. I hate to tear down a setup, once it's ready to go, but we'll do it. Trouble is, to be really effective, we're going to have to run two stories. There's Sloan's escape to be covered—"

"I get it!" Stormy said excitedly. "Have the story

of Bayliss' resignation right under the story of Sloan's getaway. Then people will realize why Bayliss quit—was forced to quit."

"You've caught the general idea," Kate said tersely. "Gosh all hemlock! Why do these stories seem to break at the last minute?" She snatched a dummy of page four from a near-by table and studied it intently, then started to give orders: "All right, Quad. Rip out that story about the calf-branding contest over in Pimena County and the one about that dog that delivers the mail over in Dashville. We can run those next week. Then set two heads: 'Deputy Bayliss Leaves' and 'Sloan Breaks Jail.' Caps, sixteen-point bold. No subheads. No room for 'em. Hurry! I'll slash out a story on Sloan and fix up this story of Stormy's—"

"What needs fixing on my story?" Stormy demanded.

"It needs cutting, you spelt two words wrong, and one or two of your phrases aren't suitable for a family newspaper. Oh, don't worry. I'll say practically everything you've said."

"Could Horace and I run the press?" Stormy suggested.

Kate shook her head. "You've done enough harm for one day, causing all this extra work." She smiled. "I'm glad you did, though." She started toward the office, walking fast.

"Guess I'll wander outside, then," Stormy said. "I just thought of something else."

Kate turned sharply at the entrance to the corridor. "No more stories, mind you," she warned. "We won't tear down any more setups for anything short of a murder—and if you come rushing in at the last moment with another story—"

"Don't worry, lady," Stormy grinned. "I don't crave to see my name featured on page one. Besides, you and Quad would probably expect me to write the story myself. I'm convinced I'm no writer—"

"You sure make a heap of news, though," Quad cut in.

"Stormy—seriously," Kate persisted, "what are you figuring on doing? I want to know. If it's anything that concerns the paper, I have a right to know."

"It's nothing much," Stormy said. "I'm just going over to see Gage Freeman and see if he won't call . . ." He hesitated.

"Won't call who?" Kate demanded. "Or what?"

"I've decided not to tell you," Stormy smiled, "until I see if the idea works out. If it does, I'll let you in on it fast enough."

"Oh, you!" Kate said impatiently. She brushed past him and headed for the office. Quad turned and busied himself at a type form. Stormy strolled out of the building, noticing as he passed the office that Kate was already seated at his desk, writing rapidly. He proceeded out to Main Street, then crossed over, heading in the direction of Gage Freeman's general store.

"Now if I can only make Gage see things my way," Stormy mused, "maybe we can make a move toward roping and hawg-tying one low-down coyote named Rufe Harper. That hombre's been needing his comeuppance for some time, and if I can put a bur under his saddle, I aim to do it. He's been ridin' high too long!"

14. CAMEO SLOAN'S RETURN

Rufe Harper's Anvil Ranch was situated some twenty miles in a northwesterly direction from Carnival, the buildings being located on a stretch of high ground, surrounded by cottonwood trees, not far from the banks of the Paladino River, which wended a lazy course between the foothills of the Carnival Mountains. After leaving Harper's holdings the stream flowed past—and through—the Ladder-R and 30-Bar outfits and eventually, after curving close to the town of Carnival, made a sluggish way across the Mexican border, where it seeped into, and finally became lost, in a spot of semidesert country.

This, of course, was far south of the Anvil; the Anvil had plenty of good grazing country, and it was acknowledged, by those who knew, to be the best-located spread in the section. With sufficient water and good grass to bank upon, Harper had no problems where the raising of beef stock was concerned. His problems were, rather, of a different sort, and at present he sat pondering them in the bunkhouse, where he and most of his crew were just finishing supper.

The bunkhouse was a long, narrow building of rock-and-adobe construction. One wall was lined with bunks. Down the center of the room ran a table about twenty-five feet in length, flanked on either side with diners seated on benches. Kerosene lamps, equipped with metal reflectors, cast light from two walls. At one end of the room was a doorway opening into the kitchen, where Doughy Breen, the ranch cook, impatiently rattled dirty dishes and wished the crew would hurry up with its coffee cups.

Rufe Harper usually lived in town; when he stayed at the ranch he bunked with his men, the big ranch house on the property being employed as little more than a storehouse. He made it a firm rule, also, to visit the ranch about once a week to check up on affairs and see that his foreman, 'Brose Echardt, was tending to business. When he ate with his men he always sat at the head of the table.

To his right was seated Echardt, to his left, Squint Amber. Other punchers, among them Steve Gooch and Muley Porter, were strung along at either side. The puncher named Larry Moulton had already left the table and was standing smoking in the open doorway, his back to the others. Blue smoke commenced to drift above the table as the men lighted cigarettes. Harper hadn't spoken for some time; Echardt finally broke the silence:

"One thing I didn't mention, Rufe," Echardt said. "Those Rafter-O cows should be able to move in a day or so. The new brands are healed enough."

Harper nodded. "I'll leave that to your judgment, 'Brose. What brand did you use this time?"

"Made the Rafter-O into a Diamond-O. We'll make out a bill of sale in the name of James Orwick."

Harper frowned. "I wish you could have made a better change in that brand. There's not much difference in a Rafter-O and a Diamond-O. If old Hoddy Oliver ever got wind of where his cows are going, he might—"

"Shucks!" Echardt broke in. "We don't need to worry about that. By the time those cows are shifted into the next county it won't even make much difference if we hadn't changed the brands."

Harper shrugged. "Okay. I'll leave it to your judgment, 'Brose," he repeated.

While they were talking the punchers had gradually drifted away from the table. A card game had been started in one corner; a couple of the men had stretched out in bunks. Three of them were seated in chairs tilted against the wall, smoking and reading ancient magazines and newspapers. Except for Doughy Breen, clearing away the remnants of the supper dishes, Harper and Echardt were left alone at the long table.

Larry Moulton turned back from the doorway. "Rider coming," he announced tersely. "Coming fast."

Within a few moments the staccato beat of rapidly drumming hoofs could be heard by the

162

men at the table. "Wonder who it is." Echardt frowned. "All the boys are in who should be in."

"Somebody from Carnival, maybe," Harper commented.

The hoofbeats came nearer; there came the sound of scattering earth and gravel as the horse was pulled to a stop. Moulton, at the doorway, said, "It looks like Bartz."

The other men in the bunkhouse looked up; the card game came to a momentary halt. Footsteps sounded at the door, then a beetle-browed man named Bartz entered the bunkhouse. He wasn't on the ranch pay roll, but often did odd jobs for Harper in Carnival.

"What you doing here, Bartz?" Harper asked.

"Something came up," Bartz panted, wearied by his hard ride. "We figured you should know about it. I got here as fast as I could."

"All right," Harper said sharply, "out with it."

"Maybe it don't amount to nothing," Bartz said, "but Gage Freeman sent a message to the Bonanza to tell you there was to be a special meeting of the town council tonight."

"What!" Harper exclaimed. "A special meeting! What for? What's it about?"

"I ain't the least idea," Bartz replied. "The message was give to Joe Wiley at the bar. Joe told Freeman's messenger you'd left for here. But we thought you'd best be told about it as soon as possible."

"As soon as possible!" Harper said angrily. He took out his watch. "Dammit! It's nigh eight o'clock now. Where in hell you been?"

Bartz stiffened. "I've been riding like hell since shortly before six o'clock, when the message came into the Bonanza Bar. Right now my bronc isn't good for anything but crowbait, I'm betting. I figure you owe me a horse."

"You'll get it," Harper said shortly, "if I decide this is on the up-and-up. You mean to say Freeman didn't send word until six o'clock?"

"Ten minutes to six when his clerk came in the Bonanza," Bartz responded promptly.

"I don't like the looks of this," Echardt growled.

"*You* don't like the looks of it?" Harper exploded. "How do you think I feel?"

"I know, boss, I know," Echardt said soothingly. "Want I should saddle up your bronc?"

"Jeez, yes!" Harper swore, leaping up from the table. Then he sat down again as Echardt started to rise. "No, let it go. It's too late for me to go to town now. The meeting would be over before I got there."

"Look here," Echardt said suddenly, "ain't there a rule, or something, that says a council meeting can't be held unless you—the mayor—are there? If that's so, whatever they do won't be legal."

"By God, you're right!" Harper brightened, then his face darkened again. "No, that rule just says I have to be informed of any meeting that's called. The same rule provides for me informing the council chairman if I'm going out of town. That was something that damned Freeman insisted on when we made the ruling. I forgot to tell him when I started out here, like I usually do. Goddam that Cameo Sloan, anyway!"

"Sloan?" Echardt queried blankly. "What's he got to do with this meeting that's been called?"

"If it wasn't for Sloan, I wouldn't have come out here tonight. I figured when he escaped he'd head straight for here. Where is he?"

"Like I told you," Echardt said, "we ain't seen hide nor hair of him."

"Did Cameo make a getaway?" Bartz asked eagerly.

Harper scowled at the man and nodded. "You didn't hear anything about it in town, eh?" he asked.

Bartz shook his head. "I thought he was still in the jug. I didn't see Bayliss this afternoon, or I'd have asked about Cameo."

"Cameo made a getaway sometime last night," Harper growled. "I don't reckon Bayliss would be the one to advertise the fact." He paused. "Knight knew about it, though. Apparently he hasn't said anything to anybody. I wonder why?" His scowl deepened. "I don't know whether I like that or not. I wonder if he knows where Cameo is. Damn Cameo! Damn Bayliss! Damn Knight!"

"Amen to that," Echardt nodded gloomily.

"Seems like our luck has turned against us lately."

"It'll turn back again," Harper promised savagely. "I've got a scheme or two up my sleeve—"

"Look, Rufe," Bartz broke in, "I ain't had no supper yet."

"What do you want me to do, burst into tears?" Harper asked sarcastically. He peeled a five-dollar bill from a roll and handed it to Bartz. "That's for your ride. If you've ruined your horse, I'll see you get another. If Doughy will give you your supper, it's all right with me."

Bartz said "Thanks" and headed toward the kitchen. A moment later a burst of profanity was heard from Doughy Breen. "You think I'm going to get meals at all hours?" Doughy was complaining in a high voice.

"You, Doughy!" Rufe Harper lifted his voice in a snarl. "You'll get meals any time you're asked for 'em on this outfit—or you won't be cooking for any outfit. Now shut up and give Bartz a bait!"

There were no further remarks from the kitchen.

Harper slouched sullenly in his chair. "Damn'd if I ever saw such an outfit," he said peevishly. "Nobody wants to do anything."

"That's not fair, Rufe," Echardt protested. "I don't reckon you got any kick on our crew. They do their work—"

"And get well paid for it," Harper flashed.

"They get paid for keeping their mouths shut," Echardt pointed out meaningly. "Aside from

Sloan, who all of a sudden got too big for his britches, the boys have worked like a team, for your benefit as well as theirs. As for Doughy—hell! Did you ever see a ranch cook that wasn't always kicking and complaining about something?"

"I know, I know." Harper forced a thin smile and tossed a long black cigar across the table to the foreman, then stuck one in his own mouth and lighted it. "You're right, 'Brose. It's just that I'm edgy, wondering about that special meeting that Freeman called."

Echardt struck a match and put the flame to his smoke. The other men in the room had returned to their various pursuits. "It looks right queer, at that," Echardt conceded, "but it won't do you any good to worry about it now, Rufe. What's done is done, and if worse comes to worst, I reckon we can undo it. Whatever it is, you can find out about it in the morning, when you go back to town. Ten to one you'll learn it's nothing for us to worry about. Freeman has been agitating for a long time to get some new sidewalks laid on east Main Street. Maybe that's what the meeting's about."

"That might be it, all right," Harper nodded. "Right now the thing that bothers me most is what has become of Cameo."

"Maybe he's pulled out of the country," Echardt suggested.

"I somehow doubt it. Cameo knows too much

about us to quit now. The double-crossing son! If he hadn't escaped from jail, I figured to—" Harper paused abruptly.

Echardt looked steadily at him a moment. "You don't need to go on, Rufe. I know what you mean. A gun barrel pushed between the bars of Cameo's cell some night would prevent him ever spilling what he knows about us. That's why you were so mad when he escaped, and come high-tailing it out here."

"Well, can you blame me?" Harper burst out wrathfully. "Cameo was commencing to think he could run my job better than I could. I thought he'd learned his lesson after Knight gun-whipped him, but the lesson didn't stick. The fool had to try to kill Knight—after I'd given him orders to return to the ranch. Do you wonder I'm through with him?"

"Not at all," Echardt said promptly. "Incidentally, with Cameo gone, we're a man short on the crew. How about putting Bartz on the pay roll?"

"That's up to you," Harper said shortly. "If you think he'll fit in, we can use him. I'm more interested in filling another job."

"Whose?"

"Pudge Bayliss'. It's time we got rid of Bayliss, 'Brose. He's so dumb he don't know how high is up. He served our purpose for a long spell, but now he's become the laughingstock of Carnival. We've got to get a new deputy sheriff in there."

"You got anybody particular in mind?"

Harper exhaled a cloud of gray cigar smoke. "How'd you like to be deputy sheriff in Carnival, 'Brose?"

Echardt looked pleased, then the expression vanished. "We-ell . . ." he commenced.

"If it's money that's bothering you, forget it. You'll be ahead in the long run. Instead of just money from cows, I'll cut you in on Pyramid profits too."

Echardt smiled. "I'm your man, Rufe."

"Good. We'll work it out in time. I can't get rid of Bayliss all at once. I'll have to pull a few wires. But we'll do it. With you as deputy, and if I can get control of the *Banner*, there's nothing can stop us."

"Why you so keen to run a newspaper, Rufe?" the foreman asked curiously. "And why does it have to be the *Banner*?"

"The *Banner* is established in this county," Harper explained. "Folks know it and trust to what it tells 'em. In short, it molds popular opinion. Y'know, 'Brose"—Harper grew confidential—"that paper could be made larger. With that behind me, I could run for political office—oh, I mean something bigger than this puny mayor's job; that's peanuts. I mean something big."

"You mean you'd run for governor of the state?" Echardt looked awed.

"Eventually. Someday whoever owns the

Carnival *Banner* can sway a heap of opinion in this state. I aim to have a hand in that. People who stick with me are going to get rich along with me—"

He halted suddenly as a voice from the doorway interrupted the conversation. Harper swung around in his chair, then leaped to his feet. The other men were staring toward the doorway now too. Cameo Sloan stood there, holding to the side of the doorjamb for support. He looked exhausted; the strip of court plaster on his cheek was dirty; a smear of printer's ink still remained on one cheekbone and extended up into his black hair.

Harper cursed him in a low, monotonous voice, ending with, "Where in hell you been since last night?"

"Been on my way here," Sloan replied wearily. He stepped into the room and sank down on a straight-backed chair. "I could use some chow, Rufe."

"You could use some common sense now and then too," Harper rasped. "What do you mean, you been on your way here?"

"I've been walking. Did you ever try to walk these hills? Couldn't get a horse when I slipped out of Bayliss' hoosegow. There wasn't none near the jail. I didn't dare stick around town, so I walked. Hid in the brush part of—"

"Damn you, Cameo," Harper said, "you've lost

your nerve. Anybody with guts could have picked up a bronc someplace. Knight has just knocked all the nerve plumb out of you."

"If I had my guns—" Sloan commenced.

"You had your guns—had 'em trained on Knight—then you let a fool woman knock you out with a jar of ink. Cripes a'mighty! You used to be some use to me, but I told you Saturday I was through with you. What you doing here?"

"What would I be doing here?" Sloan demanded resentfully. "I want a horse and guns and food. I figure you owe me that much and more. That's all I'm asking to keep my mouth shut, then I'll get out if you want to call it quits."

"And you aim to do some talking if I don't give you what you want?" Harper said dangerously, stepping close to Sloan.

Sloan started to rise from his chair. "It wouldn't be healthy for you if I talked," he said meaningly. "I could—"

That was as far as he got. Harper straightened the man up with his first punch, then swung a hard left to Sloan's middle. Sloan sank to the floor, gasping with pain. Harper reached down, seized Sloan by the collar, jerked him erect. Again his fists pounded brutally against Sloan's jaw and middle. Sloan groaned, sagged, and pitched to the floor a second time. There wasn't any movement in his body now.

Harper stood glowering over him. "You double-crossing bustard!" he raged. His booted right foot crashed heavily against Sloan's defenseless ribs. Then he whirled to face the other men. "You all heard him threatening to rat on us. Anybody got any objections to what I did?"

None of the men spoke; apparently they felt Cameo had received his due. Harper went on, "All right, 'Brose, tie him up and keep a guard over him in one of the barns. I'm not through with the sneakin' son yet—not by a long shot!"

15. THE NEW MARSHAL

Stormy, Quad, and Kate were just finishing supper in the hotel dining room. It was after seven-thirty the same evening. Kate put down her coffee cup. "Anyway," she commented, "we did get the pages one and four run-off started. It's nice to relax a few minutes. I swore Horace to secrecy regarding the Bayliss resignation story. We wouldn't want that news to get out until the *Banner* is published."

A few diners remained at other tables. Two waitresses were clearing away dishes. Kate continued, while Quad and Stormy lighted smokes. "Thanks for a good dinner, Stormy, but I'd feel better if you'd tell me just what's in the wind for tonight. All you've said is there's to be a special meeting of the town council. When I ask why Gage Freeman called a special meeting, all you do is grin. What's back of it?"

Quad puffed out a cloud of gray smoke. "Yeah, I've been wondering just what you're pulling now," he said puzzledly. "Why do Miss Kate and I have to be there?"

"Town meetings are open to the public," Stormy chuckled. "I just thought a couple of the town's citizens should be on hand."

"Look here," Kate asked suspiciously, "is there

a story in this? Are you going to make me sorry we started the last run. I'd like to know what you and Gage Freeman are up to. You and he are thicker than—"

"Anything Gage and I cook up," Stormy cut in, "is for the good of Carnival. Yes, there might be a story in it, but it's not so important it can't be held over until next week. I'm not saying now just what it is, because I don't know how the council will vote on the proposition. The rest of the council might knock Gage's idea into a cocked hat."

"Gage's idea, eh?" Kate said narrowly. "You didn't have anything to do with it, of course."

"Only in a small way," Stormy said modestly. "I just pointed out what was needed and made a couple of suggestions."

"I'm getting so I don't know whether to trust you or not," Kate stated flatly. "If you're doing something that should be in tomorrow's paper, I'll never forgive you."

"Don't give it a thought," Stormy smiled. "But come on, we'd better be getting across to the Town Hall."

He helped Kate slip into her light coat, then, after paying the bill at the desk in the hotel lobby, the three crossed the street diagonally in the direction of the Town Hall, a one-story flat-roofed building standing four doors east of the Yucca Livery, between Fitz's Barbershop and the

Photograph Gallery. Stormy opened one of the wide double doors and they entered.

Lighted oil lamps were suspended from the ceiling and cast a none-too-bright illumination over the big bare room. At the far end was a table and about a dozen straight-backed chairs. More chairs of the same type were placed in rows facing the table. While town meetings were open to the public, there was only a handful of citizens present, and they sat smoking in rather bored fashion, waiting for the meeting to open.

Near the table stood the members of the town council: Gage Freeman, chairman; Ethan Whitlock, the gray-haired proprietor of the hotel; Carl Burton, bald-headed and spare, who ran the local feed store; grizzled George Jarvis, who sold guns and hardware; a short, dumpy man named Otto Schmidt, owner of Schmidt's Clothing Store; Clem Ireland, who dealt in real estate; and Dr. Beriah Glover. With the exception of Whitlock and Schmidt, Stormy had already met the members of the council. Freeman took care of the necessary introductions, then Kate, Stormy, and Quad found seats in the front row of chairs. The council members seated themselves near the table, and Gage Freeman rapped for silence to open the meeting.

There were one or two preliminaries to get out of the way before Freeman got down to business. As he started to talk Beriah Glover rose to ask:

"Was Rufe Harper informed of this special meeting? There's a town ordinance that says the mayor of Carnival must be notified of all meetings, Gage, if you'll remember. When Harper was elected he insisted on that."

"I remember," Freeman said somewhat grimly. "And if you'll remember, Clem, there's also a rule to the effect that Mayor Harper is to notify me, as chairman, if he leaves town suddenly. I sent a messenger to find the mayor in the proper legal way, but the bartender at the Bonanza said Harper had left for his ranch and didn't say when he'd be back. So I don't reckon we're breaking any laws. That satisfy you?"

"That more than satisfies me," Glover chuckled. "You wouldn't by any chance have waited until the time was right to call this meeting, would you?"

There was some laughter at this. When it had died down, Freeman smiled thinly. "It just happened to fit in our—that is to say, it just happened to happen that way. Now, if there are no further objections, I'll be gettin' on. I know you're all curious as to why I called this meetin'."

Someone scratched a match to light a cigar. Freeman went on, "For a long time I've felt Carnival didn't have proper protection from a law-and-order standpoint. Ordinarily a deputy sheriff stationed here could take care of anything that came up and we'd be well protected. But of late I just can't feel that Deputy Sheriff Bayliss was adequate. If any of you members disagree with me, I'd like to hear from you now."

He waited. No one said anything. Freeman continued, "I'm not saying anything against Bayliss' honesty. He just didn't attend to business as he should. Why he didn't is neither here nor there. But suppose Bayliss was to leave and another deputy of Mayor Harper's choosing was to take over? That would bring about a situation I, for one, wouldn't care for."

"Me neither," George Jarvis put in. Others nodded.

Carl Burton asked, "You figuring we should write to the county seat and ask the sheriff to appoint someone in Bayliss' place?"

Freeman shook his head and said dryly, "I think the Bayliss matter will work itself out before long. What I'm asking you to do, gentlemen, is to appoint a town marshal. How do you feel about the idea?"

There was silence for a moment, then Ethan Whitlock queried, "Who you got in mind? I think it's a right good idea if we can find the right man."

"I'll tell you who I have in mind," Freeman replied. "A man who has made news from the instant he arrived in Carnival; a man who has shown that he has the proper guts—er—attitude to handle such a job; the man who is going to continue to make, and publish, the news in our town—J. S. Knight, otherwise known as Stormy Knight."

There was some applause at the mention of Stormy's name. Kate gave a small gasp and turned to him. "Stormy," she said furiously in a low voice, "you maneuvered this. Oh, you chucklehead, haven't you enough to do now?"

"I just want the proper authority to do what I may have to do," Stormy whispered back.

"But you're always getting into scrapes now—" Kate started to protest. The applause died down and she remained silent.

Gage Freeman continued, "We had a marshal here, back a good many years ago, before this town was large enough to have a deputy appointed, as you all know—and we certainly had a more peaceful time of it than we've had the past couple of years. There's nothing more I can add, except I'd like to see Stormy Knight made marshal of Carnival. He's got my vote right now. The rest is up to you." Gage paused and waited for the next remarks.

Several of the men looked curiously at Stormy. Ethan Whitlock asked after a moment, "Does Mr. Knight want the job? Will he take it if we vote him in?"

"I'll let Stormy answer that," Freeman replied.

Stormy rose. "It's my feeling that Carnival should have a marshal. If you gentlemen have enough confidence in me to offer me the job, I'll be glad to take it."

"But you have the *Banner* to publish," Whitlock said. "Can you spare the time?"

Stormy smiled. "With Miss Sanford and Quad Wrangel and Horace Brigham running things, I'm commencing to think they can get along without me—for a while, at least, until things here have settled down a mite."

"That suits me," Whitlock nodded. Stormy sat down and received an exasperated glance from Kate.

"Some people," Kate whispered fiercely, "don't know when they're well off. You won't be satisfied until you get yourself killed. You know the newspaper needs all your time."

"You wouldn't be ribbing me, would you?" Stormy grinned. "I'm just trying to make sure we'll continue to have a newspaper—"

He broke off as Clem Ireland asked, "Mr. Knight, have you ever had any experience in law enforcement?"

Stormy said "Yes" without enlarging on the subject. Ireland waited a few moments, then nodded as though satisfied.

Otto Schmidt had a question. In a thick Teutonic accent he inquired, "Of how much money do we pay to Mr. Knight for the marshal being?"

Gage Freeman replied, "For the time being, Mr. Knight is willing to serve without salary.

Any expenses incurred will, of course, be borne by the town of Carnival, as is right and natural."

"Too generous he is," Schmidt protested. "I myself am willing to the donation make—"

"Not necessary," Stormy broke in. "Thanks just the same."

George Jarvis asked, "Gage, you mentioned expenses. Does that mean that Carnival will have to provide an office and jail for the marshal?"

Freeman shook his head. "For the present it is planned to use the office and jail of the deputy sheriff."

"Do you think Bayliss will stand for that?" Carl Burton queried.

"If you ask me"—Freeman smiled dryly— "Bayliss has stood for a heck of a lot since he's been here." He added, "Much to my disgust. However, we'll worry about that question if it comes up. I don't contemplate any trouble—nor does Stormy. Now, if there aren't any more questions, we'll put the matter to a vote."

The voting took but a minute or so, and Stormy was appointed town marshal of Carnival unanimously. He rose and said, "Thank you," as the council members crowded around to shake his hand, after which Gage Freeman administered the oath of office. At its conclusion Freeman took a tarnished metal badge from his pocket and pinned it to Stormy's vest. "This has been layin' in a drawer in my store since the last marshal took it off. Lucky we still had it."

Clem Ireland said slyly, "It's nice you remembered to bring it, Gage. Y'know, this whole business has a sort of cut-and-dried appearance. But I'm not kicking. I'm willing to leave it to you and Stormy."

The meeting commenced to break up. The scattering of townspeople who had attended hurried out to spread the news about Carnival's new marshal. The various council members departed for their homes. Freeman started gathering up his papers and extinguishing the oil lamps, while Kate, Stormy, and Quad moved to the sidewalk outside to wait for him to finish.

It was dark along Main Street; only a few lights shone here and there. Overhead the indigo sky was fairly powdered with stars. Back in the hills a coyote yip-yipped, and the sound carried clearly in the night silence.

Kate said, "All right, Stormy, now you're in it, I'll congratulate you and wish you luck—but heaven help you if you don't bring Quad and me every scrap of news that comes your way. If you don't, we'll—we'll—"

"We'll run you through the press with the paper stock," Quad chuckled. "Frankly, Miss Kate, I think this is a good thing. Stormy needs that badge for his own protection. There've been attempts on his life. Bayliss failed to do anything about it. Now Stormy has the authority to do as he sees fit."

"That's the idea exactly," Stormy said earnestly. "And, Kate, don't think the paper is going to get rid of me so easily. I aim to use my office part of the time, at least—to keep an eye on you, if nothing else. This marshal job is just something I felt to be necessary, and between you and me I don't think it's going to last long or take up too much of my time."

"With Bayliss gone," Kate said moodily, "I'm afraid it will take up all of your time."

Stormy smiled. "We might have a new deputy here shortly. When he comes I expect to put the burden of law enforcement on his shoulders."

Kate laughed ruefully. "You're sure optimistic, cowboy. I'll be surprised if we see a new deputy in Carnival for some time to come. The fact that you sent a telegram to the governor doesn't mean he'll do anything about it."

"You're wrong. Maybe you'd like to lay a little bet on that. I'll give you odds," Stormy proposed.

Kate looked narrowly at him in the dim light. "Darn it! You're too ready to bet. You know something I don't know."

"That's how I got to be a newspaper publisher," Stormy grinned.

Before Kate could reply, Gage Freeman emerged from the building, locked the doors, and descended the wooden steps. "I was hoping you'd wait, Kate," he said, falling into step as the four strolled along Main Street. "I forgot to tell you before. Ada will arrive in the morning."

"That's good," Kate nodded. "I won't have to impose on you and Mrs. Freeman."

"No imposition—you know that."

"Thanks, Gage. You've both been good to me." She paused to explain to Stormy and Quad, "Ada is Mrs. Freeman's widowed sister. She's coming to keep house for me, so I won't be alone in my home."

"That's a right good idea," Stormy nodded.

They walked on. At the corner of Main and Ogden, Freeman said, "Kate and I turn off here. Well, see you tomorrow, Stormy—Quad. Stormy, I'll rest easier knowing you're wearing that badge."

"Glad you feel that way, Gage. So long; good night, Kate."

"Good night."

Stormy and Quad continued on toward the center of town. "We'll drop into the Pegasus," Stormy said. "The sooner that news gets around that I'm marshal here, the better I'll like it. There's no place like a saloon for spreading news."

"You forget the *Banner*," Quad reminded.

"The *Banner* won't be out until tomorrow."

"You wouldn't be looking for trouble, would you?" Quad smiled.

Stormy shook his head. "Trouble's here. All I want is to inform certain people that I aim to put it down."

But no trouble was due to break that night. Stormy and Quad imbibed a couple of bottles of beer in One-Horse Shea's saloon, talked with various customers, and decided to turn in, Quad going to his cot in the *Banner* building, while Stormy made his way to the hotel.

16. HARPER GETS A SHOCK

It was still fairly early when Harper, accompanied by 'Brose Echardt, Squint Amber, and Steve Gooch, rode into Carnival. Not being certain just what Gage Freeman's special meeting of the town council portended, Harper had deemed it wise to have with him a few of his gunmen, in the event trouble of some sort arose.

The men stopped first at the Bonanza Bar for a drink. When his glass was emptied, Harper asked the bartender, "Joe, what time did Freeman send word last night he was calling a special meeting of the council?"

" 'Bout a quarter or ten to six. I shot Bartz right along to the Anvil, so you'd know."

"I know; he brought word all right. You didn't go to the meeting, did you?"

Joe Wiley shook his bullethead. "I half thought I should go, mebbe," he confessed, "but last night was Toddy's night off and I had to tend bar alone. I didn't figure you'd want me to close up the Bonanza. Anyway, there was nothing I could do."

"That's the trouble," Harper snapped. "Nobody ever does anything unless I tell them. You'd think they didn't have brains."

Wiley shrugged his shoulders. "You always tell

us just to obey orders and that you'll do all the thinking necessary," he pointed out.

Harper said, "Oh hell!" in a disgusted tone, then added, "I don't suppose you even found out what was done at the meeting."

"I know, all right," Wiley said. "You're not going to like it, either, but it's too late to—"

"What in hell happened?" Harper demanded impatiently.

"The meeting," Wiley explained, "was held for the purpose of appointing a town marshal. Knight got the job."

Harper ripped out an oath. There was further profanity on the part of his henchmen. Echardt growled, "That Knight is sure sticking his neck out. Me, I'm gettin' a cravin' to swing a sharp ax—one that'll finish him for all time."

The men had another drink. Harper cooled down after a time. "This may not be so bad as it looked at first," he stated philosophically. "Knight won't be able to swing much weight in Carnival, if we watch ourselves. His jurisdiction won't extend beyond the town limits. Deputy Bayliss will be the superior officer in this neck of the range, and I can handle Bayliss." He put down his glass. "You boys wait here. There isn't much we can do about Knight's appointment now, but I aim to drift across to Freeman's general store and tell Gage what I think of his methods—pulling this special meeting when I'm away."

He strode out of the barroom, spurs clanging angrily across the board flooring.

About the same time Stormy, having unlocked the jail office and then finished his breakfast at the hotel, was strolling in the direction of the *Banner* building when he saw Harper leave the Bonanza Bar and cut across the street toward Freeman's store. Stormy quickened step.

"Harper probably just learned there's a new marshal in Carnival," Stormy chuckled, "and has gone to make a protest to Gage Freeman. Reckon I'd better drop in on the conversation."

He hurried along, the morning sun glinting brightly on his marshal's badge which he had, the previous night, spent some time in polishing. Men nodded to Stormy as he passed, and doubtless some of them wished to detain and congratulate him on his new appointment, but it was plain to see that Marshal Knight was in a hurry.

Stormy reached Freeman's store, lightly ascended the steps to the porch, and stepped inside. It was too early yet for a run of trade. As Stormy entered he saw Harper talking angrily, across one of the long counters, to Freeman, who had a defiant expression on his face.

"—and there isn't any use denying you slipped one over on me," Harper was saying.

"That's whatever," Freeman replied, tight-lipped. "I and the other members of the council felt we should appoint a marshal. I sent word—or tried to—to you to inform you the meeting had been called. If you choose to run out without saying when you'll return, that's not my business— Oh, here's Marshal Knight now."

Harper swung around, his topaz eyes glinting angrily. "Feeling pretty cocky this morning, I suppose."

"I can't kick." Stormy smiled.

"First you aim to run a newspaper, then you turn to law enforcement," Harper sneered. "If you don't look out, you'll have more than you can handle."

"That sort of sounded like a threat," Stormy said quietly.

"Take it any way you like," Harper snapped. "You can't run this town, you know."

"*You've* tried to. Why shouldn't I take a whirl at it?"

"You're crazy, Knight. I've always acted for Carnival's best interests. And you're not going to get away with this, if I can stop you. Freeman, I'm demanding that you call another meeting of the council right now. This appointment was a mistake. It's not too late to undo it."

"I'm afraid it is," Freeman replied. "Stormy got a unanimous vote. I don't reckon the council is in the mood to change its mind so soon. Cripes! You talk like you were against law enforcement in Carnival."

"We have Deputy Bayliss. He's an honest, efficient peace officer and capable of handling any crime—" Harper broke off. "By the way, what does Bayliss have to say to this?"

"I haven't seen him since the council meeting," Freeman evaded.

Stormy chuckled. "What would you expect him to say, Harper?"

"There's only one thing he can say," Harper said hotly. "It's a slur on his integrity. I say it's an insult to the finest law-enforcement officer Carnival has ever been privileged to have, and—"

"Save it," Stormy said. "So far no protest has been heard from Bayliss, so I guess what goes on here isn't worrying him much."

"He's too modest for his own good," Harper scowled. He glared at Stormy. "Don't you get too big for your britches, Knight. That badge don't mean a thing. You get too uppity and you're li'ble to get all that polish knocked off."

"Wouldn't like to try it now, would you?" Stormy invited softly.

"I'll not only try it, but I'll do it—when the right time comes," Harper snapped. "As for you, Freeman, I'm not forgetting your part in this either. You and I have something to settle one of these days soon."

"Sounds like a threat to me, Gage," Stormy chuckled. "If you want to charge him, I'll put him under arrest."

"Arrest!" Harper's yellow eyes snapped sparks. "Arrest me? *Me?* You're crazier'n I thought you were, Knight." He started to say more, then, anger overcoming him, he turned and plunged out of the store.

Stormy eyed Freeman amusedly. "I'd say Harper was mad."

Freeman nodded, serious-faced. "It was sure a shock to him. You'll have to watch out for Rufe Harper from now on."

Stormy laughed. "He's due for a still bigger shock when the *Banner* comes out. Well, see you later, Gage."

He strolled out of the store and across to the newspaper building. The noise of the press assailed his ears even before he'd reached the printing shop. Kate, Horace, and Quad were busily engaged on the final run. They were too occupied to talk much. After a time Stormy departed, promising to return and help fold the newspapers when the last printing was finished.

The remainder of the morning he moved about town, making new acquaintances and furthering old ones. After dinner at the hotel dining room he crossed over to the jail office, locked the door, and left a note on it to the effect that he could be found at the *Banner* building if needed.

By one o'clock the press had been stopped and Stormy, Kate, Quad, and Horace started folding the newspapers. By three o'clock the last paper had been folded, and, seizing a bunch, Horace darted outside to distribute them at various points about town. Quad looked at Stormy. "If you don't mind," Quad said, "I'm going to drift across to the Pegasus for a bucket of suds."

Stormy nodded. "Go to it. You've worked hard, Quad—and thanks for helping along on this business."

Kate grabbed a number of the newspapers, as did Stormy. They made their way to the office. Kate dropped into the desk chair with a sigh of relief, while Stormy sat on the table. The next few minutes were devoted to scanning the *Banner.* A thrill of elation ran through Stormy as he glanced through the still-damp paper, at the various stories. This was something he had helped make. Kate said after a few minutes, "I think Dad would have been proud of this issue." Stormy realized it was her way of thanking him.

"Who ever thought I'd become a publisher?" Stormy chuckled. "Of course it was you and Quad who really did this."

Kate shook her head. "Not entirely, cowboy. I was ready to give up. You came along and—well, the credit is yours."

"Let's forget that part. This is just a beginning. Someday we'll get that power press your dad wanted. We'll do things with the *Banner.* But something comes first." His lips tightened. "I'm going to learn who was responsible for your dad's death. That satchel with the money has to be found."

"And we never have learned who placed that bill of sale in your pocket—the one with my name forged to it—that gave you the *Banner*."

"That's the biggest—but least important—mystery. But we'll clear that up too—"

"Here comes Rufe Harper," Kate interrupted suddenly.

Harper barged into the office, his face white with anger. "You, Knight," he raged, shaking a folded newspaper before Stormy's face, "you're responsible for this!"

"For what?" Stormy asked quietly, though he knew.

Harper opened the paper, pointed a shaking finger to the story on the fourth page. "This—this about Bayliss. You'd never have dared pull this marshal business, only you knew he'd resigned."

"Certain I knew," Stormy replied coolly. "I think it's a right good thing he left."

"You hounded him out of town," Harper accused. "He'd never have resigned if you hadn't forced him. Ill health and bad eyesight. Bah! Somehow you threw a scare into him."

Stormy cocked a quizzical black eyebrow at Harper. "Remember what you said about Bayliss this morning?" he asked mockingly. "An honest, efficient peace officer. Capable of handling any crime. The finest officer Carnival ever had—integrity—modesty—" He broke off. "Surely, Harper, you wouldn't think me capable of throwing a scare into such a lion, would you?"

Harper's yellow eyes blazed. One hand started involuntarily toward his gun, then, with a quick glance at Kate, he withdrew it and, with an effort, managed to check his temper. "All right, Knight," he said steadily. "I'll admit you outguessed me this time, but when a new deputy is appointed you may not be so important in this town. I'm going to send a telegram at once to the county seat, requesting the sheriff to send a deputy here pronto!" He stiffly lifted his hat to Kate, turned, and strode out of the office.

"Whew!" Stormy whistled amusedly. "Harper acted like he was sort of upset."

Kate shook her head. "It's no laughing matter, Stormy. I saw murder in Harper's eyes for a moment. You're going to have to watch out for him—particularly if he pulls wires to get a deputy of his own choosing here."

"He won't," Stormy grinned. "If the sheriff bothers to reply to his telegram, Harper will learn that a deputy has already been appointed. That will be his third shock of the day."

"Pretty sure of that, aren't you?" Kate said, looking curiously at him.

Stormy nodded. "Unless something bigger comes up, our lead story for next week can be

193

devoted to the deputy who's coming here. His name is Sam Delaney. And of course I'll expect a few lines on my appointment as marshal."

"Stormy! How do you know so much?" Kate exclaimed. "Are you sure? Where did you learn—"

"When you've been in the newspaper business as long as I have," Stormy grinned, "you'll realize you have to know more than the rest of the people. No, I'm not going to explain anything more now. You can take it for granted what I say is true."

People commenced dropping into the office to buy copies of the *Banner*. Horace returned and got another bunch of papers which he was to deliver through the residential district. The shadows commenced to lengthen along Main Street. Quad returned sober but smelling very beery. He picked up a couple of copies of the newspaper and announced he was going to get his supper.

When he had left Stormy said, "Just about closing-up time, Kate. How about having supper with me at the T-Bone Restaurant or hotel, whichever you say? We really should celebrate getting out the paper, you know."

Kate shook her head. "I'd like it, Stormy, but I've got to get home. Mrs. Freeman's sister will be getting supper for me. I would have asked you and Quad to come too, only I hated to put company on Ada her first night. But we'll do it again."

"That would be fine."

"I'll be leaving just as soon as Horace returns. He gets his supper after the papers are delivered, then returns here and cleans up, sweeps, and so on. When that's done he locks up and goes home. It makes a long day for him, but Wednesdays he never has to come in until noon. Tomorrow we'll wrap and address the out-of-town copies of the *Banner.* After that there's nothing to do but start on next Tuesday's issue." Kate sighed wearily, but there was a certain contentment in her voice. "It's work, but I love it."

"You run along now," Stormy said. "I'll wait for Horace."

Kate looked gratefully at him and said she guessed she'd do just that. She picked up her coat, said good-by, and left by the rear door of the print shop.

17. A TIGHT SPOT

Horace returned about a quarter to seven and found Stormy sitting in the office. Stormy had lighted a lamp and was glancing through a file of old copies of the *Banner.* Horace looked rather startled when he saw Stormy at the desk. "My gosh, Mr. Knight!" he said. "Now that it's dark you shouldn't be sitting there where somebody could see you through the front window. Mr. Sanford, when he worked nights, always hung a couple of blankets over that window."

"It was as serious as that, eh?" Stormy frowned.

"Mr. Sanford didn't believe in taking chances after somebody sent a shot through here one night."

"I hadn't heard that before."

"I don't reckon Mr. Sanford ever told anybody, for fear of worrying Kate. Only that I saw him knocking out the broken pane, to make it look like an accident, I wouldn't have known. He told me not to say anything."

"I'll be more careful next time," Stormy nodded. "Thanks for letting me know. You're ready to start cleaning up, eh, Horace? Not afraid somebody might take a shot at you?"

Horace grinned widely. "There wouldn't be any reason for that, Mr. Knight."

Stormy laughed and rose from the chair. "All right, I'll leave the *Banner* property in your hands while I go to eat. If Quad isn't back by the time you've finished, be sure you lock up before going home."

"Oh, sure, I never forgot yet."

Stormy said, "So long," and headed for the street.

After supper he entered the Pegasus for a drink. Quad was standing at the bar with a bottle of beer in front of him. Stormy ordered the same. One-Horse Shea served him and said, "Nice job you did on the newspaper, Stormy."

"You can thank Miss Sanford and Quad for that," Stormy said. "They're the ones that make the wheels go round."

One-Horse moved along the bar to serve other customers. Quad said with a tight smile, "Half expected to see me get plastered, didn't you, now that the paper's been got out?"

"I didn't say that," Stormy replied.

"You were thinking it, though."

"I was hoping you wouldn't," Stormy admitted.

"Don't worry, I won't. I'm off the hard stuff— for a time, anyway. It's when I commence to get tired of a job that I start hitting it up."

Stormy smiled. "We'll have to think up some way to keep you interested, Quad. The *Banner* needs you."

Feeling reassured, he announced his intention

197

of strolling around town. Quad asked, "Heading anyplace in particular?"

"I figured to look in on the Pyramid," Stormy answered. "I want to see just what sort of gambling parlor Harper runs."

"Want I should go with you?"

Stormy shook his head. "I'd prefer to go it alone, Quad. Don't worry, I don't aim to get into any scraps."

"Okay. I'll be drifting back to my cot before long. You said Horace was redding up the place?"

Stormy nodded. "Don't feel in a rush to get back. I reckon the kid will lock up all right. . . . Well, see you tomorrow, if not before."

He left the Pegasus and stood on the sidewalk a few minutes, glancing both ways along the street. Yellow rectangles of light splashed the dusty roadway here and there, where lamps gleamed from windows. Directly across, a light still burned in the *Banner* office, and the front door stood wide open. Stormy frowned. "I wonder . . ." he muttered, then started across the street.

Reaching the open door of the building, Stormy slipped silently inside. A light burned in the office. From the print shop, beyond the office wall, came the vigorous swish-swish of Horace's broom. After a moment the sweeping stopped. Stormy peered around the corner of the corridor where it opened into the print shop and saw Horace stuffing scrap paper, oily rags, and other

198

rubbish into a tall wire basket. The boy whistled softly as he moved about his work.

The rear door of the print shop was open on the alley. An oil lamp, suspended in a bracket on the back wall, failed to light the print shop thoroughly, but Stormy could see that the oil-and-ink-stained floor had had a thorough sweeping. Stormy peeked still farther around the corner. Now he could see the closet, built between the side wall of the building and the office partition. The tall paper rack standing near that side wall cast a shadow on Quad's cot, with its neatly folded blankets, which stood in front of the closet.

Horace finally picked up the wire basket of rubbish and lugged it out to the alley. The instant his back was turned Stormy tiptoed across the floor to Quad's cot and sat down. He rolled and lighted a cigarette. It was plain that Horace hadn't heard him. The print shop grew lighter. Stormy arose and saw that Horace was standing out in the alley. He'd set fire to the rubbish in the basket and stood watching the flames which threw a bright light through the wide rear window of the shop.

"It could have been this way," Stormy muttered, nodding his head with a certain satisfaction. "Maybe I've hit on something."

He continued on his way toward the alley doorway and had nearly reached the threshold before Horace heard him. The boy glanced suddenly around, startled, then he relaxed. "Oh, it's you, Mr. Knight. Sort of gave me a start, you did; I didn't hear you come in."

"Reckon you were too busy," Stormy smiled. "You nearly through cleaning up? That's good." The two stood a minute gazing at the burning paper in the basket. Stormy went on: "You want to make sure that fire's completely out before you leave. We wouldn't want the building to catch fire."

"I'm mighty careful. That was one thing Mr. Sanford drilled into me." The boy sobered. "Just think, a week ago tonight he was alive."

"That's another matter to be squared, one of these days."

Horace said, "You think he was murdered, don't you?"

"If I'm not far off my base, the *Banner* will be running a story to that effect before you're much older. But we won't talk about that now, Horace. . . . Well, be sure to lock up when you leave. I'll see you tomorrow."

"Good night, Mr. Knight."

Stormy made his way back to Main Street, pondering certain matters in his mind. He told himself finally, "I think . . . I think it could have been worked that way. Now if I can only get some proof."

He walked about town for a time. Except for a

few saloons and a couple of restaurants, everything was closed. Harper's Pyramid Gambling Saloon was open, of course. Stormy had glanced through the entrance once, but as it was too early for much activity, he'd postponed his visit until later.

An hour passed. The next time Stormy walked by the *Banner* building, all was dark. Stormy kept on, in the direction of the Pyramid, his high heels making hollow sounds on the wooden sidewalks as he progressed. Now and then a pedestrian passed and spoke. There were but few people on the street.

He reached the Pyramid, looked in through the open, double-doored entrance. The Pyramid was a big, barnlike structure with a long bar running the length of one side wall, where two perspiring bartenders strove mightily to keep up with the thirsty demands of the crowd. The remainder of the floor was given over to the games—chuck-a-luck, blackjack, keno, the wheel, roulette, faro; there were four or five tables of poker, stud, and draw. The games were presided over by sharp-faced professional gamblers in Harper's pay.

At the rear of the building was a partitioned-off room which served as Harper's living quarters and office. A veritable bedlam filled the Pyramid: the clicking of chips, the whirr of the wheel, voices of the croupiers. Men swore, laughed, talked loudly, and bitterly cursed their luck. The room was swimming with tobacco smoke. Cigar and cigarette butts were scattered underfoot. A strong odor of man sweat filled the nostrils. The clients of the Pyramid were mostly towns-people; many were cowmen; also there were prospectors and a handful of miners.

As Stormy strode through the doorway Rufe Harper, standing at the bar, turned and saw him. Harper's face went hard, his body stiffened, then, quite suddenly, he relaxed and approached Stormy, a smile on his face, hand outstretched.

Stormy pretended to not see the hand. "Thought I'd drop in and look your place over, Harper."

"Glad you did," Harper said with forced cordiality. "I wanted to talk to you, anyway." He smiled a bit sheepishly. "Maybe I owe you an apology for blowing up the way I did today. I've had a lot of business worries of late, and it's made me short-tempered. I've been thinking things over. There's no reason you and I can't be friends."

"That's the way you feel about it, eh?" Stormy said quietly.

"Exactly. I had a telegram from the sheriff right after supper. It seems he's already appointed a new deputy for Carnival. You didn't know that, did you?" He looked narrowly at Stormy.

"The sheriff didn't send any telegram to me," Stormy said evasively. He commenced to understand now this sudden friendliness on Harper's part; with an unknown deputy due to arrive, Harper had decided to tread softly until he saw how the ground lay.

"Like you to meet my manager, Fox Pelton," Harper was saying. He raised his voice. "Fox! Hey, Fox! Come over here."

A beady-eyed man with large ears and a pointed nose threaded his way through the throng. He wore a silk shirt and "town clothes." A diamond sparkled on one finger. Harper said, "Fox, I don't think you've met Marshal Knight. This is Fox Pelton, my manager, Stormy."

Pelton's manner was suave, sleek. His hand, when it grasped Stormy's, felt like a dead fish. Stormy definitely did not like the man. Pelton said, "Can we serve you a drink, Marshal?"

"Thanks, no," Stormy replied. "I had one at the Pegasus a spell back. I'll just look around and get acquainted with your layout."

"Fine," Harper said, though it was plain he didn't care for the idea. "Fox can go with you and introduce you to our employees."

"Not necessary," Stormy smiled. "I won't get lost. And I wouldn't want to interrupt any of your men." Before Harper could protest, Stormy started to push his way through the crowd.

Harper swore under his breath and said something, low-voiced, to Pelton. Pelton nodded and went to a burly ruffian who acted as one of two bouncers in the Pyramid. The bouncer listened carefully, then hurried out the front doorway. Pelton rejoined Harper, and the two returned to the bar, where they narrowly watched Stormy as the marshal made his way from table to table.

Half an hour later Stormy had learned what he wanted to know. He came pushing through the throng, his face scornfully contemptuous. Pelton and Harper were still at the bar. They swung around to face Stormy as he approached.

Stormy said crisply, "All right, Harper, you can close up now."

Harper's jaw dropped. "Close the Pyramid? What do you mean? There's no closing limit in Carnival."

"You've already reached it, so you're wrong. Your games are crooked as a dog's hind leg. You've installed lead frets on one of your roulette wheels; the dice at one of your tables are loaded; that wheel is connected to a spring under the table—"

"You're crazy, Knight—" Harper commenced.

"—and I don't like the technique of one of your faro dealers. I didn't check into your poker games, but I'd lay odds they're using marked cards."

Several of the clients in Stormy's vicinity had paused in their play and were darting inquiring glances in Harper's direction. He decided to bluff it out.

"Don't talk like a fool, Knight," he blustered. "Look here, I'll go with you and we'll check into every item you've mentioned. I'll prove you're wrong."

"I've already proved I'm right. I've had experience with this sort of thing before. You're closing up now. You can reopen again when you decide to run on the square."

"And suppose," Harper sneered, "I refuse to close?"

"That's up to you," Stormy returned calmly. "I can always put you under arrest and make the necessary charges."

"You wouldn't dare arrest me. I'm the mayor in Carnival—"

"I don't give a damn," Stormy said testily, "who or what you are. Now, either you close up or you're coming down to the hoosegow with me. Think fast! What do you want to do?"

Fox Pelton's right hand had commenced to edge inside his coat. Stormy caught the movement. Instantly his forty four Colt's gun flashed into view, covering both men.

"Keep your hands away from that underarm weapon, Pelton," Stormy snapped, "or I'll blast you to hell! Looks like you're itching to occupy a cell with Harper."

A loud laugh suddenly roared from Harper's lips. "Knight," he said, "I don't think you're going to arrest anybody. This looks better and better.

You've been wanting a showdown. Well, it's here. Take my advice and put that gun away pronto, or you might get hurt."

A voice spoke behind Stormy: "Put that hawg leg away, Knight." The tones were low, vicious.

Stormy swung around, still keeping Harper and Pelton covered. Then he realized he was in a mighty tight spot.

Standing just behind him, drawn guns in hands, stood 'Brose Echardt, Squint Amber, and Steve Gooch.

Echardt spoke again. "Put it away, Knight. You're covered complete!"

18. LAW ENFORCEMENT

Stormy made no move to comply with the order. He realized he was outnumbered, but, he told himself grimly, he'd be damned if he'd back down. A tense silence had fallen over the Pyramid. Men left their games and craned necks to see what was going on. After a few minutes snickers ran through the crowd: there were men present who felt Stormy was nothing but a kill-joy, out to spoil their fun.

Harper spoke again. "You see, it's no use, Knight. You're covered. You can avoid trouble if you'll just use your head. Put your gun away and I'll tell the boys to lay off."

"You're resisting the law, Harper," Stormy said grimly. "You may get me, but I'll get you first."

"Who said anything about getting you?" Harper asked in assumed surprise. "Hell, I haven't even got my gun out of holster—"

"You know what I mean," Stormy said tersely. "And I'm not lowering my gun. Get that straight."

"How about it, chief?" Squint Amber asked in ugly tones.

"You shut up, Squint," Harper said testily. "This can be settled peaceful." He turned back to Stormy. "Now use your head a mite, instead of butting it against a stone wall. This is no shooting affair. My men are just protecting me. Put your gun away and we'll talk this over. See, I'm giving you a chance. I don't want trouble here. I stand for law enforcement. This can all be settled—"

"That's enough, Harper," Stormy cut in. His left hand reached around to a hip pocket, produced a pair of handcuffs. "I'm going to put these on you. If you're smart you'll call off your dogs and submit to this law enforcement you're talking about. Hold out your mitts!"

"You stubborn fool!" Harper fairly yelled his exasperation. "You'll get killed if you try to go through with—"

"Put those mitts out, Harper," Stormy said steadily, moving a step nearer. "You're coming with me."

"On your own head be it," Harper snarled in ugly tones. "I tried to warn you what you were up against, but if you can't use sense—"

And that was as far as he got when a new voice broke in from the direction of the entrance—a lazy, drawling voice that, nevertheless, carried a strong tone of authority:

"All you hombres go easy. I reckon Stormy's going to call the tune, after all."

Gasps of astonishment left the lips of Harper and his henchmen. Stormy shot a quick glance toward the doorway, and his face lighted up. "Sam! Sam Delaney!" he exclaimed.

Quad was there too, a rather ridiculous-looking Quad with his funny derby hat. But there wasn't anything ludicrous about the sawed-off, double-barreled shotgun Quad cradled in his right arm. Standing next to Quad, six-shooter in hand, was a skinny-framed, slouchy-appearing, black-haired man with a battered sombrero stuck on the back of his head and a deputy sheriff's badge of office pinned to his vest.

"All you hombres put them guns away," Deputy Sam Delaney was saying somewhat peevishly. "If Stormy wants to play, let him have his way, or I'm goin' to be forced to spill a mite of lead."

"What the devil is this?" Harper stormed. "Who are you?"

"Name's Delaney," the deputy said in his tired voice. "Appointed here. Got my credentials, signed by Sheriff Jackson, in my pocket, if you insist on seein' 'em."

"You're the new deputy?"

"That's what I'm tryin' to tell y'all," Delaney said complainingly. "Can't you understand plain American *habla?*"

"I can and I do," Harper said promptly. "Glad to know you, Delaney. I'm Rufe Harper, mayor of Carnival. This fool"—gesturing toward Stormy—"has got some crazy notion—"

"Must be you got that notion." Delaney yawned. "Never yet heard anybody call Stormy Knight a fool—not and get away with it. What you don't

209

seem to understand, Mister Harper, is that you're playin' with dynamite when you buck him."

"I tell you I'm the mayor—" Harper commenced.

"I don't give two damns," Delaney said boredly, "even if you're the czar of all the Rooshians. Whatever it is, I'm backing Stormy's play. . . . Stormy, if you need my authority to go through with what you started, you got it." The words ended in another jawbreaking yawn.

"Thanks, Sam." Stormy swung on Harper's men. "All you hombres drop your guns—now!" There was a rattle of hardware as the weapons struck the floor. "You're all under arrest," Stormy went on. "Keep 'em covered, Sam—Quad. Harper, hold out your mitts. These bracelets are going to look nice on your wrists."

A howl of rage ascended to the rafters, but Stormy was adamant. An instant later the handcuffs were on Harper's wrists. "You're heading for the hoosegow, just like I warned you you'd be," Stormy continued. "Pelton, Amber, Echardt, and Gooch are going with you."

There were more protests, but the prisoners were finally started out the door. Stormy turned to face the astounded crowd. "The Pyramid's closing up for the night. You hombres get out."

Pelton called over his shoulder to one of the gamblers to lock up and take care of the cash. Men came streaming out of the building to follow Stormy, Sam Delaney, and Quad along

Main Street as they escorted their angry prisoners toward the jail.

"Somebody's going to suffer for this, somebody's going to suffer for this," Harper kept saying wrathfully, over and over.

"Sounds like he's already started to suffer," Delaney drawled.

Reaching the jail office, Stormy turned to the crowd that had followed them down the street. "All right, men," he said, "you can scatter off home now. The fun's over." Reluctantly the crowd started to disperse. Stormy unlocked the office door. Quad found and lighted a lamp. The prisoners were taken back and placed in separate cells. By this time they were speechless with indignation. Harper finally broke down, just as Stormy and his friends were leaving, and commenced talking again.

"You can't do this to me," he lamented. "I'm the legally elected mayor of Carnival."

Stormy chuckled. "Who says we can't?"

Harper's manner became humble. "Look, Knight, I'll admit I acted hastily. Get Judge Turner over here and we'll plead guilty to a charge of disturbing the peace, or something, and pay a fine. I'll concede you were within your rights. I lost my temper. But we can't stay here all night. You'd make Carnival a laughingstock if the county heard you'd put your mayor in jail. Folks would wonder what sort of administration—"

"The county will hear it, all right. Too late to stop news now."

"But will you get Turner here, or won't you?" Harper said.

"I'll think about it," Stormy replied shortly. Taking the oil lamp, he headed back to his office, followed by Quad and Delaney, then shut the door between the office and block of cells.

Placing the lamp on his desk, he stuck out his hand to Sam Delaney. "Cripes! It's good to see you again. How in time did you get here so soon?"

"I knew from your telegram that I'd be hearing from Sheriff Jackson, so I was packed and ready to drift when his wire arrived, appointin' me to Carnival. Caught the first train to the county seat and saw Jackson. He didn't seem to know what it was all about, except he'd had instructions. Course I knew what wires you'd pulled."

"The sheriff must have moved faster than I hoped for," Stormy put in.

"From the county seat I headed for here. There wasn't any passenger train due that would have got here until tomorrow, but I grabbed a freight and rode the caboose. Landed here a little over an hour ago."

"And none too soon," Stormy said. "Gosh! I wouldn't have been surprised if you didn't get here for a week or so. Went to the trouble of getting myself appointed marshal, just so Carnival would have an officer to handle any trouble that might come up. By the way, where'd you pick up Quad?"

Delaney yawned and explained: "When I dropped off the freight I headed for your hotel. Signed up there and dropped my luggage, then asked where I could find you. The clerk didn't know, but he said I might find you at the news-paper office. I found the *Banner* building from his instructions. It was all dark, but I figured you might be in the back someplace. I rattled the doorknob some, and the next thing I knew, Quad had flung open the door and was holding a scatter-gun on me."

"Hell!" Quad said sheepishly. "I didn't know who it was. I'd turned in and was asleep. Didn't know but what the whole thing might be a trick of some sort. Sam said he was the deputy sheriff. I didn't know whether he was or not. He said he was looking for you, Stormy, so until I was sure of things, I decided to come along and bring my shotgun. I knew you'd said you were going to the Pyramid, so we headed for there first—"

"And found Stormy in trouble," Delaney drawled, "as he usually is. Say, what's this about you owning a newspaper?"

"It's true," Stormy grinned. "At least I'm half owner. The *Banner* is the basis of part of the trouble here. Rufe Harper wants to run it, and I can't see it that way. But I'll give you the whole story eventually. What you think we ought to do about those prisoners we put in cells?"

"Let 'em rot there until the ants carry 'em out through the keyhole, for all I care," Delaney said. "What you got in mind?"

"They could get out on bail tomorrow, then I could have 'em brought to trial eventually. There'd be certain expenses to the town that-a-way. Personally, I'd just as soon turn 'em loose, now that I've done to Harper what I said I would. There are certain things I'd like to find out about those hombres. So long as they're tangled with the law, they might not make any false moves. That's one thing I want 'em to do—and the sooner the better. Harper said he was ready to plead guilty to disturbing the peace, if I'd get the justice here to accept a fine."

"You arrested 'em," Delaney yawned. "It's up to you."

Stormy glanced at his watch. "Quarter to twelve. Quad, you know a lot about folks in this town. What do you know about Judge Turner?"

"Not much. I've seen him. Sort of a crusty old guy."

"Know where he lives?"

Quad shook his head. "Gage Freeman would know."

"I tell you," Stormy continued, "you slope over and get instructions from Gage. Then see Turner and tell him that Rufe Harper wants to get out of jail. If Turner won't be bothered, that answers the question."

Quad left his shotgun standing in a corner of the office and hurried outside. While he was gone, Stormy sketched briefly for Sam Delaney the situation in Carnival and related the various incidents that had taken place. The sleepy look commenced to vanish from Delaney's eyes.

"Damn'd if you haven't run into a mess of something," he said. "Instead of just one mystery, there's three—"

"Maybe you realize now," Stormy interrupted, "why I wanted a deputy I could trust in Carnival."

Delaney nodded shortly. "Three mysteries . . . why did somebody want you to publish the newspaper? How could James Sanford be murdered when he was locked inside his place? What became of the satchel with the three thousand? Look, Stormy, you're sure it was murder?"

"Damned sure," Stormy replied firmly.

"You got any clues to back up your belief?"

"One or two things. I'll tell you about them, Sam, when I've got things straightened out more in my own mind—"

He broke off as steps sounded outside the office. Quad entered, followed by Carnival's justice of the peace, Judge Hame Turner. Turner was a tall thin man with a frosty manner, silvered hair, and keen blue eyes. The men shook hands. Delaney was introduced as the new deputy sheriff. Turner explained that Quad had already told him about the jailing of Harper and his associates.

"I'm darned sorry to be getting you out so late, Judge Turner. Not that Harper demanding to see you made any difference, but I figured it might be easy to collect fines right now. If this went to trial, Harper would hire some shyster lawyer who might drag out the trial for weeks. I figured Carnival might be ahead financially if we did it this way," Stormy said.

"Quite right," Turner said shortly. "Bring in your prisoners. I'll establish court right here." He seated himself at the deputy's desk.

The prisoners were brought in. Harper's eyes lighted when he saw Judge Turner. "I'm glad to see you, Turner," he commenced. "This is an outrage and I'm not—"

"Judge Turner to you, Harper," the justice said icily. "Please remember this is now a court of law. I came here because I understood you and your friends wanted to plead guilty to disturbing the peace. If my impression is wrong, I'll close court and this business can go through in the regular way."

He waited. Harper didn't say anything more. He glanced at his henchmen. They too were silent. Turner continued, "The court is now ready to hear evidence. Marshal Knight, are you ready?"

Stormy told briefly what had happened. Quad and Sam Delaney told their stories. When they were finished Turner turned to Harper. "Do you wish to deny what has been offered as testimony in this court?"

Harper said wrathfully, "Any man says my games are crooked is a liar! Why, dammit, I—"

"Harper, watch your language," Turner said frostily. "Must I remind you again this is a court of law?"

"All right," Harper growled. "I deny what Knight says about my games not being on the square."

Turner turned to Stormy. "Marshal Knight, are you bringing charges relative to the integrity of the various games played in the Pyramid Gambling Saloon?"

Stormy hesitated, then shook his head. "Such charges would be difficult to prove now," he pointed out. "There were enough men left in the Pyramid to destroy such crooked equipment as existed. It would be only my word against that of Harper and his employees."

The judge swung back to Harper. "Am I to understand you do not deny the other charges made by Marshal Knight?"

Harper paused. Finally he said sulkily, "All right, I give in. I reckon me and my boys did sort of lose our tempers for a few minutes."

"You're very fortunate," Turner said dryly, "you didn't lose anything else. A temper is a bad thing to have but a costly thing to lose. . . . The evidence having been heard, I charge you five defendants with resisting an officer, while said officer was pursuing his legal and proper duties, as he saw them. Rufus Harper, guilty or not guilty?"

"Guilty, goddammit!" Harper exclaimed bitterly.

"What?" Turner snapped.

"Guilty."

"Fox Pelton?"

"Guilty, your honor."

Turner beamed icily. "Pelton, you sound as though you had been in court before." Pelton flushed. Turner continued, "Ambrose Echardt?"

"Guilty," came the reluctant growl.

Turner turned his gaze on Squint Amber. "Uh—er—Amber," Turner said, "this court cannot accept nicknames. What's your Christian name?"

"Huh?" Amber's eyes widened. "Aw, I don't go to any particular church, judge."

"I'm not talking about your religion. What's your given name, your first name?" Turner said testily.

"Oh we-ell . . . aw . . ." Amber's face grew red, and he lowered his squinty eyes in embarrassment.

"Come, come, Amber," Turner said sharply. "Don't you understand me? Your given name, your Christian name, your— Well, what did they call you when you were a boy?"

"Aw, what difference does it make?" Amber snarled. "Everybody calls me Squint."

"Amber," Turner said sternly, "would you like to be cited for contempt?"

"All right, all right," Amber blurted. "The name's Fauntleroy." He looked miserable.

There was an instant of dazed silence. Even the judge looked rather shocked. Stormy and his friends smiled. Steve Gooch let out a loud guffaw which he endeavored too late to suppress. Even Harper looked at his employee with a certain amazement. Turner quickly recovered himself.

"Fauntleroy Amber," he said with twitching lips, "do you plead guilty or not guilty?"

"Guilty," Amber mumbled.

"Stephen Gooch?"

"Guilty, Judge."

Turner considered a moment, then said tartly, "You are each fined twenty-five dollars for resisting an officer of the law. Rufus Harper is fined an additional twenty-five for contempt of court."

"What!" Harper exclaimed. "Contempt of court? Why? What did I—"

"Your language when you first came in here," Turner explained. "I do not like profanity in a court of law. It sounds" the judge didn't even crack a smile "like hell!"

Harper started a second protest but thought better of it. It was plain to see, he considered, that Turner was out to make it tough for him, if possible.

"In the absence of the regular clerk," the justice went on, "I stand ready to accept the money to cover your fines. I hope you have it with you."

"I'm paying for the crowd," Harper growled. He drew out a thick roll and peeled off one hundred and fifty dollars in greenbacks, which he threw down on the desk. Turner quickly scribbled a receipt for the money, then stood up. "Court's closed," he announced briefly. "You're free to depart any time you care to."

The erstwhile prisoners hurried toward the door and stepped out to the street. Only Harper paused, just as he was leaving, his yellow eyes blazing hatred. "From now on, Knight," he snarled, "I hope you understand it's war."

"What do you think we've been doing since I got here," Stormy grinned, "picking wildflowers?"

Harper cursed and hurried out to the darkened street.

The instant the door closed behind him, Hame Turner burst into laughter. "Great Jehovah!" he snorted. "Can you imagine a name like that for a tough gunman—Fauntleroy Amber!"

"It's enough to make anybody feel tough," Quad commented.

Turner nodded. "Parents should give more thought to the names they inflict on offspring. Well, gentlemen, I'll be getting along home again."

"Thanks for coming over, judge," Stormy said.

"I'm glad to come any time, under such circumstances," Turner replied. "The town can use this money." He said good night, donned his hat, and left the office. Stormy closed the door after him.

"Maybe," Sam Delaney drawled, "this will teach your friend Harper a lesson."

"I don't care about teaching him a lesson so much as I do about bringing him out in the open," Stormy said seriously. "When he gets mad enough he's going to start pressing his luck. When that happens, he's sure to make a mistake. Then we can nab him and his whole dirty crew. Carnival's a good town, but there are too many hombres in Harper's employ who think a carnival is just a place to raise hell and do as they like. This town isn't that kind of carnival."

"Enough ca'tridges burned in the right direction can prove that point, too," Delaney drawled thoughtfully.

The three men talked a few minutes longer, then Quad announced he was going to head back for his cot in the *Banner* building.

"I reckon we can all use some shut-eye," Stormy nodded. "Sam, you might as well sleep at the hotel tonight. There's a cot here, but you'll have to get some blankets tomorrow. Besides, I want to *habla* with you a mite and hear if you've had any news from the gang in Texas. And we might find a drink."

Delaney nodded. "Suits me. But I'm more interested in getting all the details on what's going on in Carnival. I've a hunch there'll be a lot of powder smoke drifting before this situation is cleared up."

19. A DEBT TO BE PAID

The next morning, following breakfast, Stormy turned over the keys of the deputy sheriff's office and jail to Delaney, then strolled around town with the newly appointed peace officer and introduced him to various merchants and townspeople. The two men arrived at the *Banner* about ten o'clock, and Sam was introduced to Kate, who was busily engaged in addressing wrappers for out-of-town *Banner* subscribers.

Kate shook hands with the deputy, who eyed her admiringly. "Now I'm commencin' to understand," he drawled, "why Stormy so sudden got interested in publishing a newspaper. Me, I don't know how good he is at publishin' news, but I've sure seen him make a lot in my time, Miss Kate."

Kate colored and smiled. "You men talk as though you'd known each other for years."

"Sometimes it seems longer'n that, miss," Delaney said. "Back there in Texas we sure—"

Stormy cut in quickly, "She's fishing for information, Sam, so there's no use telling her about all those bank robberies and train holdups we pulled, down near Eagle Pass."

"We can't even tell her," Sam said lazily, "about the time you and I held up the stagecoach and stole the driver's whip?"

"Gosh no!" Stormy exclaimed, grinning. "Don't even mention such desperate crimes."

"You two!" Kate laughed. "Look, I don't bluff worth a cent, so don't start running any long whizzers on me. I'm darn glad you're here, Sam. Stormy said when you arrived he'd turn over all the law enforcement to you and stick to his newspaper."

"Hey," Stormy cried in some alarm, "I didn't say I'd give up being a marshal entirely. I've got to have some excitement."

"Like, for instance, last night's?" Kate smiled.

"You heard about Harper and his gang?"

"It's all over town, I'd say," Kate replied, "judging from the number of people who have been in this office asking what happened after you put those men in jail."

"We got Judge Turner over and he fined 'em," Stormy laughed. "Even Fauntleroy was fined."

"Fauntleroy?" Kate looked blank. "Who's he?"

"Fauntleroy Amber." Kate started smiling, and Stormy told her the story of last night's happenings. When he had finished she exclaimed:

"What a piece of news that will make in next Tuesday's edition! Quad gave me some of the details, and I've already started to write it up, but he neglected to mention Fauntleroy. You know, Sam, I'd planned to give you the big story in next week's issue. Your appointment here is news, and folks will want to know where you're from

223

and so on, but I think you'll admit that headlines that read 'Mayor Harper Arrested' make much bigger news."

"That's all right with me, Miss Kate. I'm not craving space in your newspaper." He touched fingers to the brim of his sombrero. "Well, I'd best be pushing along. I want to look the town over some more. Glad to have made your acquaintance, ma'am."

"And I yours, Sam. Drop in often. And if you get any news items, be sure and let us have them."

"I'll do that. . . . By the way Stormy, you mentioned a fellow named Cameo Sloan escaping from the jail last Sunday night. Want I should get on his trail?"

Stormy considered a minute, then shook his head. "Let it go for the time being. Just mosey around and see what you can pick up here and there. Keep your eyes open. I was talking to Hoddy Oliver a couple of days back—he owns the Rafter-O, eighteen miles from here. He complains some of his cows are missing. You might check into that, after you've got settled around."

"Good. I'll keep it in mind." Turning, Delaney strode indolently out to the street.

Kate faced Stormy. "So that's our new deputy?"

"Don't let his sleepy appearance fool you, Kate. He's hell on wheels with a six-shooter, and he'd go through a lot for me—as I would for him."

Kate looked serious as she dropped into the desk chair. "Sit down a minute, Stormy—see, I brought a chair in here for visitors—I want to talk to you."

Stormy tossed his hat on the table. "What's on your mind, lady?"

"Stormy, there's something queer going on. You're the town marshal and Sam Delaney's the deputy sheriff. He should outrank you—yet he acts as though he were taking orders from you."

"Maybe he is," Stormy said soberly. "Look, Kate, we're not going any deeper into the subject. There's a lot going on that you don't know, but I'm not giving out any information yet."

"Why?" Kate demanded.

"It might be dangerous for you if you knew what I do."

"How dangerous?"

"Suppose Harper took a notion to kidnap you. He might even try to torture information out of you. Right now what you don't know won't hurt you."

Kate smiled. "He might take a notion to kidnap me anyway."

"I aim to prevent that, if possible, but if he did, he couldn't get information you didn't have to give him. See what I mean?"

Kate nodded. "All right. I'll leave it to you. Stormy, more people have complimented me on this last issue of the *Banner*. We got seven new subscriptions this morning."

"That's great. Y'know, I've been doing some thinking about the paper. Why couldn't we make it twice a week, instead of just once?"

"Whoa, cowboy! We can't go too fast, you know. The paper will have to grow with the town, and county."

"You mean we couldn't get enough news to fill two issues?"

"That's partly the reason. Back about four years it commenced to look as though Dad would start issuing twice a week. That was when the Carnival Mine was running great guns. Then the mine petered out, all at once. There's scarcely any mining done now. Prospectors pick up a little silver back in the hills from time to time, but I'm afraid Carnival's big mining days are over. Anyway, this is good cow country. I like that better. In time more and more people will move here to take the place of the mining people who have left."

Stormy nodded. "I reckon I understand. Sometimes I do wonder where the news comes from for each week's issue."

"It's not too difficult. We have to keep our eyes open—and our ears—and pick up whatever we can. People bring in notices of deaths and births and marriages. This morning I got a story about old Joel McManus being kicked by a horse. His leg was broken. We can always do stories about old residents and newcomers to town. We exchange stories with other papers in the state. Then we subscribe to a filler service that comes from Chicago—"

"Filler service?"

Kate nodded. "The company in Chicago sends us a list of items we can use—everything from national news to jokes. The story in this week's issue, about the number of people dying yearly from snake bite in India, was from the filler company. So was the one about Navaho rugs finding a market in the East. Oh, I'm not worrying about filling the paper. This story about Harper being arrested and fined will increase circulation, I'm betting. Then there'll be stories about you being appointed marshal and about Sam Delaney."

"Why don't we publish the paper on Saturday instead of Tuesday? That's when most people come to town."

"Dad always said that most big news took place on Saturday and Sunday, so it was best to bring out the paper about Tuesday. I'm not sure I always agree with that idea, though."

"Sometime we'll publish the paper twice a week."

"That's the spirit, cowboy," Kate laughed, then sobered suddenly. "If we have a paper to publish. You know Dad borrowed three thousand on the *Banner*. On my way here this morning I was cutting through Mr. Trent's yard, to come in the back door, and—"

"You mean Banker Morgan Trent? Is his house—"

"Right across the alley, back of us, here. I always take a short cut through to Beaumont Street by way of his yard."

Stormy looked thoughtful. "Yeah, seems like I remember you mentioning that once before. What about it?"

"Well, Mr. Trent was out in his yard when I came through. I could see he hated to speak about it, but he reminded me of that three-thousand-dollar debt. According to the note Dad gave, the bank can demand payment thirty days from the date of the note— Stormy! You're not listening to me."

"Sorry, Kate, I was thinking about something. I got what you said, though. Trent wants his money, I take it."

"He warned me he might have to ask for it. He says money is short right now."

"That's news to me, but maybe money is scarce. I'm no banker."

"But, Stormy, what are we to do?"

Stormy scratched his head thoughtfully, his mind still far from the present subject. "Pay him, of course," he said finally.

Kate sighed. "I do wish you'd pay attention.

Now where arc we to raise three thousand dollars in—let's see—less than three weeks? The *Banner*'s bank account is only about two hundred dollars—"

"Two hundred seven dollars and three cents." Stormy suddenly came back to the present. "At least it was."

"How do you know that?" Kate asked, surprised.

"Cripes! I forgot to tell you, Kate. My money came from home Monday. I deposited fifteen hundred dollars to the *Banner*'s account, after Trent told me your signature was good for drawing money out."

"You did!" Kate's long-lashed eyes widened. "I'll be darned! But even that won't be enough."

Stormy got to his feet. "Come on, we'll drift down and pay Trent his money. I didn't put all my cash in the *Banner* account. I started an account of my own. There'll be enough to take up that note."

"But, Stormy—"

"But me no buts. You want that note paid off, don't you? Anyway, whether you do or not, I do. I'm half owner of this newspaper, and I don't like the idea of it being in debt. Come on, let's get started. It's nearly noon, anyway, and then we can have dinner together. Quad can take care of things while we're out."

Ten minutes later they were in Morgan Trent's private office at the bank. "Well, well," Trent boomed pompously, "what brings you two here?"

He shook hands with Stormy and added to Kate, "You're becoming more charming every day, young lady. Now if it weren't for Mrs. Trent, and if I were younger, I might . . ." He didn't complete the sentence but winked jovially at Stormy, then indicated two chairs near his desk.

"Thank you, Mr. Trent," Kate said, smiling.

"But our young marshal takes up most of your time, I suppose," Trent ran on. "By the way, Marshal Knight, let me congratulate you on the manner in which you handled our mayor. It's rumored he was fined by Judge Turner. We need a firm hand here. That Pyramid has always been a sink of iniquity. Perhaps now Harper will realize he's not the boss in Carnival. It's regrettable, of course, that Carnival's own mayor had to be placed behind bars—a blemish on our civic virtue, as it were—but as I was saying to Mrs. Trent, only this morning, it will show people we are not ashamed to uncover dishonesty, regardless where it hides. As I say, Marshal Knight—"

"Mr. Trent," Stormy cut in, "we don't want to borrow any more of your time than necessary. The fact is, we've come to take up that note Kate's father signed."

Trent's face dropped. "You—you mean you want to repay the three thousand dollars?"

"And the interest." Stormy nodded.

Trent heaved a long sigh. "Kate, my dear girl, I wouldn't have had this happen for anything.

This puts me in the light of pressing for payment. I'm afraid you misunderstood my remarks of this morning."

"You said," Kate pointed out quietly, "that money was tight at present and that you might have to call on me."

Trent shook his head and smiled sadly. "But not that tight, Kate. I wouldn't want to press an old friend. I merely pointed out the matter, in case you didn't know your father had borrowed the money. I'm rather clumsy, I fear. No, you just let that note run as long as you like."

"That's right decent of you, Mr. Trent," Stormy put in, "but I think we'd better pay up."

"But can you spare the money?" Trent asked. "I think the *Banner* account is only something better than seventeen hundred dollars."

"Have you forgotten I opened a personal account?" Stormy said.

"You want to draw on that?" Trent looked surprised.

Stormy nodded. "We want to wipe that note off the books."

"But it's so unnecessary—" Trent commenced.

"We'll feel better with it paid off," Kate interrupted.

Trent surrendered. "Of course you will. Just a minute. I'll have my cashier figure the interest to date and bring in the proper papers."

He rose from his desk and opened a door leading

into the rear half of the bank room, back of the cashier's cage. "Jennings," he commenced, "let me have that Sanford note and—" He stopped short upon hearing a much louder voice:

". . . and you tell Trent I can't wait all day."

Trent moved hastily out of the office, closing the door behind him. Kate and Stormy eyed each other.

Stormy said, "That sounded like Rufe Harper's voice."

"It was," Kate replied. "I'd like to know what he wanted. I wish Trent hadn't closed this office door."

"You and me both," Stormy nodded. "Harper sounded like he was used to getting in here any time it suited his fancy."

The minutes passed. Stormy glanced around the office. It was rather showily furnished. The desk was of mahogany; the chairs were upholstered. One door led to the lobby of the bank. A door in one side wall opened on the bank proper. Behind the desk a clothes closet stood with its door ajar. Stormy rose from his seat, crossed the room, and opened the closet door. He glanced inside but saw nothing except Trent's hat and a fancy vest hanging on the hooks within. He left the door as it was and returned to the chair.

Kate looked curiously at him. "You wouldn't be snoopy, would you?" she smiled.

Stormy grinned. "I just thought I might see some

of the bank's extra money laying on the floor of that closet. Y'see, from the way Trent talked, money isn't tight at all. He sort of gave me the impression there was money to burn."

"That's certainly not the way he talked to me this morning," Kate said. "Something must have happened to change his tune."

Trent arrived after a time, bearing papers in his hands. He apologized for keeping them waiting. "One of our local cattlemen wanted to see me—buttonholed me, couldn't get away from the cuss."

"Sounded like Rufe Harper's voice," Stormy said bluntly.

"Harper? Mayor Harper? No, it wasn't Harper." Trent eyed Stormy rather sharply, stroking his sideburns meanwhile. "Now you mention it," he said at last, "I do seem to remember seeing Harper standing in the lobby, talking to someone. I'm not sure. . . . Anyway, Miss Kate, here's the note your father signed. Now if you and Marshal Knight will sign these withdrawal slips . . ."

The note had been redeemed. Trent said to Stormy, "I presume you realize this just about wipes out your personal account as well as the *Banner* money. I just want to make it clear that you two mustn't want for anything. If you find you need money, or if the *Banner* should require some financing, I'll be more than pleased to oblige. I personally think that now is the time to broaden your business. The *Banner* should have a larger audience. Instead of four, it would be nice to see Carnival able to boast of an eight-page paper. I'm sure you could develop such a project, Marshal Knight. . . ."

Kate and Stormy managed to escape after a time. "As I've thought more than once," Kate smiled, "Mr. Trent must have been born during a high wind." She and Stormy were out on the sidewalk now. They crossed the street and headed toward the hotel dining room.

All through dinner Stormy was unusually silent. Kate said finally, "There's no law that compels you to talk, of course, but—"

"I'm sorry, Kate," Stormy said contritely. "I've been thinking about Trent. After what he said this morning I thought he was anxious to have that note taken up. Then when we go to pay it he acts like he doesn't want the money. How do you figure it?"

"Maybe," Kate speculated, "he just wanted to see if we had the money to pay."

"He must have known that much. Maybe all that talk was just bluff and he really did want the money. He might want to see us broke."

"But why should he?"

Stormy shrugged. "Why should he deny he was talking to Rufe Harper?"

"That was funny, wasn't it? I— Stormy, are we really broke?"

"We're not rolling in millions," Stormy said

dryly. "You know what we have in the bank. But don't worry. We'll pull through."

"We'd better," Kate said soberly. "I have to order more paper stock and ink this week."

"In other words," Stormy smiled, "I've got to try just that much harder to find that satchel of money that was stolen from your dad. Kate, what else did Trent have to say when you met him out in his yard this morning?"

Kate pondered. "Well, I told you what he said about the note. I don't know as he said anything else—wait a minute, he did mention having seen Quad in the print room quite early a couple of mornings. He could see right through the rear window, you know."

"I doubt he could see much, unless he crossed the alley and came close. But what about Quad?"

"Nothing much. Trent just mentioned that Quad got to work early. I explained that Quad had been sleeping at the shop, that we thought it safer, after what had happened one time."

"Did he ask if Quad was armed?"

"Now that you mention it, he did. I told him Quad always kept a shotgun handy. . . . Stormy, what's on your mind?"

"My hair," Stormy grinned.

"All right, put me off if you like. But at least tell me what you were looking for in Trent's office closet when he stepped out of the room."

"A hand satchel," Stormy confessed.

"You mean the one that was stolen from Dad?"

Stormy nodded. "The same. Not that I expected to find the money in it, of course."

"Stormy! You're not suspecting Trent of a hand in that business, are you?"

"Kate, until they're proved innocent, I'm going to suspect dang nigh every man in this town. And I think you'll admit there's a distinctly fishy air about Mr. Morgan Trent at times."

"But, Stormy, he was friendly to Father."

"So, probably, was Rufe Harper at one time. Men change, you know."

Kate looked troubled. "I hate to think it—about Trent. He's so looked up to in Carnival. . . . Oh well, he's not proved guilty yet. Come on, I've got to get back to the *Banner.* There's work to do."

"There's plenty work to do," Stormy said seriously, "but you and I aren't talking about the same sort of work."

20. "IT'S MY JOB!"

The remainder of that day and the next passed without serious incident. Harper had reopened the Pyramid, Wednesday evening, but so far as Stormy and Sam Delaney could determine in their visits the first night and the following, the games were being operated squarely. Judging from the sour looks on the faces of the professional gamblers, the house wasn't raking in its usual profits.

Since the night of his arrest Harper had passed Stormy several times in Carnival, but, beyond a cold nod of recognition, had had nothing to say; this was not at all to Stormy's liking: he had hoped to force Harper into some sort of rash move. However, Harper was, apparently, too smart to do anything without first laying careful plans, and Stormy was forced impatiently to bide his time until something definite was effected upon which lawful action could be based.

Friday morning, about ten o'clock, Stormy strolled into the *Banner* office and found Kate seated at the desk, polishing her story of Harper's arrest. She handed the sheets of paper to Stormy. He read them through and nodded approvingly. Kate said, "Think that will do for our lead story?"

"It couldn't be better. It will land like a

bombshell on Harper, I'm thinking. I've a hunch he thinks he's too big in Carnival for anything like this to appear. Course most of the town knows about it now, anyway, but I just wish the paper could be published right off—"

"Want a daily newspaper now, do you?" Kate's eyes danced.

"It would be a right good idea, if we could handle it."

"We will, cowboy, you see. One of these days we'll give Carnival a real honest-to-goodness newspaper. Meanwhile we'll do with what we have."

Stormy changed the subject. "Say, Mrs. Thomas is a right good cook."

"You liked Ada's supper, then?"

"It was darn nice of you to invite Sam and Quad and me last evening. I haven't had home cooking like that in a dog's age, and— Hey, what's the matter?" Kate had commenced to smile.

Kate explained. "Apparently Quad likes her— and her cooking—too. Ada told me this morning. Quad asked if he could call on her tonight."

"No!"

"Yes. First thing this morning Quad went out and bought a new shirt and necktie."

Stormy chuckled. "Think anything will come of it?"

Kate shrugged her slim shoulders. "*Quién sabe?*

Who knows? I do know, so Mrs. Freeman tells me, that Ada has been dreadfully lonesome since her husband died five years ago. And she seemed pleased that Quad had asked to call."

"I'll be darned. Think of Quad— Maybe, Kate, this is the sort of interest he needs to keep him straight and hold him on the job. I was thinking, later, if things go all right, we might cut Quad in on a share of the *Banner*'s profits."

Kate nodded. "I think that's a good idea, if things work out the way we want them to."

"Say, Kate"—Stormy flushed a trifle—"I got an idea when I woke up this morning."

"Hope it didn't give you a headache," Kate smiled.

"It darned near did, at that. Look, I've been reading some of the big city newspapers they have at the hotel, and several of them have a whole column of short paragraphs written by one man— I mean one man on each paper. The paragraphs are sort of short and snappy. Like there was one called 'Casual Comments, by Joe Castor.' Another writer called himself 'The Rapier.' His writing was very sharp and sarcastic. Then there was another—"

"What you're getting at, Stormy," Kate broke in, "you'd like us to have a regular columnist, like the Chicago and Kansas City papers—and other large towns."

"Is that what you call 'em—columnists?

Anyway, you get the idea. It's a good way to get news into people who don't want to spend too much time reading."

"We'll have one someday. But we couldn't afford it now, Stormy."

"It might be we could get around that. I notice all the big papers have a weather report. That started me thinking. What would you think of a column by a writer who called himself 'The Weather Man'? It was a name that just—well, just sort of came to me." Stormy tried to appear casual.

Kate eyed him suspiciously. Weather? Stormy? She smiled suddenly. "All right, let's see what you've written."

Sheepishly Stormy extracted a sheaf of papers, covered with penciled writing, from his pocket and extended them to the girl. She glanced at the first sheet, then at Stormy, saying, "I do believe you've been bitten by the writing bug."

Stormy flushed. "Well, it is sort of fun to see your sayings in print."

"I've been thinking that same thing for a good many years now," Kate admitted. She read the first item on the page:

When the mayor of our promising city is hailed before the justice of the peace and fined for resisting an officer, it is a distinct reflection on the people of Carnival. It's

240

not too early now to commence thinking about our next election. The *Banner*'s nomination for the job is Gage Freeman. He should win in a breeze.

Kate glanced up at Stormy. "Not bad. Darn good! I think Gage would make a good mayor, too." She read on:

Recent storms seem to have swept two prominent (?) men out of Carnival. Whatever became of Cameo Sloan and Pudge Bayliss? Does anyone care?

Kate looked thoughtfully at Stormy. "Maybe you've hit on something that will appeal to our readers. I like this stuff."

"Thanks. Most of it, of course, is aimed at Harper and his gang, but I've sprinkled in other items about townspeople I've picked up here and there."

Kate read on, smiling at a human-interest bit that had to do about a small boy buying eggs for his mother. There was a rather humorous paragraph about a pair of nocturnal fighting tomcats. Then another slap at Harper:

The Pyramid Gambling Saloon reopened Wednesday night. To give the devil his due, it is rumored the house isn't raking in its customary winnings of late. Could it be that Mayor Harper is giving citizens a break?

Kate read other items:

The thunder and lightning expected at the Pyramid last Tuesday night fortunately failed to materialize. Mayor Harper and his cohorts admit they were caught without their slickers.

The next paragraph read:

Recently, when asked about the weather in Carnival, Judge Hame Turner said, "Fine!" (To the tune of one hundred fifty dollars.)

Kate turned to another sheet. An item halfway down the page caught her eye:

Whoever heard of a gun-totin', rip-tearin', plenty-tough badman being named Fauntleroy? The *Banner* simply refuses to believe it! Are you certain you gave the judge the right name, Mister Amber?

Kate snickered. "You're sure rubbing it in, Stormy." She went on to further remarks anent Harper's employees:

The two plug-uglies who masquerade under the name of bouncers in the Pyramid have worked up for themselves quite a reputation as fighters. To date they have managed to throw out and beat up every gullible victim who was so rash as to protest his losses at the Pyramid's various games of chance. Unless these two manly exponents of the art of assault-and-battery decide to seek a more healthy climate, they may get caught in the approaching storm.

Her smile broadened as she read on down the page. The last paragraph ran:

Weather report: Cloudy in the vicinity of the Pyramid; unsettled in the Bonanza; considerable precipitation in all the bars.

Kate raised her eyes. "But not a watery precipitation, I take it. Stormy, it's good—all of it!"

"Will you print it?" he asked eagerly.

"Will *we* print it!" she corrected. "I'll head the column 'The Weather Man Reports' and run a short editorial note to the effect that this is now a weekly feature of the Carnival *Banner*."

"A weekly feature?" Stormy's face fell. "Gosh, I don't know if I can write—"

"Yes, you can," Kate contradicted. "You've

started something; now you've got to go through with it. Wait 'til Quad sees what I give him to set up. Golly! This sort of thing is just what we need to help fight Harper. You've told me yourself that ridicule is sometimes as effective as force." She sobered suddenly. "But, Stormy, this is going to raise merry—"

"Careful! Don't say it," Stormy said. "I know what you mean. It's going to hit Harper right between the eyes."

"This is farther than the *Banner* has ever gone before. Don't you realize this is dynamite?"

"Sure I do," Stormy nodded eagerly. "The sooner the explosion comes, the sooner we get things settled."

Kate's heart thrilled at his courage. She rose suddenly, placed her hands on his shoulders. The next instant Stormy felt her lips warm on his own.

"Hey—" Stormy gasped in surprise.

"It doesn't mean anything." Kate blushed furiously. "It's just a reward for—"

"The heck it doesn't mean anything," Stormy said enthusiastically, and gathered her into his arms.

"Darn it," Kate murmured, "I knew I was running a risk—" The rest of the words were smothered against his mouth.

Sometime later they were aroused by the sounds of Quad's voice, approaching the office doorway: "Miss Kate, can I have a look at your dummy? Oh, excuse me!"

"You can take it from me, he's no dummy," Kate murmured drowsily. "Er—I—I mean—" She hastily disengaged herself from Stormy's arms, her features crimson, her tawny hair tumbled over one eye. "Oh yes, Quad. You mean the dummy I made up for page two?"

But Quad had retired discreetly to the print room.

Stormy moved toward the girl again. Kate said, "No, Stormy, no! People can look right in this window and see us from outside. You'd better go away and—and—do your marshaling job for a while. I'm busy."

Stormy said blissfully, "The Weather Man reports, 'Fair and warmer, with blue skies—' "

"Stop talking nonsense," Kate said.

She got rid of him after a time.

That was on Friday. The following Tuesday the *Banner* was published with flaring headlines, telling the story of Harper's arrest, as well as with Stormy's new column, which made an instant hit with readers. In no time at all the news was all over Carnival. Men could be seen standing on sidewalks, reading and chuckling over Stormy's pithy paragraphs. Drinkers in saloons grinned idiotically every time someone mentioned the name Fauntleroy.

Repercussions came almost immediately:

The two bouncers in the Pyramid decided to take the hint, and when last seen were riding hastily out of town, their few worldly possessions tied to saddles behind. Next Rufe Harper came storming into the *Banner* office, his face white with anger, his yellow eyes blazing.

Stormy had been expecting this and was waiting in the office with Kate when Harper rushed in. "You looking for somebody?" Stormy asked coolly.

"You know damn well I am," Harper raged. "I—"

"Take it easy, Harper," Stormy snapped. "If you've got business with me, state it and then get out!"

"I've got business with you, all right—both of you," Harper snarled. He shook a rolled copy of the *Banner* in Stormy's face. "This time you've gone too far."

"Shucks! We've just started," Stormy grinned. "I hope to have something even better next week."

"Unless you retract every word you've said about me and my Pyramid," Harper threatened, "there won't be any newspaper next week."

"Retract it?" Stormy asked. "How do you expect us to do that?" He added, "Even if we wanted to."

"You can get busy right now, print up another paper, leaving my name out of it. I won't have that business about me being arrested and fined—"

"Mr. Harper," Kate put in icily, "it requires just about a week to prepare the *Banner* for printing. We can't—"

"I don't care how long it takes," Harper fumed. "You'll both get busy right now. You haven't sent any copies out of town yet, and—"

"Look, Harper," Stormy said coldly, "get it through your head that the *Banner* stands as is— and we stand back of it. We're not changing anything and we're not bringing out a new issue just to please you. If you don't like that, there are two things you can do."

"What's that?" Harper demanded.

"Well"—and there was a distinct challenge in Stormy's tones—"I've heard of editors being threatened with a gun. Have you thought of that?"

"I've a good notion to—" Harper paused.

"Or," Stormy continued smoothly, "if you think you have a case, you can hire a lawyer and sue the *Banner* for libel. But I don't advise that. We've proof of every statement we've made in the paper, and you'd just be throwing money away. Now make up your mind quick what you want to do and then clear out. We've work to do."

Harper was fairly trembling with rage. He stood glaring at Stormy. "Cripes a'mighty!" he thundered. "If this paper gets circulated around, you'll make me a laughingstock in the county— a fool."

"No, Harper," Stormy contradicted with a thin smile, "we didn't make you a laughingstock and a fool. The paper just pointed out that fact. And I still insist you're a fool if you continue what you're trying to do here."

Harper bared his teeth in a snarl. His right hand dropped to gun butt—then an amazed gasp left his lips. As though by magic, Stormy's forty-four had leaped into his right fist and its muzzle was bearing directly on Harper's middle.

"Go ahead, Harper," Stormy said quietly, "pull your iron if you want action."

"Stormy!" Kate cried. "Harper! You can't—"

A gunshot from down the street someplace interrupted the words. Then came two more explosions, close together. They sounded like the reports from a forty-five six-shooter. Sudden wild yells ascended along Main Street.

Harper stiffened, glanced over his shoulder, then back at Stormy. Stormy said swiftly, "Who's doing that shooting, Harper?"

Harper said, "I don't know. Put your gun away, Knight, and we'll go—"

"Don't lie to me," Stormy snapped.

"I tell you I don't—"

Stormy commenced to believe Harper was telling the truth. "I'll go see for myself." Jabbing the muzzle of his forty-four hard into Harper's middle, he backed the man toward the doorway, then with a deft movement of his left hand he reached down, plucked Harper's gun from its holster, and tossed it out to the dusty roadway. "I don't aim to be shot in the back when I leave," he said tersely, and leaped toward the sidewalk to join the men running past in the direction of the Bonanza Bar.

Gage Freeman came plunging up as Stormy reached the street. "It's Squint Amber," Freeman panted. "He's gone hawg-wild—shot old Vink Tanner—"

"Who's Vink Tanner?"

"Just a harmless old bum who hangs around town. Been here as long as I can remember. Vink was ridin' Amber about that Fauntleroy name— as a lot of others were. Amber lost his temper and pumped lead into Tanner—"

Stormy leaped past Freeman, talking as he moved. "Where's Amber now?"

"Holed up in the Bonanza Bar," Freeman replied. "He's threatening to kill anybody who comes near him."

At that instant Sam Delaney came sprinting along the sidewalk. "What's up?" he yelled.

Stormy jerked out the necessary words. Delaney nodded. "I'll go put him under arrest."

Stormy shook his head. "It's my job, Sam! You stick near and keep Harper and his coyotes off my back if the going gets rough."

Without awaiting a reply, he broke into a run that carried him toward the Bonanza Bar.

21. OUTLAWED!

A crowd had gathered in front of the Bonanza Bar. It parted as Stormy approached, with Sam Delaney coming swiftly at his rear. Stormy saw several of Harper's men. He singled out 'Brose Echardt and asked:

"Amber inside that saloon?"

Echardt glared sullenly at Stormy but didn't reply.

"I don't want to ask you again, Echardt," Stormy snapped.

"Yeah, he's in there." Echardt laughed harshly. "Nobody but a damn fool would go after him, though. He's—"

"He's gone plumb loco, Marshal Knight!" a man yelled. "Drove us all out of the Bonanza at the point of his gun. Pore ol' Vink Tanner is in there too—hurt bad. Amber wouldn't let none of us get him to a doctor."

Sam Delaney, at Stormy's shoulder, said, "I'd like to take him off your hands, Stormy."

Stormy shook his head. "It's my job," he said again. "Sam, I just remembered I left Kate with Harper. Maybe you'd better go back."

"She's all right," Delaney replied. "Gage Freeman is with her. I saw Harper leave your office."

Another shot sounded inside the Bonanza,

then the sound of shattered glass. Joe Wiley, who operated the saloon for Harper, was standing near and groaned. "Jeesis! There goes our mirror. Can't you stop him, Marshal? Amber's gone crazy."

There came further crashing of glass. It sounded like bottles and glasses being destroyed. Wiley pawed at Stormy's arm. "There goes the stock. For Gawd's sake, Knight—"

Stormy shook him off. "Do you suppose I give a damn about your stock?"

Harper came pushing through the crowd, a sneer on his lips. "What's the matter, lost your nerve, Knight? Maybe this town better appoint a new marshal."

Stormy paid no attention. He was studying the swinging doors of the entrance, getting the layout, as he remembered it, firmly in his mind. He'd been in the Bonanza only once, and that for only a minute. He wanted to move fast, once he'd pushed through those swinging doors.

"Yep," Harper jeered, "our brave marshal has lost his nerve."

Still Stormy didn't reply. Sam Delaney growled, "Harper, you'd best keep your trap shut."

A sudden cheer went up from the crowd. Stormy had started toward the broad front steps that led the way to the Bonanza porch. Abruptly he changed his mind and swung off at an angle. And just in time: through the swinging doors of the entrance came three fast shots, fired as quickly as Squint Amber could pull trigger on his forty-five!

Excited yells ascended from the crowd as it scattered frantically to get out of the line of fire. A trio of splintered holes had appeared in one of the swinging doors, which swung violently for a moment and then came to rest.

Catlike, Stormy vaulted over the porch rail and came down with scarcely a sound. For an instant he flattened himself against the front wall of the building, then commenced to edge cautiously toward the entrance. In the street the crowd held its breath. Harper was watching with gleaming, triumphant eyes, a sneering smile on his lips.

Stormy was almost to the entrance before he spoke, the words sounding clearly along the now silent street: "You're under arrest, Amber. I advise you to give up."

He heard a rather startled gasp from inside; Amber hadn't realized he was so close. There came a swift scurrying of booted feet, then from near the rear of the saloon came Amber's snarled reply: "You'll never take me alive, Knight!"

"I haven't said," Stormy spoke grimly, "that I *wanted* to take you alive."

He took another quick step, then whirled swiftly through the swinging doors and inside the barroom. From behind the bar came two rafter-rocking explosions. Hot lead thudded into the wall at Stormy's back. He had a quick glimpse of Amber's hateful features above the top of the bar as the man was lifting his six-shooter for another attempt. Stormy flipped a quick shot sidewise as he dived for the shelter of an overturned table. He was moving too fast for accuracy—hadn't even expected to hit Amber—but the shot served its purpose as it ripped into the already shattered bar mirror! Amber ducked down, out of sight, behind the long counter.

The barroom was a shambles. Tables and chairs were overturned, glasses and bottles scattered across the floor. A strong odor of spilled liquor assailed Stormy's nostrils. Some yards away, sprawled like a limp bundle of tattered clothing, was the inert, bewhiskered form of Vink Tanner. Stormy judged the old derelict was already dead.

From behind his table top Stormy warned, "You'd better give up, Amber. You'll never get out of this. You're outlawed."

Amber didn't reply. Stormy could hear him breathing heavily and wondered if Amber could be reloading, there, in the protection of the bar. Had Stormy been certain he was, he would have rushed the man, but such procedure was too risky, otherwise. Stormy spoke again: "You'd better surrender, Amber."

"Only a fool would say that," Amber snarled back, and followed up with an obscene curse.

Stormy persisted quietly, "I'll see that you get a

fair trial. If you'll tell who killed Sanford, it will help—" An exclamation of surprise burst from Amber's lips; plainly the man hadn't expected Stormy to take that tack. Stormy continued: "How about it, Amber? Ready to make a clean breast of things?"

Amber swore at him. Stormy raised his six-shooter and sent two swift shots winging through the front of the bar at about the point from which Amber's voice had last come.

A yelp of mingled pain and astonishment greeted the effort. Stormy judged he had at least winged the man.

"Nicked you a mite, eh, Fauntleroy?" Stormy taunted. "That's only the begin—"

The words were interrupted as Amber rose swiftly from behind the bar and unleashed a stream of orange fire from his Colt. Splinters from the edge of the table behind which Stormy was sheltered flew off into space.

"You dirty bustard!" Amber half screamed as he once more ducked out of sight.

Again Stormy sent a shot crashing through the front of the counter, but this time was rewarded for his efforts with only a harsh laugh and a sneered, "Missed me a mile, law man!"

Stormy mused, "That's four shots I've blown away," and deftly replenished the spent shells in his cylinder. A minute dragged past with no activity from either man.

Amber finally became impatient. "Why don't you come and get me, you lousy son?"

Stormy didn't reply. Another sixty seconds ticked off. Stormy glanced around. A shattered whisky bottle lay near at hand. He picked up a small scrap of broken glass and tossed it down near the end of the bar, where there was a passage between counter and wall.

Then, with one swift leap, Stormy crossed the room and bounded to the top of the bar, gun in hand.

The ruse had worked: hearing the tinkle of the bit of glass as it landed on the floor, Amber had whirled to a crouching position, facing toward the end of the bar, thinking Stormy was approaching in that direction. Even as Stormy vaulted to the top of the long counter, Amber swung around to face him, one arm dangling useless at his side. A curse was ripped from his lips as the gun in his other hand spurted living flame and smoke.

Stormy felt the breeze of the bullet fan his cheek as it whined past. The forty-four in his hand jerked twice. Through the swirling powder smoke Stormy saw Amber commence to wilt. The man's legs sagged. Quite suddenly he pitched sidewise against the back wall, then slid to the floor to lay without motion.

Stormy dropped to the floor behind the bar, his booted feet slipping over broken glass and spilled whisky, and bent above Amber's huddled form. The outlaw's eyes were closed, but he was still breathing in a sort of labored fashion. A wide crimson stain was spreading rapidly on the breast of Amber's gray woolen shirt.

Stormy reached down and plucked the six-shooter from Amber's unresisting fingers and stuck the weapon in the waistband of his trousers. Then, stepping over the unconscious body, he rounded the bar and examined Vink Tanner. A feeling of pity swept through Stormy as he straightened out the frail old form and felt for a heartbeat. There wasn't any. Tanner was dead.

Going to the swinging-doored entrance, Stormy stepped out on the saloon porch. In the street the crowd still waited with bated breath. A sudden cheer greeted Stormy's appearance, and the gathering swept toward him. Stormy held up one hand.

"You all better stay out," he said. The crowd halted. Stormy searched for and found Deputy Sam Delaney's grinning face. "You might send for Doc Glover, Sam."

"I already did," Delaney replied. "Sent for him right after you went in. He should be here any minute." He started to ascend the porch steps.

Rufe Harper, followed by 'Brose Echardt, broke from the crowd. "Vink Tanner still alive?" Harper asked.

Stormy shook his head. "No. Amber is, though. I can't say how long he'll last."

Harper looked disappointed as he and Echardt followed Stormy and Delaney inside the saloon. As they entered Stormy said icily, "Harper, didn't you hear me tell the crowd to stay out? What do you want here?"

"I'm within my rights, Knight," Harper growled. "Maybe you've forgotten I own the Bonanza. Echardt is my foreman. I've asked him to come."

"All right, stay," Stormy conceded reluctantly. He started to say more, but a sudden outburst from Harper interrupted the words:

"Jeesis almighty!" Harper exploded. "Look at this place. It's ruined! Damn that Amber. I'll— What got into him? Did he go plumb insane?"

"Just about, Rufe," Echardt scowled. "All the boys were kidding him, more or less, about that Fauntleroy name. Then the rest of the crowd took it up. Squint sure went loco. He yanked his gun and made us all get out—even his own pals. Tanner kept needling him, and Squint filled the old buzzard full of lead. I reckon he set out to prove just how bad he could be."

Harper didn't hear the last of the words. He was striding angrily about, bewailing the damage in the place. His steps carried him around the end of the bar, where he saw Amber's unconscious body.

"Damn you!" he snarled, and sent a heavy kick

crashing against Amber's side. "I'll teach you to—"

And that was as far as he got. He felt a steely grasp on his shoulder as Stormy whirled him around and sent him flying in the direction of the doorway. "I don't give a damn who Amber is or what he has done!" Stormy exclaimed. "You aren't kicking a wounded man, Harper."

"Why, damn you, Knight!" Harper started to return, then stopped at the look in Stormy's eyes. "Look here, Knight. I own this place. You can't put me off my property in such a highhanded manner."

"Get out!" Stormy snapped. "And don't come back while I'm here. You too, Echardt. This place stinks bad enough without you two. Go on, light out pronto!"

Mumbling protests, the two men headed for the doorway and passed through to the street.

"There's one sweet pair," Delaney drawled disgustedly as Harper and his foreman departed. "Imagine treating one of his own men that-a-way. And Amber hit bad, too—not that I'm sayin' Amber didn't deserve what he got."

"It was him or me," Stormy said soberly. "He deserved what he got, all right. I've a hunch he had a hand in the killing of James Sanford—but, regardless, I just couldn't stand for Harper treating him that way—"

He broke off as Dr. Glover entered. "Making

work for me, eh, Stormy?" he said. "Howdy, Sam."

"I don't know whether you can do anything or not, so far as Amber is concerned," Stormy replied. "But if there's a chance of pulling him through long enough for me to ask him a few questions, I'd like—" He broke off as the doctor started to kneel at the side of Tanner's body. "No use bothering with him, Doc. He's been dead for some time."

Glover nodded and made his way around the bar. He opened his medicine case and busied himself over the unconscious Amber. Finally he rose to his feet, shaking his head. "I don't know," he said dubiously. "Looks like you've just about finished Amber, Stormy. Course, if I could have him down to my house where I could work on him—"

"You mean he might live?" Stormy asked.

"Great Jehoshaphat, no! No chance of that. But I might be able to restore him to consciousness for a few minutes. But he'd have to be moved carefully. I've given him a shot to keep his heart pumping a while longer. There's a lot of internal bleeding that's bad, though. One bullet entered his right lung—"

"We could roll him on a tarpaulin," Sam Delaney suggested. "Four men could carry him down to your place, Doc. What do you say?"

"I'm not so sure about rolling him," Glover replied, "but you could lift him on the tarp. It's worth trying. He might be alive when you got him to my place."

Sam nodded. "I'll take care of it. Stormy, you might as well leave. Miss Sanford is waiting for you outside."

There was still a crowd gathered before the Bonanza when Stormy stepped into the open air. He glanced about, paying but small attention to the numerous questions that greeted his appearance. Neither Harper nor Echardt were to be seen, but on the edge of the throng Stormy spied Kate, standing with Quad and Gage Freeman.

He joined them and quickly replied to their eager questioning. Kate still looked somewhat shaky, but she forced a smile. "You continue to make news, cowboy. There's never any doubt about filling the *Banner*'s columns when you're around."

"You're making headlines, Stormy," Quad put in.

"They're not the sort of headlines I like," Stormy said soberly. "And I've a hunch they won't be appearing in many more issues. We've got Harper on the run now. I aim to keep things going that way, without any letup, until we've stopped him complete. Then there'll be peace in Carnival."

22. A SHOT IN THE DARK

Three days passed with no change in Squint Amber's condition. The man was still unconscious. As Doc Glover had told Stormy: "I'm double-danged if I know what's keeping him alive, but he hangs on. Maybe he'll die without regaining consciousness. I don't know any more about it than you do. Yes, I'll get in touch with you the instant there's a favorable sign. My wife is there, and I've got another woman helping her. They know what to do in case I should be out."

Friday, shortly past noon, Stormy saw Kate standing on the sidewalk in front of the *Banner* building as he came strolling along. "Hi-yuh, lady," Stormy greeted. "Loafing on the job again, eh? I reckon I'll have to hire me another editor."

"Loafing my eye!" Kate smiled. "I'm just catching a breath of fresh air before I return to your slave pen. Pretty easy for you. Nothing to do but wear a badge and walk around town, while I do the work. By the way, where's Sam? I haven't seen him for a couple of days."

"Sam's taking a ride around the country, in his capacity as deputy. That's between you and me. If anybody should ask you, you don't know."

There were several people on the street. The sun beat down strongly, making more intense the shadow between buildings. Not a cloud floated in the blue sky overhead.

"So that's why you're so busy with your marshaling all of a sudden," Kate nodded. "Well, don't forget you'll have to start writing a few items for your Weather Man column."

"I already did some scribbling this morning," Stormy said. He delved in a pocket and brought out some folded sheets of paper which he handed to the girl. "Most of these are just friendly notices about people in town. I got one in about the Pyramid—"

"What about the Pyramid?"

"Well, you know most of Harper's professionals have left him. Sam and I have kept such a close watch that Harper's been forced to operate his games on the square. Consequently he's put a limit on winnings. Folks don't like it and are laying off the games. That means the gamblers aren't making the big percentages they used to. Harper's plenty burned up, but there's nothing he can do about it."

Kate unfolded the papers and found the item he'd mentioned:

The recent gale that hit the Pyramid seems to have blown most of Harper's tinhorns out of Carnival. They probably fear the coming downpour and are, wisely, moving to greener fields. Rumor has it that the

262

Pyramid is due to close shortly. That's fair-
weather news.

"Is Harper going to close the place?" Kate
asked.

Stormy shrugged. "There's some gossip to that
effect, though Harper denies it. He's put new
stock in the Bonanza—stock which he bought
from other saloons in town—and ordered a new
bar mirror. So it looks like he doesn't intend to
give up."

Kate read another paragraph:

Last Tuesday's hail (of bullets) storm,
which mussed up the Bonanza Bar some,
must have put a crimp in Mayor Harper's
profits. However, the Bonanza has
reopened, and various imbibers report the
liquor is better than usual. That's the
spirit, Mister Mayor; you set 'em up and
we'll knock 'em down. But hold on tight:
there's a hurricane on the way!

The girl glanced at Stormy, her eyes dancing.
"Harper will be fit to be tied when this comes
out— Oh, here comes Sam now."

Stormy glanced around. Sam Delaney was just
reining his pony into the hitch rack. He doffed
his sombrero to Kate, said "Howdy, folks,"
then swung down from the saddle.

Stormy said, "Pick up any information, Sam?" Sam started to speak, glanced at Kate, then paused. "It's all right," Stormy nodded. "Kate knows how to keep her mouth shut."

Delaney said, "In the last two days I've visited and talked to all the ranchers nearby. They were all surprised to see me and—they all have cattle losses to report. Last night, after dark, I swung over to Harper's Anvil outfit and hid out in the brush where I could watch the place. I did some scouting around close to the buildings too."

"Learn anything?"

"The Anvil hires a bigger crew than I'd say was necessary for a spread that's operated on the square. And here's something queer—Harper appears to be holding somebody prisoner in one of his barns. He had a guard in front of the door all the time."

"A prisoner?" Stormy frowned. "Now who in heck could that be?"

Sam shook his head. "Darned if I know." He yawned lazily. "I didn't leave there until about three hours ago, but I never did get any definite information." He added after a few moments, "Hoddy Oliver, of the Rafter-O, seems to be the heaviest stock loser. I told him our suspicions. He's going to see the other ranchers, and if at any time we need a crew of fighting riders, they'll be waiting at Oliver's for us to say the word. Hoddy said that each ranch would contribute one cowhand, and he'll live at the Rafter-O until a call comes."

"That's a right idea, Sam," Stormy nodded. "You get any sleep at all last night?"

"Too busy trying to learn what the Anvil was doing."

"Haven't eaten today, either, I suppose."

"You hit it, cowboy."

Stormy said, "Go get your chow and then turn in on my bed at the hotel. I'll take care of your office until you've caught up on your shut-eye."

They talked a few minutes more, then Sam crawled back into the saddle and moved down the street.

A moment later Quad emerged from the T-Bone Restaurant, next door to the *Banner* building, picking his teeth. He spoke to Stormy and Kate and started to move past. Stormy said, "Just a minute, Quad."

"What's on your mind, Stormy?"

Stormy grinned. "You and I have got to come to some sort of agreement."

Quad looked serious. "What about? I haven't been hitting the bottle."

"Nobody said you had," Stormy chuckled. "But, look, for two nights now I've gone to Kate's house to pay a social call. Each time I've found you already there, visiting Ada Thomas. That way neither of us makes any headway."

"Stormy!" Kate blushed. "Now what—"

Quad laughed. "I'm commencing to see what you mean. I think you're right. Hereafter let's compare notes before we go calling."

Stormy nodded. "It's a deal."

Quad was still laughing as he entered the *Banner* building.

Kate and Stormy conversed a few minutes longer. Kate said finally, "Well, you've your job to do and I've some copy to polish. I'd better be getting back to the desk."

At that moment a woman with faded blond hair, a hard mouth, and a supercilious air walked past. She wore a tight-bodiced dress that brushed the sidewalk and carried an open black parasol to shield her from the sun's rays. In passing she cast a contemptuous glance at Stormy and spoke frigidly to Kate: "How do you do, Miss Sanford?"

Kate's brief nod was just as cool. Stormy muttered as the woman swept by, "For gosh sakes, who's that—the queen of England or something?"

"That," Kate replied tersely, "is Mrs. Banker Morgan Trent."

"You two don't appear very friendly."

"She's not very friendly with anybody in town. Being the wife of Carnival's banker, she likes to play the part of the grand lady. She doesn't play it very well. She told Dad once it was unladylike for me to work on a newspaper. We've barely been on speaking terms since."

They watched the woman as she proceeded

along the street, crossed over and entered the bank. "Mr. Trent is probably in for another hen-pecking," Kate observed.

Stormy asked casually, "Have they any children?"

Kate shook her head. "It's rumored Mrs. Trent says children are too expensive. She's money crazy, you know."

"Probably wouldn't even pay a servant, I suppose," Stormy commented casually.

"I should say not. She does her own work. That probably doesn't fit in well with her part of grand lady, but she does hate to spend a penny. . . . Stormy, why are you so interested?"

Stormy didn't reply at once. He seemed lost in thought. Finally he said, "I got an idea. Maybe it's just a shot in the dark—"

"Idea about what?" Kate asked.

Stormy cocked a black eyebrow at her. "Ask me no questions, I'll tell you no lies," he grinned. "Well, see you later, Kate." Turning, he walked swiftly down the street.

"That man!" Kate said in exasperation as she turned into the *Banner* office. "Lord, how I love him!"

That night Stormy and Sam Delaney were seated in the hotel restaurant eating supper when a small boy entered with a message. "You're Marshal Knight, ain't you?" he asked.

"You hit it right on the nose, son," Stormy nodded.

"Dr. Glover says you're to come to his house right away, and not to lose no time," the urchin said.

"It must be about Amber," Delaney said as they both got to their feet. "Want me to go with you, Stormy?"

Stormy shook his head. "Finish your supper. You've had a busy two days as it is. I'll see you later." Seizing his sombrero, he hurried from the hotel.

Three minutes later he was at Glover's residence. Mrs. Glover, a pleasant-faced, gray-haired woman, met him at the door. "Beriah said for you to go right in," she said, indicating a doorway a short distance down the front hall.

Stormy entered to find Dr. Glover just straightening up from administering a hypodermic to Squint Amber, who was stretched out on a narrow bed. "Is he awake, Doc?" Stormy asked.

"You can see for yourself," Glover replied, stepping back and adjusting an oil lamp on a nearby table. Across the room curtains fluttered in the breeze through an open window. "You can call it awake, if you like. His eyes are open, but I can't get him to say anything. He can't last much longer. Pulse thready as the devil. Once, just before you got here, I thought he was already gone, but he's picked up a mite again."

Stormy approached the wasted form stretched on the bed. Amber's eyes were already glazing, but they seemed to follow Stormy's movements. "Do you know me, Amber?" he asked.

A flicker of hate appeared in the swiftly dulling eyes. Stormy continued, "Don't hold it against me, Amber. You know you had it coming, don't you?"

"Mebbe—I did," the words came feebly. "Come to—think of it—I ain't—kickin'."

"Look, Amber," Stormy said. "You might as well clear your conscience before you go."

"Ain't got—no conscience," the man answered defiantly.

"Harper can't help you now," Stormy persisted. "He wouldn't if he could—"

Surprisingly, Amber broke in again. "He went back on Cameo—Sloan, too." A long sigh left his lips; he closed his eyes for a moment, then opened them again. "All right—I'll talk. What— you want—to know?"

"About Sanford. That was murder, wasn't it? I think I know who killed him. You tell me if I'm right."

"You're plenty smart, Knight"—a ghost of a scornful smile curved the pallid lips—"if you figured—that out. If you're right—I'll tell any- thing—you want to know."

Through the open window came a sudden, warning shout. Stormy whirled. He caught a brief glimpse of a face just beyond the curtained opening. The savage, shocking roar of a forty-five deafened his ears. Then both face and gun disappeared from view. Stormy thumbed one swift shot from the vicinity of his hip, but knew he had missed.

Leaping to the window, he plunged through, landing on the earth, outside, gun in hand. In the dim light from the stars he saw a man stop some distance away, turn, and unleash a brilliant stream of orange fire. Then from nearer the house came two swift shots. The first man groaned. Stormy heard the thud as the man struck the ground.

Then came Sam Delaney's cool, drawling tones: "Reckon I got him."

"That you, Sam?" Stormy asked.

"It's me." They came together in the darkness and moved on to the silent figure stretched on the earth. They stooped down. Delaney scratched a match. Stormy said, "Cripes! It's Fox Pelton."

"I thought it looked like him," Delaney returned. "After you left the hotel I got to thinking it might be some sort of trick, so I come trailin' you. I saw this hombre peekin' in the window of Doc Glover's house. Then I see him raise a gun. I let out a yell to warn you, but I reckon I was too late. Anyway, he didn't hit you, did he?"

Stormy said bitterly, "I don't think he was trying to hit me. I've been a damn fool, Sam. I should have thought of this."

"Thought of what?"

Stormy explained, "Harper's probably had somebody keeping an eye on Doc's house ever since Amber was brought here—"

He broke off as Glover called to them through the open window. They hurried to approach. Stormy said, "What about Amber, Doc?"

"Amber's dead," Glover said. "That shot got him right through the head. Luckily it missed you, Stormy."

"Lucky, hell," Stormy growled. "That shot was meant for Amber. Pelton was killing off evidence."

"Who?" Glover asked.

"Fox Pelton—you know, the manager of the Pyramid. Sam just killed him."

"It's good riddance, I'd say," Glover grunted.

By this time men had come running from all directions, attracted by the noise of the shots. Stormy said, "Sam, you stay here and clean up this business. I'm going to see if I can find Harper. We'll see what he has to say about this."

But by the time Stormy returned to the center of town and entered the Bonanza Bar, he was told by Joe Wiley that Rufe Harper had left for his ranch some time before. Wiley added, "Somebody said there was some shootin' a short time back. You know anything about it, Marshal Knight?"

"Yeah, some," Stormy replied grimly. "You'll be able to read about it in the *Banner*." Without saying more, he turned and walked out of the Bonanza.

Before he reached the doorway Wiley called after him, "Hell! Your newspaper won't be out until next Tuesday."

Stormy paused in the entrance. "You and all the rest of Harper's coyotes can count yourselves lucky if you're alive to do any reading by the time Tuesday comes. There's a showdown coming fast!"

23. A HORNETS' NEST

It was about two o'clock the following afternoon when Stormy drew rein and dismounted from his buckskin gelding before the hitch rack of the deputy sheriff's office. Sam Delaney, who was sitting in a tilted back chair on the small porch, looked up with a trace of surprise. "You figurin' to ride someplace?" he queried indolently.

"My pony's getting too fat for his own good," Stormy replied. "Thought I'd exercise him a mite."

"That the only reason you're forkin' your saddle?"

"Not entirely," Stormy admitted. "I decided to ride out and take a look-see around the Anvil spread. Harper hasn't returned to town yet, so he must still be out there. Besides, I'm curious about that prisoner you said they were holding."

"I didn't see said prisoner, remember," Delaney drawled. "I just know they seemed to keep a guard posted in front of one of the barns. What—or who—was inside, I haven't the least idea. Maybe it was just a prime piece of horse-flesh they'd stolen someplace."

"I don't think so," Stormy said thoughtfully. "Anyway, I aim to snoop around there some. You can handle the law enforcement in town while I'm gone." He stepped down from the porch. "Well, I'll be seeing you eventually."

"So long," Sam yawned. "Don't stop any lead slugs."

Five minutes later Stormy was guiding his pony along the trail that ran from Carnival to Harper's Anvil outfit. To the west ran the Carnival Mountains, the colorful peaks reflecting brightly in the strong afternoon sunshine. Prickly pear, yucca, and mesquite grew along either side of the trail. A few miles farther on the cacti gave way to grass. Here and there were out-croppings of rusty-red and grayish-blue granite. Yellows were to be seen too.

Stormy spurred the pony on. When he judged he was within ten miles or so of the Anvil Ranch, he reined his mount off the trail and picked a more leisurely course through the rolling foothills. "This is sure good cow country," Stormy mused. In time he came to the cottonwood-lined banks of the Paladino River. Here he paused just long enough to get a drink and water the pony, before again mounting and striking out more directly for the Anvil.

An hour later he was hidden in the brush on a small ridge overlooking the Harper outfit. Here he produced his binoculars and proceeded to look over the grounds. He could see men moving between the bunkhouse and the other buildings. Once he saw Harper emerge from the bunkhouse, speak to one of the hands a moment, then again retire inside. There was a sizable corral, well filled with horses. "Sure is a large crew for an ordinary-size spread," Stormy muttered. He shifted the field glasses and focused them on a faded red barn, a short distance from the bunkhouse. The door of the barn was closed, and seated on a bench against the door sat a man with a rifle close at hand.

"That's the guard Sam mentioned," Stormy mused. "Now I wonder who Harper is holding prisoner in that barn? Come dark, maybe I'll find out."

The sun dropped behind the Carnival Mountains after a time. It grew darker. One by one the stars commenced to appear. Stormy rose to his feet and, after tightening his cinch, again climbed into his saddle. "Time to move up, horse," he murmured. "And if you make any noise, I'm through with you for life."

The full moon had lifted above the eastern horizon by the time Stormy once more dismounted, this time in a thick clump of mesquite not more than seventy-five yards from the bunkhouse. Tossing the reins over a low limb, he started toward the building on foot, moving with all the stealth of an Apache and taking advantage of every bit of shadow that offered concealment.

He was approaching the bunkhouse from the

rear and was almost there when he caught the sound of rapidly approaching hoofbeats. Knowing that the men within the building would have their attention concentrated on the coming rider, Stormy straightened up and broke into a run that carried him to a point just below an open window of the bunkhouse, from which streamed a broad rectangle of yellow light.

He could hear men's voices now, as the horseman pulled to a stop near the door in the front. He heard somebody say, "It's Larry Moulton." Then, as Moulton entered the bunkhouse, Stormy heard Rufe Harper ask, "What's doing in town, Larry? I've been expecting somebody to come out all day."

"Hell," Moulton replied, "we've been expecting you to come in all day. There's news—"

"Spill it," Harper snapped testily. "Don't stand there blowing wind."

"To begin with," Moulton related, "Fox Pelton is dead, but he rubbed out Squint Amber first." There were excited exclamations at this. Moulton told what had happened.

Harper laughed triumphantly. "We can spare Pelton. Now I'll feel safe in town again. Didn't feel secure there, while Amber was still alive. He might have spilled something—"

"Maybe you'll credit me with some brains now, Rufe," 'Brose Echardt's voice broke in. "Remember it was me suggested that you put

Pelton to watching Doc Glover's house when they took Squint there."

Harper disregarded the words. A new thought had struck his mind. "Say"—and he sounded worried—"you don't suppose Amber spilled anything to Knight before Pelton killed him, do you?"

"Use your noodle, Rufe," Echardt said. "If that had happened, Knight and Delaney would have been out here today."

"They were both in town, I reckon," Moulton put in. "I know Delaney was seated on his porch most of the day. I didn't see Knight, but he was probably working on his newspaper."

Harper commenced to recover his nerve. "I just wish that damn Knight had of showed up here," he sneered.

Echardt said, "You wouldn't dared do nothing if he had come here. Don't forget he wears a badge."

"T'hell with him and his badge both," Harper growled. "If I ever got a chance at him out here, there wouldn't be enough left of his carcass to prove he'd ever been here." He turned back to Moulton. "Any business to speak of in town?"

"The Bonanza's open. Joe Wiley took it on himself to close up the Pyramid last night."

Harper cursed. "What's the idea?"

Moulton said, "Well, you weren't on hand to run the business. 'Sides, there's only about five of your tinhorns left. Joe figured they might steal anything they took in."

Harper swore some more. "Muley," he ordered one of the other men, "you go saddle up for me. I've got to get to Carnival. Every minute the Pyramid stays closed I lose money."

"I ain't so sure of that," Echardt contradicted. "Your profits ain't been so good lately. Say, Rufe, what you going to do about Sloan? We can't keep him in that barn forever."

That brought another burst of profanity from Harper. "I don't dare release him. He knows too much about us. Maybe"—and Harper laughed nastily—"he'll just die a natural death, if we keep him tied up long enough."

Outside, crouched beneath the window, Stormy was taking it all in. Sloan! Cameo Sloan! That's who the prisoner was. A sudden thought came to Stormy: if he could help Sloan effect an escape, the man would make a good witness against Harper. There might be no limit on the testimony he'd be able to give regarding the nefarious activities of his former chief. Sloan had been Harper's right-hand man, too. Stormy told himself, I've simply got to get Sloan away from here.

While he huddled against the bunkhouse back wall, trying to formulate plans, a horse was brought up for Harper. A minute later Stormy heard the man say, "S'long," and shortly after hoofbeats were drumming toward the trail that led to Carnival.

Stormy waited a time, listening, hoping to pick up something definite from the conversation going on inside the bunkhouse, after Harper had departed, but the talk was only on general subjects, and within a little while a card game was started that seemed to occupy the Anvil crew's sole interest.

Stormy's thoughts returned to Sloan. He'd have to have a horse to make a getaway. It would be pretty risky going to the corral to rope one. Then, too, there was the matter of getting a saddle and rigging up— Stormy paused and cursed himself for an idiot. Why hadn't he thought of it before? Larry Moulton's saddled horse still stood in front of the bunkhouse; it hadn't been taken to the corral.

Stormy rose slightly and edged around the corner of the building, made his way past the end, then peered cautiously toward the entrance of the bunkhouse. The bunkhouse door was closed, but in the light from the windows Stormy saw a chestnut gelding, its reins hanging to the earth, standing not far from the bunkhouse steps.

Stormy edged forward, seized the reins, and slowly led the horse away. Its hoofs sounded only dully on the ground, and within a few minutes Stormy had brought the horse some distance from the bunkhouse without the animal being missed. Five minutes passed before he threw the reins over a limb, beside those of his own pony, in the clump of mesquite.

Stormy drew a long breath. So far, so good. He glanced toward the barn where Sloan was held prisoner. It wasn't quite so far off as the bunkhouse was, but stood to the right more. Stormy paused a moment to consider the situation. There was one guard before the door of the barn; he'd have to be disposed of too. "Well," Stormy reminded himself, "the sooner I get started, the better off I'll be." He grinned in the half shadow. "Or will I?" Pausing but a moment more, he turned his steps in the direction of the barn where Cameo Sloan was held captive.

Seated before the door of the barn, the cowhand named Bartz leaned back on his bench and reflected that working for Harper wasn't all it was cracked up to be. Instead of getting some nice money for rustling cows from other outfits, here he was sitting guard over a prisoner that was tied up tight anyway. By this time the poker game was probably going in the bunkhouse, too. . . . Bartz abruptly ceased his musings as he saw someone appear around the corner of the barn. He seized his rifle and got to his feet.

Casually Stormy sauntered nearer. The moon was at his back. He said, "Got a match, feller?"

"Sure." Bartz relaxed and lowered the rifle.

Then he paused. "Hey, who are you? You ain't no Anvil hand—"

That was as far as he got. Stormy closed in fast, brushing aside the barrel of the rifle in Bartz's hands. His six-shooter described a short arc in the air; the barrel descended against Bartz's head. Bartz grunted and slumped to the ground without another sound. Stormy caught the rifle as it fell, to prevent its clattering against the earth.

Moving swiftly, Stormy lifted the bench away from the barn door. The door wasn't locked and swung easily back under his hand. He stepped into the Stygian darkness within. A voice came feebly to him through the gloom. "Who's there?"

"You there, Sloan? This is Stormy Knight."

"Knight! God, I'm glad you're here." A half sob broke from Sloan's lips. "They've kept me tied here," he whined. "Didn't give me half enough to eat. Harper aims to kill me, I know he does."

"Don't talk so loud," Stormy hissed. He heard Bartz stirring outside. Following the direction indicated by Sloan's voice, he crossed the floor and knelt at Sloan's side. The man was stretched prone, with hands and feet bound. Stormy reached for his barlow knife. "Once I get you out of this, you're going to talk plenty, Sloan," he whispered, working at the captive's bonds. "Otherwise I don't aim to help you."

"I'll talk," Sloan promised brokenly. "Anything

you want to know. Harper's treated me like a dog. He and the rest of the crew have been stealing the country blind. They rebrand stock, forge bills of sale, and drive cows to other counties."

"Save that until later." Stormy cut through the last of the rawhide thongs and helped Sloan to his feet. "We've got to make a run for it. I've horses hidden in the brush."

"I'll try." Sloan swayed and clutched at Stormy's arm. "I'm weak and stiff. My legs have been cramped so long—"

He broke off as Stormy clamped one hand over his mouth. In front of the barn Bartz was on his feet again, stumbling around like drunken man in a half stupor. Up near the bunk-house Larry Moulton was making a great outcry over the discovery that his horse was missing. He yelled, "Bartz! Hey, Bartz! Did you take my bronc? Hey, you down near the barn, Bartz!"

The words penetrated Bartz's dazed mind, served to rouse him to consciousness of what was happening. He raised his voice in a frantic yell: "Fellers, come a runnin'! Somebody's here! Sloan's gettin' away!"

"Dammit," Stormy swore, "either that Bartz has a mighty thick skull or I didn't hit him hard enough. Come on, Sloan, you've simply got to make your legs move. We've got to get out of here plenty pronto!"

He grabbed Sloan and half carried him to the door. As they reached the open air Stormy saw Bartz just raising his rifle. Stormy shoved Sloan to one side; his forty-four roared savagely in the night. Bartz gave a loud cry of anguish, whirled around, and pitched to the earth.

Men came running from the bunkhouse, bright orange spurts of flame darting from their hands. Bullets commenced to whine around and kick up dust at Stormy's feet. He seized Sloan by the arm. "Run, you coyote, run, if you want to get out of this. We've messed into a hornets' nest, looks like. There's hell to pay and no pitch hot!"

24. LEADEN DEATH

The moon had passed under a cloud now, making more bright the savage flashes from the six-shooters. Sloan staggered a few paces, with Stormy pulling him on. Then the man tripped, twisting out of Stormy's grasp as he fell heavily to the earth.

Stormy swore as he stooped to help Sloan up again. "C'mon, you fool!" he panted. "This is no time to get lead in your shoes!"

He paused suddenly as his hand, groping for Sloan's arm, touched the side of Sloan's head. There seemed to be a sort of hole there. Then Stormy understood as his hand came away wet and sticky from the touch of the warm lifeblood.

"The lead wasn't in your shoes, after all," Stormy muttered as he again broke into a run.

Men were dashing toward him from the right, shooting as they moved. Stormy flipped two quick shots toward them and lengthened his stride. He heard a cry of pain as a man went down.

Bullets buzzed around like angry bees. He felt the sombrero jerk on his head and knew a slug had passed dangerously close. He had but one thought in mind now. Escape!

That mesquite clump where he had left his horse couldn't be much farther. He was breathing hard, but found consolation in the thought that the men behind him were finding the going fully as difficult as they pounded over the rough, uneven terrain. They weren't gaining on Stormy, but he wasn't drawing away much either. And they continued shooting.

At any moment one of their slugs might find his body. "Damn the luck!" Stormy gritted. "I've just got to make my getaway. I know too much to have them stop me now!"

Again he sent a shot winging toward his pursuers. Whether he hit anyone or not, he didn't know, as he sped on. Suddenly the welcome clump of mesquite loomed through the gloom. The next instant Stormy had seized his pony's reins, vaulted into the saddle, turned the horse, and plunged in his spurs.

He fired his last cartridge as the gelding straightened out in a long, distance-devouring stride that carried Stormy swiftly toward the trail that ran to Carnival. Behind him the baffled shouts of the Anvil men still rang in his ears.

"Whew!" Stormy whistled with relief as the buckskin pony settled into a steady gait. "That was close." He reloaded his forty-four as he rode. A grin crossed his face as he pounded along through the night. "The Weather Man reports a blizzard—a blizzard of hot lead—in the vicinity of the Anvil Ranch." Then a frown creased his features. "At least one man was killed; probably two. I sure wish I could have got Sloan away alive."

He was five miles from the Anvil holdings before he pulled the pony to a halt. The little beast was breathing hard, its withers flecked with foam. Stormy patted its neck. "You sure covered that stretch in record time, horse. Catch your breath a mite before we move on. Then we'll take it easier."

It was after one o'clock in the morning when he arrived in Carnival. The streets were dark and empty, with only a couple of lights showing. The Bonanza Bar was still open. The Pyramid was closed. Farther down the street a lamp burned in Sam Delaney's office.

Delaney came to the door as Stormy reached the hitch rack and stepped wearily down. "Stormy?" he queried, peering through the darkness.

"It's me, Sam," Stormy replied, reaching the porch.

"You look like you might have something to tell," Delaney observed, drawing Stormy into the office and closing the door. He pulled down the shade at the window and turned up the lampwick. "I was about to turn in, but thought I'd stay up a mite longer— Hell! that's blood on your hand!"

Stormy glanced at his left hand. Dried blood smeared his fingers. He laughed shortly. "It's not mine. Cameo Sloan's blood."

"Sloan's, eh?" Sam said. "Was he the captive?"

Stormy nodded. "I'll tell it in a minute. I want to wash this off first."

"You'll find a bucket of water in the corner there. Towel on that nail just above."

While Stormy was washing his hands he asked, "Anything special doing in town while I was gone?"

"The usual Saturday crowd, but it seemed a mite deader'n usual. The Pyramid wasn't open, for one thing—that is, it wasn't until about ten o'clock, when Harper came dashing into town and opened it up. He had to tend his own bar. Couldn't locate his bartenders, and only two of his tinhorns were on hand. He closed about an hour ago. I stuck around all the time he was open and he wasn't liking it a bit. Finally said something about the town getting deader all the time and shut up for the night."

"We've slowed him down, all right," Stormy nodded. "Now that we've showed his games are crooked, folks won't trust him even when he runs them on the square. Consequently, business is poor."

"And I aim to keep it that way, where Harper is concerned. . . . But what happened to you? I note there's a hole in the front of your sombrero."

"Probably one in the back, too, where the bullet went out." Stormy smiled. He dried his hands and dropped into a chair. "Yes, Cameo

Sloan was the prisoner Harper was holding. I did my best to get him away, but my best wasn't quite good enough." Stormy rolled and lighted a cigarette and, while he smoked, told Delaney what had happened at the Anvil Ranch.

". . . so when Sloan went down with a slug in his head," Stormy concluded, "I couldn't see any use of staying any longer, so I high-tailed it out of there as fast as my bronc would carry me— and believe me, Sam, it was none too fast for comfort. Those waddies were really throwing lead."

Sam smiled and said lazily, "Had quite an excitin' time of it, didn't you? Do you think those rannies recognized you?"

"I doubt it. The moon passed under a cloud and the light wasn't too good. That Bartz hombre might have recognized me, but I'm pretty sure my bullet finished him. Gosh, did that Bartz have a hard skull! I nigh bent my forty-four barrel over his conk, and in five minutes he was up again."

"His hat probably saved him some. Your gun barrel softened him up, anyway, you can count on that. . . . Do you think if you'd made a stand and showed those hombres your badge, they'd have quit?"

Stormy shook his head. "I thought of it, but they weren't in any mood to listen to that sort of reasoning. Being outnumbered the way I was, I judged it was best to slope fast. So far I haven't regretted my decision."

"I reckon you were right," Sam nodded. "Anyway, you've got enough on Harper for an arrest now?"

Stormy cocked a quizzical black eyebrow at the deputy. "Oh yeah? That's what I thought at first, too. Now I'm not so sure."

"But, Stormy," Sam pointed out, "Sloan told you that Harper and his crew were rustling from all the outfits around here—"

"Sure he did," Stormy broke in. "But Sloan's dead now. I'd look like a fool if I arrested Harper and took a dead man's evidence into court. It would be Harper's word against the word of a man who wouldn't be on hand to swear to the testimony. Harper could call me a liar and get away with it—in court."

Sam's eyes narrowed. "I'm commencing to see what you mean . . ." He paused, then, "Look here, you can arrest him on another charge. After all, Harper was harboring an escaped prisoner."

"Holding an escaped prisoner," Stormy pointed out.

"What's the difference?" Sam wanted to know.

"Just this," Stormy explained. "If I took Harper to jail on such a charge, he'd soon get out on bail. He'd claim that he had captured Sloan, after Sloan's escape from the hoosegow, and intended to turn him over to the law. You and I would know such a statement was a lie—but we'd have one hell of a time proving Harper was a liar."

Sam swore softly. "Looks like Harper's got us stopped, doesn't it?"

"Not stopped—just slowed down, Sam. Oh, we could make a lot of trouble for Harper on what we know—but I want to know more. When I get him in a corner I want to have so much proof against him that he won't be able to wiggle loose."

"You're correct, no doubt about it. You going to say anything to Harper about your visit to the Anvil?"

Stormy shook his head. "I'm not going to mention it at all. Those hombres may guess it was me out there—or they may not. So long as they don't know, it will worry them. I'll let them stew in their own juice for a spell. Anything that annoys Harper and his crowd helps us just that much."

The two men smoked in silence for a time. Finally Stormy rose to his feet. "Well, I'd better be putting my bronc in the livery and heading over to the hotel. Bed's going to seem plumb welcome."

Sam accompanied him to the door. "You don't figure there's much we can do about Harper right off, then?"

"I'm afraid not. If he'd only make some move I

could catch him up on—but he doesn't. Anyway, Sam, we've got one consolation."

"What's that?"

"Harper's fighting a losing battle right now. He's going to have to face that fact sooner or later. When he does that he'll lose his head and make a mistake—someplace along the line. That's all I ask—just one mistake. Then we've got him."

Delaney yawned. "Maybe we could force his hand in some way."

"I've been thinking of that too. Oh well, it will work out eventually. Good night."

"So long, Stormy. See you *mañana*."

The door closed behind him as Stormy rounded the end of the hitch rack and climbed into his saddle.

25. QUAD COMES ACROSS

The next day was Sunday, which meant little activity in Carnival. The stores and shops along Main were closed, though most of the saloons were open for business. Few people were abroad. Drunks slept off their hang-overs; family men puttered about their houses or sat in stiff-collared domesticity on their verandas and wished the breeze would stir a bit of fresh air through the cottonwood trees that lined the residential section. The two churches, located at either end of Beaumont Street, had drawn their customary attendance in the morning, but now they too were closed.

Around two in the afternoon Stormy found the door of the *Banner* building open. He went in and discovered Kate and Quad working in the print room. Quad was setting type. Kate sat frowning over a partly completed dummy of page one.

"Just a couple of heathens," Stormy greeted them, "working on Sunday."

Kate glanced up and brushed a lock of hair out of her eyes. Quad said "Hello" and continued with what he was doing. "The better the day, the better the deed." Kate smiled. "We just had to catch up a little, while we could, Stormy. Later on, when we get settled around, there'll be no Sunday work. But Quad and I just thought we'd put in a couple of hours, while we had a chance. . . . Oh, by the way, you're eating supper at my house tonight. Ada has promised us a chicken."

"Good. Too bad Quad can't come too," Stormy grinned.

Quad glanced sharply over his shoulder. "Who says I can't come?" he demanded. "Ada invited me first."

"Seems to me you set right well with Ada Thomas," Stormy chuckled.

"I don't think she hates me any," Quad returned. "Anyway, it was really me who got the chicken. I traded a month's subscription to the *Banner* for it."

Kate said suddenly, "Where were you last night, Stormy?"

"Just riding around," Stormy said idly. "I thought I'd give Quad a free rein with Ada Thomas at your house."

"Is that so?" Quad retorted. "Well, if I was Miss Kate I'd ask what other house you were hanging around—where they shoot holes through the crown of your Stet hat."

Kate frowned with sudden concern. "Stormy! What happened?"

Stormy smiled. "Don't let Quad upset you, Kate.

I just punched those holes in my sombrero for better ventilation."

"Do you expect me to believe that?" Kate asked scornfully.

Stormy said cheerfully, "Nope. Want me to make up another one for you?"

"Oh, you!" Kate said exasperatedly. "So long as you're here, why don't you think up a couple of items for your column?"

"That's an idea. It'll fill time until you're ready to go home."

Stormy retired to the office, sat down at the desk, and chewed on the end of a pencil. He rolled two cigarettes, smoked them, one after the other. Eventually he started writing.

Kate came in after a time. Stormy glanced up, then got to his feet. "Sit down and take a look at these paragraphs," he said.

Kate seated herself at the desk and took up the sheets of paper. Stormy dropped into the nearby straight-backed chair. Kate read:

Fresh breezes from the northwest bring a rumor that Cameo Sloan has been staying at the Anvil Ranch. How about it, Mister Mayor?

Kate looked quickly at Stormy. "Is Sloan out at the Anvil?"

"I just put that in to needle Harper a mite,"

Stormy replied. "You'll see another item about the Anvil farther on. They don't mean much, but I'll bet they bother Harper a heap."

"Do you think Sloan is at the Anvil?"

"I know he was. His body is still there, for all I know."

"His body?"

Stormy nodded. "I was out there last night. They were holding Sloan prisoner. I tried to help him escape. . . ." Starting at that point, Stormy told the girl of his previous night's adventures. Much of the color had left Kate's face by the time he was finished.

"Stormy," she half whispered, "they might have killed you. Where is this going to end?"

"Right here in Carnival," Stormy replied. "*When* it will end is the thing that interests me. And don't worry your head about it. We're getting along all okay. . . . Take a look at that other item about the Anvil."

Kate glanced down the sheet and found it:

The weather was quite foggy in the vicinity of the Anvil Ranch a few nights ago. The *Banner* wonders could that fog have been created by gun smoke?

"You see," Stormy explained, "they don't know who it was that went out there last night. Harper is going to suspect me, of course, but he'll wonder why I haven't done anything about Sloan when he reads this. I'll bet they held a couple of burial parties out there this morning."

Quad entered the office, bearing a sheet of paper filled with written notations. "Here's the list of supplies we have to order, Miss Kate. It's quite long, but I held it down as well as possible."

"All right, Quad. I'll get busy and order first thing tomorrow."

Quad nodded. "And if you're not coming back in the print room again, I'll start to clean up. Got to shave and change my shirt."

"Go ahead, Quad. I'm through out there for the day."

After he had departed, Kate picked up the supply list and started studying it. Suddenly she frowned.

Stormy said, "What's wrong? Can't we afford what he's ordering?"

Kate glanced at him a second, then looked back at the paper. "It's going to take money, but that's not what's bothering me. It's Quad's writing. I've seen it someplace before. He writes a rather peculiar hand and— I've got it! Stormy, have you that bill of sale with you—you know, the forged bill giving you the *Banner*? The one you found in your pocket?"

"Yeah. Why? You don't think Quad—"

"Let me see it—quick!" The girl's face was colored with excitement.

Stormy produced his wallet, removed the bill of sale and handed it to Kate, then bent close to her shoulder while Kate placed the bill of sale alongside Quad's order list, to compare the handwriting.

"It's the same writing!" Kate exclaimed. "See—how he puts that little quirlicue on the s— and look at the way the *t* is crossed on a sharp angle. And there's this capital letter—"

"It's Quad, all right," Stormy nodded. "Well, I'll be everlastingly—" He broke off, raised his voice, and called to the back room, "Quad, come here!"

"Can't come right now," Quad called back. "I'm shaving."

"I don't care," Stormy yelled, "if you're pulling your own teeth. You get in here. It's important!"

They heard Quad say something to himself as he came along the corridor and turned into the office, one side of his face still covered with lather. "What's got into you two?" he growled. "Is it so important you can't wait to tell me?"

"You're the one that's going to do the talking," Stormy said tersely. "We just called you in to inspect a couple of samples of handwriting."

"Take a look at these, Quad," Kate said, indicating the bill of sale and the order list.

Quad bent above her shoulder, then he stepped back suddenly, his features crimsoning. "I'm a double-dyed idiot!" he said sheepishly. "All right, I did it. Now you know."

"But, Quad," Kate persisted, "why—why?"

"We-ell"—Quad shuffled his feet uncomfortably—"it'll maybe take a few minutes to explain and make you understand—"

"We've got all the time in the world," Stormy cut in. "So come across, Quad, come across."

"Well, to start with," Quad said, "I happened to see a copy of the *Banner* in Denver. How it ever got way up there, I don't know, but there it was—"

"Why shouldn't the *Banner* reach Denver?" Kate asked indignantly. "Our paper spreads news all around."

"That's enough, Snip," Stormy cut in dryly. "You're not trying to sell him a subscription. Let Quad talk."

Quad continued. "I was getting pretty tired of my Denver job. I'm used to booming around a lot—anyway, I used to be that way." His color deepened. "I looked the *Banner* over. I liked the make-up and the way James Sanford handled his editorial. Thinks I, I'd like to work on a paper like that. So I quit my job and drew what pay I had coming—"

"And headed for here," Kate put in. "To ask Dad for a job."

"Those were my intentions," Quad answered, "but I got tangled up in some two-handed drinking and didn't get started as soon as I expected. To make a long story short, I went broke and had to bum my way here. And then—well, you know what happened just about the time I arrived. Your dad was shot and it looked like Harper would get the paper. I didn't think I'd care to work for Harper. But I did like the way Stormy sized up when he and Harper had a few words. I thought, now if only this Knight feller would buy the paper, everything would be fine. But Stormy didn't look like he'd be interested in newspapers."

"So you took it on yourself to work up my interest, eh?" Stormy said ironically.

"Something like that," Quad confessed. "That day, Miss Kate, after your dad was taken to the undertaker's, I saw you come out of there. Then I got an idea. Why shouldn't a pretty girl like that become interested in a handsome young gaffer like Stormy Knight?"

"Spare us our blushes," Kate said.

"You got to admit I guessed right," Quad said.

"Just a regular little Dan Cupid, aren't you, Quad?" Stormy smiled.

"That was the general idea. But I didn't know how to get you two to meet," Quad continued. "But I was broke. I had to have a job. I think better when I'm in a desperate fix like that. Suddenly I hit on the idea of starting a rumor around town that Stormy was to buy the paper. He didn't seem to take the hint, though. Then I got another idea: I wrote out that bill of sale and signed Kate's name to it. I knew that would get you two together, then I figured when that happened Stormy would play Sir Galahad and come to the rescue of the lady in distress."

"You're a student of human nature if I ever saw one, Quad," Stormy said, shaking his head incredulously. "You certainly called the turn. But how did you get that paper in my pocket without me knowing?"

Quad explained: "When I wrote it out I figured I'd be able to slip it in your pocket when you weren't looking, but somehow I couldn't ever seem to get close enough to you. Then I got a break. You remember that night in the Pegasus when you were shot at and then chased the fellow up the alley?"

"And he hit me on the head and knocked me cold!" Stormy exclaimed. "So that was when—"

"That was it," Quad nodded. "A lot of us followed you out of the saloon. I got to you first and slipped the paper into your pocket. Later, when you regained consciousness, you found it, and it all seemed like quite a mystery. . . ."

Quad paused, beads of perspiration standing out on his forehead. He looked anxiously from Stormy to Kate and back to Stormy again, as hey stood staring at him, eyes wide with amazement. "Look," Quad said in some trepidation, "you two aren't going to be sore, are you?"

"And you did all that—got me mixed into this

mess," Stormy said sternly, "just so you could wangle a job for yourself."

Quad gulped. "I reckon that's the way it is. But I don't think things are too bad. They've worked out right well and—and I'd like to stay here. I hope you two won't be mad."

Stormy grinned. "Mad, you jughead! You'd better go finish shaving right now, before Kate kisses the rest of the lather off your face. You really fixed it up pretty nice for her."

"Oh, is that so?" Kate retorted, smiling. "How about yourself?"

"Haven't heard me doing any kicking have you?" Stormy laughed. "I'm danged thankful Quad did as he did."

"Everything's all right, then?" Quad beamed.

Stormy clutched his hand hard. Kate said, "We owe you a debt, Quad, it's going to be hard to pay."

Quad was covered with confusion. "I guess I'll go back and finish scraping my face," he said, backing through the office doorway.

When he had left, Kate said fervently, "Darn the luck!"

"What's the matter?" from Stormy.

"There's a peach of a story and we can't use it in the paper."

Stormy nodded. "No, it wouldn't do to let Harper know just how come I got into the newspaper business. But we'll publish it someday, you see. . . . Next Tuesday's issue is just about set up now, isn't it?"

Kate nodded. "Trouble is, nowadays, news happens so fast that I'm never sure what's going to remain in the form and be printed and what isn't."

"Page one all set?"

"I'm on the dummy now. Why? You going to bring in some important news?"

"I don't know for sure," Stormy said slowly. "No"—in reply to another query—"I don't plan to have anything in about my visit to the Anvil last night, but there's a mighty big piece of news coming up soon."

"What?" Kate asked.

"Sometime shortly," Stormy replied, "I'm going to name the man who killed your father—and tell just how it was done."

"Stormy! Do you know how—who—"

"I've got it pretty well worked out, Kate. There's one or two things don't quite dovetail yet, but I'll have it soon."

"But, Stormy, tell me—"

Stormy shook his head. "I'm not going to say anything more, Kate, until I get everything straightened out in my own mind. When that happens—well, you'll see fireworks then, and the *Banner* will carry the biggest story it ever carried!"

26. MORGAN TRENT'S STORY

It was shortly after nine o'clock the following morning when Stormy entered the *Banner* office to find Kate seated at the desk. "Mornin', beautiful," he greeted, doffing his sombrero. "Carnival is certainly lucky today."

Kate swiveled around in her chair. "Hello, Stormy," she smiled. "But just why is Carnival lucky today?"

"All the nice sunshine outside," Stormy explained, "and you as a citizen to add to the beauty."

"Go along with your palaver," Kate laughed. "If that's all you came here to say, I haven't time to listen. We're about to start the run, for tomorrow's issue, of pages two and three, and I've got to get back and help Quad and Horace—"

"Quad and Horace are going to have to do without your help for a spell," Stormy cut in. "You're going to the bank with me. I've already told Sam Delaney what's up; he's going to meet us there."

"But why am I going? What are you going for?" Kate suddenly sobered; her hazel eyes widened. "Stormy, have you learned something new?"

"Nothing new. I just figured it was time to let

303

you in on what I already know. What you said last night after supper, about needing money to continue publishing with, convinced me it was time to act. I could see you were worried. You don't need to worry about money matters."

"Stormy! Have you a line on that missing satchel?"

"Ask me no questions, I'll tell you no lies," Stormy grinned. "Go tell Quad you'll be away for a spell. He and Horace can get along without you better than I can."

It wasn't yet ten o'clock when they picked up Sam Delaney lounging against the tie rail in front of the Stockmen and Miners' Bank. Sam lazily doffed his Stetson to Kate, and the three entered the building, where Stormy told the cashier behind the grilled window they wanted to see Morgan Trent. The cashier went to the door leading to Trent's office from the back of the bank, knocked, stuck his head in a moment, then returned. "Mr. Trent will see you. Just step into his office."

Stormy started through the swinging gate at the end of the counter, but the clerk shook his head and indicated the other door to Trent's office, the one that opened from the lobby, marked PRIVATE. "Mr. Trent likes his callers to use that door," he explained.

Before they could reach it the door was swung open and Morgan Trent greeted them: "Well, well, this is a welcome surprise. Come in, Kate—Marshal Knight. And Deputy Delaney too." A shade of surprised annoyance crossed his features as he mentioned Delaney's name, but it quickly passed and he ushered his visitors into the office, closed the door, and pointed out chairs for them. He settled behind his large flat-topped desk and demanded crisply, "Well, what can I do for you?"

"Mr. Trent," Stormy said quietly, "we've come to see what you can tell us about the killing of James Sanford and your connection with Rufe Harper."

"What!" Trent's jaw dropped. Then he forced a feeble smile. "That's no subject for jesting, Knight." Onc hand nervously stroked his side-burns. "Come, come! What's the real reason for this call? You see, I'm quite busy this morning, so—"

"That bluff won't work," Stormy cut in. "You see, Trent, I located the satchel with the three thousand dollars."

A sudden gasp left Kate's lips: "Stormy!" Trent went white. He tried to speak; words wouldn't come. Abruptly his pompous form collapsed like a blown-up paper bag with the wind released from it, and he sagged in his chair. "It was—you—who—took—that satchel?" he mumbled helplessly.

Stormy nodded. "I'd racked my brains, trying to figure where it might be. Of course Harper

305

might have had it and destroyed the satchel, but I didn't think so. One or two things pointed to you. That feeling was strengthened the day Kate and I were here and you denied Harper was in the bank. He sounded like he was more friendly with you than folks think. A few days ago I saw your wife come in here. Figuring no one would be home at your house, I paid it a visit and entered by a rear window. I found the satchel wedged between the wall and the bed in your bedroom, Trent. Leastwise, I think it was your bedroom. It didn't look like a lady's room. I have the satchel in a safe place now—"

"So it was you took it," Trent said brokenly. "I accused my wife."

"Why not Harper or one of his gang?" Delaney asked.

"Harper didn't know I had it. He's been sorely puzzled."

"Double-crossing your own crowd, eh?" Stormy said.

Trent swallowed hard. "Gentlemen—Kate—I swear to you I didn't know your father would be killed. It was to be only a robbery, they told me. I was forced to it—" His voice broke; he raised his hands to his face.

Stormy said, "Pull yourself together, Trent. I'll do the talking. You fill in the gaps and tell me if I'm wrong. I've figured out pretty well just what happened, but there were one or two other

306

things I didn't understand—still don't. I wanted it all clear before I acted. One thing I didn't understand was how you could be mixed up with a coyote like Harper. Folks in Carnival think pretty well of you. So far as I could learn, you've always been honest."

"I have, I have," Trent half sobbed. "I've had the respect of Carnival. I'm a member of the church—"

"I'm afraid that won't help you now," Stormy said, steely voiced. "I'll get on with my story . . ." He paused. "Kate, some of this about your dad isn't going to be pleasant to hear. Maybe you should—"

"Don't think of me, Stormy," Kate cut in. "Just tell us all you can."

Stormy nodded. "To begin with, Harper knew that James Sanford would have a satchel containing three thousand dollars with him that morning. That information he got from Trent here. Harper figured if he could kill Mr. Sanford and take the money, Kate would have to sell the *Banner*, which Harper wanted to take over. The whole thing was planned to make it look like suicide. So far as the missing money was concerned, if it couldn't be found, and if both doors of the *Banner* building were locked, folks would think there had never been any satchel or money. The word of Gage Freeman, who saw Mr. Sanford arrive at the office with the satchel, would be disregarded. Isn't that the way Harper planned, Trent?"

Trent lowered his hands from his face. "That's the way it was, only—"

"Save it for later," Stormy interrupted. "The night before the murder Horace Brigham was cleaning out the building, as it is known he always does Tuesday evening, after the paper has been issued. Horace has both front and rear doors open. While Horace was busy out in the alley, disposing of trash, the murderer entered the front door and concealed himself in that closet in the print shop. Oh, it could be done. I practically did it myself one evening, and Horace didn't know I was there until I came right up to him. Also, after I'd looked that closet over, I found a cigarette butt in the closet, where it had been stepped on. Now, no one enters a closet just to smoke a cigarette."

Stormy smiled thinly. "I'm reminding myself I need a smoke." He deftly rolled and lighted a cigarette, then resumed, "The murderer stayed hidden in that closet until after Horace had departed and locked both doors. Then he waited there, all night, until James Sanford arrived in the morning with the satchel of money. He, Sanford, had unlocked the front door to let himself in. The back door was still locked from the night before. When Mr. Sanford arrived and sat at his desk, the murderer tiptoed to the front and softly closed and locked the front door. Incidentally, Gage Freeman happened to glance across the street at the moment the door was being closed. Naturally he thought Sanford did it."

Stormy drew deeply on his cigarette. "I can only surmise what happened next, but this is the way I see it: After closing the front door, without being overheard by Mr. Sanford, the killer stepped into the office and spoke to him. Surprised, Mr. Sanford whirled around in his desk chair. Now, it was well known that he had a short time before purchased a double-action thirty-eight-caliber revolver, a design that's not common in Carnival. Maybe the killer asked to have a look at the weapon, on the pretense he contemplated getting one. Or perhaps Mr. Sanford reached into the desk drawer for the gun the instant he saw the murderer. At any rate, the gun was in his, Sanford's, hand when the murderer fired and killed him. . . . Is all this clear to you folks so far?"

Trent just stared at Stormy. Sam Delaney nodded. Kate was white-lipped but composed. She said, "Go on, Stormy."

"When Mr. Sanford was shot," Stormy resumed, "he fell to the floor, his hand still clutching the thirty-eight. The murderer stooped down, pressed Sanford's finger against the trigger, exploding the gun and sending the bullet into the baseboard, where it wouldn't, ordinarily, be noticed. I was lucky and happened to find it the day I took charge of the *Banner*. I dug out the bullet and still have it. I saw the position in which Sanford's body lay on his office floor. I know the angle at which the thirty-eight slug entered the base-board. The way I've told you is practically the only way this thing could have happened. Do you agree with me?"

Still Trent couldn't speak. He gazed at Stormy as though hypnotized. Delaney agreed, as did Kate. The girl said, "But how could the murderer make his escape?"

"I'm coming to that," Stormy nodded. "The instant the killer exploded Mr. Sanford's gun he rose and seized the satchel containing the money, rushed through the print shop, opened the rear door, dropped the satchel into the alley, then locked the door again. The satchel was to be picked up by a confederate—though he never got it. The instant the killer had relocked the back door he rushed into his hiding place, the closet, and waited for somebody to come."

Stormy knocked the ashes from his cigarette. "Remember, that closet is located in the darkest part of the shop, set back from the paper-cutting machine and the big paper rack which stand on either side. Meanwhile people on the street have heard the shots. Harper and his men reach the door of the *Banner* building first. To give the killer plenty of time, Harper refuses to let the door be opened until Bayliss arrives. Eventually the door is opened. Harper's crew pour in first and head for the back room. Other men paused at the office to look at Mr. Sanford, dead on the floor. The instant the Harper men reach the back room they gather near the closet. The murderer quickly steps out, mingles with them, and in the excitement no one notices that he hadn't entered the building with the others. When the rest leave, he leaves with them. With both front and rear doors locked and one empty shell in Mr. Sanford's revolver, it looks like suicide."

"Well, I'll be danged—" Delaney commenced.

"Wait a minute, I'm not through yet," Stormy cut in. "Gage Freeman tells me that when the shots were heard—he insisted there were two shots, though Harper bullied folks into believing otherwise—the Harper crew, with one exception, headed toward the *Banner* building. The one exception is a man named Muley Porter. Porter jumped over the Bonanza rail—he'd been on the Bonanza porch with Harper and the others—and sprinted up Flagstaff Street, then turned into the alley that runs past the rear door of the *Banner* building. Others beside Freeman saw Muley Porter run up the alley. I've talked to a lot of folks in town. It's my belief that Porter ran into the alley to pick up a satchel of money that was to be dropped there. However, while several people remembered seeing Porter later, no one remembers him carrying a satchel. Therefore somebody else must have got the satchel. Morgan Trent lived directly back of the *Banner* building;

311

he knew the satchel was to be tossed out the rear door. He hid behind his back fence, then grabbed the satchel before Muley Porter could get there. Is that right, Trent?"

Something akin to awe had entered Trent's eyes as he listened to Stormy relate the details as though he'd been on the spot to see what had happened. Now he bowed his head in a short nod and forced a wan smile. "I don't suppose it's even going to be necessary for me to name James Sanford's murderer?"

"Let me tell you first who I think it is," Stormy said quickly. "The killer was shorter than average. On the floor of the closet where he hid there was an old newspaper. He stood on that, leaving faint footprints. He wasn't a heavy man, or they'd have been heavier footprints. The feet were small. The back of the closet is of unplaned lumber, and that rough surface had picked up a lot of dust over a number of years. The killer's shoulders had rubbed against that dust, and the mark he left was considerably below the height of my shoulders. In short, the killer was undersized. I find only one man in Harper's crew to fit that description: Squint Amber. Nor have I been able to find anyone who saw Amber on the Bonanza porch with the Harper gang that morning, though several men remembered he was in town the previous night, and he was seen some time after the murder."

"It was Amber who killed Sanford," Trent admitted. "In case you're interested, it was Amber who shot at you and knocked you on the head in the alley back of the Pegasus that night."

Stormy nodded. "I suspected that. Though it was dark in that alley, I could see it was a small man I was chasing. Well, Amber's paid for his crime, but you, Trent, have to—"

Delaney broke in admiringly, "Stormy, you're smart!"

"I'm lucky," Stormy amended. Kate couldn't speak. Her eyes looked slightly moist. Stormy went on, "Well, Trent, we're putting you under arrest."

"Grant me a few minutes," Trent said, "then I'll go with you. But first I wish to be heard. Believe me, I had no idea James Sanford was to be murdered, when that plot was arranged. As it was explained to me, Amber was simply to steal that satchel and drop it in the alley, after he'd held Sanford up and roped him into his chair. Amber was to have been masked, so Sanford wouldn't recognize him. If I could make you see—"

"Talk fast," Stormy said tersely.

"I became involved in this dirty business through my wife," Trent started. "I met Sarah on a train nearly fifteen years ago. I was infatuated. She told me she was a parson's daughter. We came here and opened the bank. Sarah commenced to get ideas she was better than the other ladies in Carnival. She lorded it over them; in addition she was money-crazy. I should have squelched her, but I wanted to avoid strife. I was successful here and had the respect of Carnival. Then, three years ago, Rufe Harper arrived in Carnival and recognized my wife."

Trent's voice dropped to a shamed whisper. "She'd been no parson's daughter. Instead Harper recognized her as a former Las Vegas honky-tonk dancer known as High Pockets Sal. To Harper it was a great joke to find Sal posing as Sarah Trent, high-and-mighty wife of the town banker. To me it was a terrible shock. I feared, if the secret became known, Carnival would lose faith in my bank."

"And Harper put pressure on you?" Stormy asked, interested.

Trent nodded. "Harper threatened to expose Sarah and me to the town unless I loaned him the money to buy the Anvil Ranch. It was more money than the bank could afford, but my wife persuaded me. Since then my life has been a hell. Harper started rustling stock. The payments he made on the loan were returns from the sale of stolen cows. But I was helpless. Had the news got out my bank was shy of money, a run on the bank would have started. Many depositors would have lost their savings. To protect my depositors and keep the accounts solvent, I accepted the money from Harper. My wife laughed at my fears and urged me to co-operate with Harper. She admires him as a go-getter."

Stormy nodded understandingly, commencing to feel sorry for the banker. Trent continued, "James Sanford never liked Harper. James fought him from the first. Harper set out to break him. When Sanford borrowed three thousand dollars from me, Harper saw his chance. You see, my wife makes herself familiar with all the bank's affairs and, at Harper's instigation, forced me to put that thirty-day clause into the note covering the loan. Then, when Sanford couldn't take up his note, after the plan to rob him went through, Harper planned to have me foreclose on the *Banner*, though Sanford had never expected me to enforce that thirty-day clause. When I foreclosed, Harper would buy the newspaper from my bank. I hated the whole idea, so I resolved secretly to snatch that satchel before Muley Porter could get it and, later, return the money to Sanford. After Sanford was murdered I was afraid to turn the money over to Kate for fear my part in the plot would be discovered. I shudder to think what would have happened had my wife known I got that satchel. Harper was greatly mystified over its disappearance and finally concluded an outsider must have stumbled on it by chance and picked it up before Porter arrived."

Trent drew a long breath. "Well, you know how things worked out. I should long ago have confessed my part, but I feared ruining the bank and my depositors." He broke off to say to Kate, "The other morning when I mentioned payment of the note, that was on my wife's urging. I had no intention of pressing you for payment. I hope you'll forgive me."

Kate nodded. "Let's just forget it, Mr. Trent."

"You're very kind to a transgressor, Kate," Trent said pitifully. He sagged in his chair, a broken man, and gazed up at Stormy. "Well, you can put me under arrest now."

Stormy and Sam exchanged glances. Kate started to speak. Stormy caught her thought. He said to the banker, "Trent, maybe I've changed my mind about arresting you. You've suffered too, apparently through no fault of your own. To a large extent, what you've done has been done to keep your bank solvent and protect your depositors. I don't say it was right, but I can't find it in my heart to condemn you. Would you be willing to testify against Harper in a court of law?"

"Lord, yes, Marshal Knight." Trent's eyes brightened.

"All right," Stormy said shortly. "Keep your mouth shut and don't leave Carnival. Go on as though nothing had happened. Come on, Kate— Sam. We'll be leaving."

For some minutes after their departure Trent just sat staring blankly into space. Finally he gave a long sigh and struggled to his feet. He got his hat and stepped out to the rear part of the bank. "Jennings," he said to his cashier, "I'm not feeling well. I'm going home for the day."

"I'm sorry, sir. You just go 'long and take it easy. But are you sure Mrs. Trent will be home to care for your needs?"

"Do you know of any reason why she shouldn't be?"

"She just left here a short time before Marshal Knight, Miss Sanford, and Deputy Delaney departed, sir."

"My wife?" Trent seemed unable to believe his ears.

"Yes, Mr. Trent. She came back here when I told her you had visitors and said she'd wait to see you. Then after a time she said something about doing some shopping and left suddenly."

Trent looked concerned. He glanced toward a chair adjacent to his office door. "Did—did she sit there?"

"Yes sir." The cashier looked surprised.

"And, no doubt, overheard the conversation that took place in my office."

"No doubt, sir. You know that door catch doesn't hold tightly. It was Mrs. Trent; I didn't think it would matter."

"All right; it can't be helped now, Jennings."

Trent's shoulders drooped as he passed through the swinging gate and made his way out of the bank.

27. BLOOD IN THE DUST

After they left the bank Kate, Stormy, and Sam Delaney headed west on Main Street. Kate said softly, "Stormy, I don't think you realize what you've done. It's grand! And going easy on Mr. Trent was—"

"Gosh, I couldn't see anything else to do," Stormy broke in. "But there's a showdown due now. We've got what we need to go ahead. We can arrest Harper."

"That means more trouble." Kate's voice was almost a wail. "I'd forgotten that part. All I was thinking of was getting back to the paper and writing a new story."

Delaney said, "I don't reckon we'll have any trouble with Harper now. It's just a matter of picking up him and his crew and putting them under arrest. We'll probably find him at the Bonanza, and before he knows what it's all about he'll be in the hoosegow."

"You sure there won't be any risk?" Kate persisted.

"Can't see why there should be," Stormy replied, with a meaning glance at Delaney.

They dropped Kate at the *Banner* building and continued on toward the Bonanza Bar. Entering the Bonanza, Sam and Stormy glanced quickly

about. There was no sign of Harper or his henchmen, though several of the usual idlers were
standing at the bar. Joe Wiley looked up as
Stormy and his companion entered.

"What'll it be, gents?" Wiley growled.

"We're not drinking," Stormy said. "We're
looking for Rufe Harper."

Wiley's eyes slipped sidewise. "I don't know
where Rufe is," he evaded.

"Better think twice, Wiley," Stormy said icily.

"I tell you I don't know, Knight," Wiley snarled.
"If you and the deputy ain't drinking, I can't do
nothing for you."

Delaney yawned boredly. "Reckon we better
toss him in the hoosegow, Stormy?"

"Might as well, if he won't speak up," Stormy
nodded. "The Bonanza is due to be closed
anyway. Harper has run his course, and we're
bound to catch up with him plumb soon."

"Wait, wait," Wiley said fearfully. "I just
happened to remember something. Mrs. Trent—
you know, the banker's wife—she sent word in to
Rufe, a spell back, that she wanted to see him.
Rufe and the boys left. I saw them talking to her
out on Flagstaff Street"—Wiley jerked a thumb
toward a side window—"but I don't know what it
was about. Didn't pay any attention. Haven't
seen Rufe since, but he and the boys must be
someplace around town."

"How long ago was this?" Stormy snapped.

"Twenty minutes to a half hour."

Stormy said, "Come on, Sam." The two left the Bonanza.

On the sidewalk they glanced up Flagstaff Street but saw no one in sight. Delaney finally said, "You know, I fixed it with Gage Freeman about letting Hoddy Oliver know when the time was ripe to round up such waddies as are still at the Anvil. Freeman's clerk is a good rider and can be trusted. I've a hunch it's about time we sent word to the Rafter-O, so Oliver can get his boys organized."

"That's a right idea, Sam. Better let Gage know."

"I'll take care of it," Delaney said. "Say, what do you suppose Trent's wife wanted to see Harper about?"

Stormy frowned, shook his head. "I don't know. I don't like it, either. We've got to locate Harper. I'll tell you what, you drift over and tell Freeman to get his clerk started for the Rafter-O. That'll give Oliver the go-ahead. I'll wait at the *Banner* for you, and we'll decide our next step."

Delaney nodded and crossed to Freeman's general store. Stormy returned to the *Banner* print room, where he found Kate talking to Quad, while Horace listened, wide-eyed.

"So you see how it is, Quad," Kate was saying swiftly. "You'll have to rip page one apart and shift the columns. I'll get at the story at once."

"Judas priest!" Quad exclaimed. "What a story! Hi, Stormy! You've really torn Carnival wide open this time. Talk about detective work! Miss Kate, play up Stormy's part strong when you write the story—make Carnival realize it's lucky to have such a man here."

"You're telling *me* what to do where Stormy's interests are concerned?" Kate smiled. "I'll take care of that, Quad. You do the composing. We'll want the biggest head we've ever used— let's see—'SANFORD MYSTERY SOLVED'—'Marshal Knight Proves Murder'— two-column spread—maybe it will run to three—boldest type in the case, Quad. Subhead, 'Mayor Harper Involved.' I'll give you more later—wait! Stormy, will you make an arrest before this issue comes out?"

"Hope to," Stormy nodded. "What about Morgan Trent?"

"We'll leave him out of it," Kate replied. "Later we may have to use something—but that will be another issue. Not the issue that has to be published tomorrow. Darn! Why do these stories always have to break at the last minute?"

"Before Quad finishes setting up the story," Stormy said, "we should be able to add that Mayor Harper is under arrest—"

He broke off as Sam Delaney came walking into the print room. "Gage Freeman got his clerk started. Hoddy Oliver should have word in a little better than two hours. It's just a short jump from the Rafter-O to the Anvil. With luck, Oliver should be delivering a bunch of prisoners tonight."

Stormy frowned. "I'm sorry you can't be on hand, with Oliver, when he drops down on the Anvil. Your authority—"

"I took care of the authority," Delaney drawled. "I deputized Oliver the day I made arrangements with him. Don't know just how legal it is, but—"

"We're set, then," Stormy smiled. "Once Oliver delivers a bunch of prisoners to us, we can forget the legal angle. Whatever comes up, I'll take care of it."

At that moment Morgan Trent came rushing in the back door of the print shop. His eyes were wild, his manner almost hysterical. "Marshal Knight!" he babbled. "There's going to be trouble. My wife overheard us talking in my office. She warned Harper. Harper and his men have made a plot to kill you. You'll have to—"

"Whoa, whoa," Stormy cut in. "Take it easy, Trent. How do you know this?"

"My wife told me, thinking that I would side with Harper to save my own skin. I couldn't do it. I've done enough wrong already. We quarreled. Violently. Never before have I laid hands on a woman, but—but this time I failed to control my temper. For a time I practically lost my mind. Everything went black—"

"Good God!" Quad groaned. "There goes the rest of page one. He's killed her—"

"Killed Sarah?" Trent's eyes widened with horror. "Heaven forbid! I slapped her face and locked her in her room. Then I came directly here." Words tumbled from his lips in an incoherent stream for a few moments. Finally Stormy got the man calmed sufficiently to tell what he knew.

"How about this plot to kill me?" Stormy asked. "Not Harper alone, surely?"

Trent shook his head. "Harper will be accompanied by 'Brose Echardt, Larry Moulton, Steve Gooch, and Muley Porter. They're going to the Pegasus and have a drink, then start a rumpus. They figure One-Horse Shea will send for you. When you arrive they'll shoot you down from the doorway. Deputy Delaney meets the same fate if he accompanies you. They figure with you out of the way they'll be able to get the newspaper away from Kate—"

"This is it," Stormy said grimly. "Come on, Sam, there's work to be done."

Kate's face had gone white. She raised one protesting hand, tried to speak, but words wouldn't come. Quad had snatched off the apron he always wore when working, seized his derby hat from a hook, then dropped at the side of his cot in the corner. He came up, holding his double-barreled shotgun.

"I'm taking a hand in this, Stormy," Quad jerked out. "There's five of them. There'll be room for me on your side."

"Good, Quad," Stormy nodded tersely. "Glad to have you."

Horace said in a quavering voice, "Could I help you, Mr. Knight?"

"You sure can, Horace, by staying here with Kate." He drew his forty-four, spun the cylinder, jammed it back in holster. "Sam—Quad! Come on! If Harper wants trouble, we'll give it to him."

Kate rushed across the room, seized Stormy's arm. "No, Stormy, no!" she cried. "Don't go out there. They'll kill all three of you. There must be a more peaceful way to settle this. There's already been too much killing. You can't go out there—"

"Kate, girl," Stormy said gently, "it's got to be this way. Can't you see? Harper has to be stopped *now*."

"But not by you," Kate pleaded. "You've risked your life enough. You've done more than your share—"

That was as far as she got. Quad's hand, on Kate's shoulder, swung her around. "Kate," Quad said furiously, "what kind of a news-paperman are you? Do you suppose your dad would act like this? Good Lord, girl! Snap out of it! Remember, come hell, come high water, the *Banner* has to be published tomorrow—and it's got to carry *all* the news. There's a real story coming up. Are you going to muff it? Tear the blazes out of page one and get ready to write a story that is a story. I'll be back to set type when this is finished." He gave her a slight shake. "See what I mean? You're going to do this for your dad. It's what he'd want you to do."

Stormy and Delaney stood staring at the man with his absurd derby hat, his double-barreled shotgun, and the smear of printer's ink across one cheek. As he talked he was, somehow, getting his idea to penetrate Kate's beginning hysteria. The girl's body stiffened suddenly. Her chin came up. She brushed at her eyes and blew her nose hard in her handkerchief. Then she forced a smile.

"You're right, Quad, right as the deuce," she said steadily. "I've been behaving like a fool. Go ahead, you three, make the news. I'll do my part." She went to Stormy, put her arms about his neck, held him close a moment, then stepped back. "Good luck—and come back soon—Quad, Sam—Stormy—"

They didn't hear the half sob that broke from her lips as they hurried toward the front of the building. Morgan Trent and Horace stood staring after them, then Trent turned to the girl.

"I'd willingly give the rest of my life to possess courage like that," Trent said simply.

Stormy and his two companions halted a moment on the sidewalk, beneath the wooden awning that stretched out from the *Banner* building. Across the street the Pegasus Saloon looked quiet. There was no one peering above the top of the swinging doors, as Stormy had half expected to see. He glanced down toward the corner of Main and Flagstaff streets.

"There they are!" Stormy snapped grimly.

Harper, accompanied by Echardt, Gooch, Porter, and Moulton, had just emerged from the Pyramid Gambling Saloon and were starting east on Main Street.

"That's where they were, eh?" Delaney drawled.

"Sweet jeesis!" Quad burst out. "They were in the Pyramid getting extra guns. Look! They're each totin' two six-shooters."

"That's no sign they can each use two," Delaney yawned. "Say the word when you're ready, Stormy."

Harper and his henchmen hadn't yet spied Stormy and his companions. They crossed Flagstaff and started toward the Pegasus.

Stormy said suddenly, "Come on, fellers. Make every shot count."

He moved out to the center of the unpaved street. Now other people along Main commenced to see that something unusual was afoot. There were two or three excited yells. Several men dashed for the protection of building corners.

By this time Harper had spotted Stormy, as had 'Brose Echardt. They spoke quickly to their men, who leaped to the center of the roadway and started at a run toward Stormy and his two companions. The opposing factions weren't more than seventy-five yards apart now.

Stormy raised his voice: "You're all under arrest, Harper! You and your men throw down your guns. Pronto now!"

A harsh laugh left Harper's lips. Stormy saw a blaze of white fire spurt from the man's right hand. The bullet flew wide overhead. Somewhere down the street a woman's high-pitched scream rent the air. There came the sound of many running feet.

Stormy laughed grimly. "It's trouble they're craving. Sam—Quad! Let's give it to them!"

He broke into a run toward Harper, the other two moving swiftly on either side. The Harper men were firing madly now, the leaden slugs kicking up dust and whining viciously all around.

Stormy felt his forty-four buck in his hand. He saw dust puff out from the right shoulder of Harper's coat. Harper swayed back but kept coming. At Stormy's left Sam Delaney thumbed two quick shots. One missed Larry Moulton; the other caught Muley Porter in the side and whirled him half around.

'Brose Echardt had dropped to one knee to level his right gun. Stormy felt something red hot burn along his ribs even as he threw a shot at Steve Gooch. He heard a thunderous double explosion from Quad's shotgun, then Moulton and Gooch were swept violently from their feet as though some gigantic scythe had cut the legs from under them.

Quad swore and fumbled for fresh shells. At that instant a shot roared from Harper's six-shooter, and Quad pitched, face down, on the earth. "Quad's down!" Stormy yelled to Sam. "Let's square things for him."

But Moulton and Gooch were also down, motionless, their blood dripping steadily into the dust. Muley Porter was out of the fight, crawling on hands and knees toward the side of the roadway, his left side stained crimson. Now only Echardt and Harper were left to face Sam and Stormy.

The guns were roaring continuously. Abruptly Sam Delaney swore, spun sidewise, and landed on his shoulder in the roadway. He strove to rise, but his strength failed and he lay still.

Even as Sam dropped, Stormy sent a bullet crashing through 'Brose Echardt's lungs. Echardt swayed on his feet a moment, then his legs jackknifed and he crashed down.

"I evened it for you, Sam," Stormy laughed grimly, and abruptly found himself flat on the earth with an agonizing pain torturing his left side. He realized, quite suddenly, that he was hit.

"That's the second time I've been nicked," he told himself dully. There didn't seem to be any strength left in his body. His brain was swimming in a sea of blood and fog and powder smoke.

Somehow he got to hands and knees and glanced up just in time to see Rufe Harper charging toward him with upraised gun. There was a wide, triumphant snarl on Harper's face as he approached.

Stormy threw his body sidewise, as Harper's gun roared. Harper swore, lifted his gun again. With a superhuman effort Stormy brought his forty-four to bear on Harper. He felt the gun jerk in his hand as Harper lost his balance and fell on top of him, bearing Stormy back to earth.

Then a great curtain of oblivion swept down and engulfed Stormy's swirling senses. . . .

28. CONCLUSION

Stormy awoke gradually to find himself stretched out in a strange bed. His body felt thin and weak, but his mind was clear. He glanced around the room. Bright sunshine was entering a window at one side where muslin curtains waved in the breeze. "I'll be danged," he muttered, and tried to raise himself. It couldn't be done. "Gosh, I'm sure puny," he mused, and was glad to sink back on his pillow.

A door opened opposite the foot of the bed and Kate entered. A joyful smile lighted her face. "Stormy!" she cried. "You've come to at last." She swiftly approached and dropped on her knees at the side of the bed.

"At last?" Stormy said resentfully. "You'd think I'd been out forever."

"It's seemed that long. Three weeks today."

"What!" A sudden surge of memories overtook him. "Cripes! The fight! Sam? Quad? Kate, tell me—"

"Take it easy, cowboy. You've had a narrow escape. Dr. Glover didn't think he could pull you through at first, but I told him he simply had to."

"The others, Kate . . . ?"

"Sam's up and around. He's at the house now—

maybe you don't know you're in my room. I had you brought here. I'll call Sam in a minute. He's been waiting, hoping to see you."

"How about Quad?"

"Quad's all right. He just had his hair parted by a bullet. Beyond a headache, he was all right in a little while. Harper's dead—but, wait, I'll call Sam."

She went to the door. Within a few minutes Sam limped in, using one crutch. His left shoulder was bandaged too.

"Hi-yuh, Sam," Stormy grinned.

"Hi-yuh, Stormy. It was a squabble, wasn't it?"

"Something to write about. You all right?"

Sam nodded. "It was shock knocked me out more than anything. You killed Harper, you know, just as he was about to finish you. Echardt, Moulton, and Gooch are dead. Muley Porter will live to serve a nice term in the pen. Hoddy Oliver rounded up eleven rustlers, not counting the cook, at the Anvil. Hoddy and his boys happened to drop down on them at the right time. There were five waddies who'd just returned from running a bunch of stolen cows up to the next county. They all talked plenty, once they were in jail."

Sam left after a time. Stormy went to sleep again. When he awoke it was night; an oil lamp burned low on a nearby table. He lifted his voice and called. Kate appeared in the doorway. "How would you like some of Ada's chicken soup?"

"Sounds like manna from heaven to me," Stormy smiled. "I'm hungry." Kate left the room, singing to herself.

Quad brought the soup. "Well, darned if it isn't hard to kill you," he laughed. Kate came in, followed by Ada, a pleasant-faced woman in the early thirties. Stormy said:

"It's good to see you again, Mrs. Thomas."

"Mrs. Wrangel, if you please," Quad grinned. "Yep, we did it last week, Stormy."

"Congrats," Stormy said. "You sure work fast when you get started, Quad."

"It was you that gave me the start," Quad said sincerely.

Ada Wrangel drew her husband out of the room, leaving Kate to feed the soup to Stormy. Stormy asked questions about the *Banner*.

Kate said, "Cowboy, I never worked so hard in my life. Yes, we got the paper out on time, the day after the fight. Quad drove me like a madman—and him with his head done up in a bandage. There was the story to write, the type to be set. Horace helped on that, and we hired a man to work the hand lever on the press. Mr. Trent offered to help. I got him to aid in reading galley proofs."

"Morgan Trent?"

Kate nodded. "He's a different man these days. By the way, his wife has left Carnival. No one knows where she's gone. Sam saw no use of holding her, and we've managed to keep Mr. Trent's name out of the papers. He sure helped getting out the issue that day—and night. We worked straight through until the paper was published the day after the fight. All the time I was nearly frantic, wondering if you'd live. You'd lost so much blood. But we simply had to get the *Banner* out. Half the town was waiting around the office to get the story. You should see how our circulation has climbed. Incidentally, I've been keeping your Weather Man column going, too, until you could return."

Stormy said gravely, "It isn't as good as mine, of course."

"I've had no complaints yet," Kate retorted. She finished feeding him and put the bowl to one side. "Gage and Mrs. Freeman are anxious to come see you when you're strong enough. Lots of others, too. Folks drive me crazy at the office, asking about you."

"So Ada and Quad got married. That's good, though I had an idea you and I would beat them to it. Never mind, they'll be green with envy when they see the governor at our wedding."

"I suppose he'll come, of course," Kate said mockingly.

"I don't know why he shouldn't. He's practically a cousin of mine. My father's cousin, as a matter of fact."

"Stormy, I had no idea . . ." Kate paused. "Sam said you'd have a story to tell me."

"It's high time I let you in on things. You see, Kate, Sam and I used to be with the Texas Rangers. Then, after we got out of the service, Sam came to this country and grabbed himself a job as a deputy. He was always writing me what good country it was, as was the governor. Well, I'd saved some money and decided to buy me a ranch. I mentioned my intentions in a letter to the governor. Meanwhile he'd heard that conditions in Carnival, under Mayor Harper's administration, weren't all they should be, so when he replied he suggested that I come to Carnival as a special investigator for him. So that's what brought me here and that's how come I could get such quick action when I wanted Sam Delaney to replace Bayliss as deputy."

"Well, I never!" The girl's eyes were shining. "And you bought a newspaper instead of a ranch."

"We'll have the ranch yet, Kate. Sam told me the Anvil will be for sale, cheap. I know stock raising. We'll take the profits from cows and give Carnival a newspaper that will be hard to beat. Eight or twelve pages, maybe."

"Oh, if we could. You're a dear—"

"Come closer to me."

The girl bent down. Stormy felt her warm

334

arms around his neck and her soft lips on his mouth. Her tawny hair tumbled down about his face. After a time he took a long breath and murmured, "The Weather Man Reports conditions sultry—"

"Stormy Knight!"

"—with no clouds, bright sun, and blue skies. In short, beautiful Kate, clearing weather!"

Center Point Large Print
600 Brooks Road / PO Box 1
Thorndike, ME 04986-0001 USA

(207) 568-3717

US & Canada:
1 800 929-9108
www.centerpointlargeprint.com